Better Than Perfect

Books by Kristina Mathews

Better Than Perfect
(More Than A Game Book #1)

Worth the Trade
(More Than A Game Book #2)

Better Than Perfect

Kristina Mathews

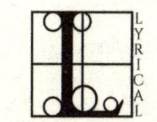

LYRICAL PRESS
Kensington Publishing Corp.
www.kensingtonbooks.com

LYRICAL PRESS books are published by

Kensington Publishing Corp.
119 West 40th Street
New York, NY 10018

Copyright © 2013 by Kristina Mathews

All rights reserved. No part of this book may be reproduced in any form or by any means without the prior written consent of the Publisher, excepting brief quotes used in reviews.

All Kensington titles, imprints, and distributed lines are available at special quantity discounts for bulk purchases for sales promotion, premiums, fund-raising, and educational or institutional use.

Special book excerpts or customized printings can also be created to fit specific needs. For details, write or phone the office of the Kensington Special Sales Manager:
Kensington Publishing Corp.
119 West 40th Street
New York, NY 10018
Attn. Special Sales Department. Phone: 1-800-221-2647.

LYRICAL PRESS and the L logo are trademarks of Kensington Publishing Corp.

ISBN-13: 978-1-61650-793-0
ISBN-10: 1-61650-793-4

First paperback edition: January 2015

10 9 8 7 6 5 4 3 2 1

Printed in the United States of America

Also available as an electronic edition:

ISBN-13: 978-1-61650-528-8
ISBN-10: 1-61650-528-1

To my best friend, who long ago swept me off my feet with his green fridge and quality toilet paper.

Chapter 1

"Pitchers and catchers report to spring training in thirteen days, twenty-one hours and seventeen minutes," Hall of Fame broadcaster Kip Michaels announced, and the crowd went wild. "Kicking off today's Fan Fest, I'd like to introduce one of our newest players. Two-time Cy Young Award winner, perennial All-Star, and the last man to pitch a perfect game. Give a warm San Francisco welcome to Johnny 'The Monk' Scottsdale."

Thirty thousand people were expected at the ballpark today. A great crowd—for a baseball game. But instead of working the count, Johnny would be working the crowd. Answering questions. Signing autographs. Putting himself out there in a way he wasn't entirely comfortable with. He was as nervous as the day he'd made his professional debut fourteen years ago. Butterflies? Try every seagull on the West Coast taking roost in his stomach.

Focus. Breathe. Let it go.

"Thank you. I'm thrilled to be here." He'd much rather face the 1927 Yankees than sit in front of a camera and a microphone talking about his game instead of playing it. "I hope I can help the team bring home a World Series Championship."

He tried to relax his shoulders. Tried to hide his nerves. The Goliaths could be his last team. His last shot at a ring. His final chance to prove himself and leave a legacy that went beyond the diamond.

After fielding a few questions about what he could bring to the team, and deflecting some praise about his success so far, Johnny was released to another part of the park to sign autographs. Little Leaguers approached with wide eyes and big league dreams. Tiny tots with painted faces squirmed with excitement about getting cotton candy while their parents shoved them forward to collect an autograph. A shy boy with a broken arm asked him to sign his cast. The look on his face was more than worth the discomfort of being in the spotlight for something other than his on-field performance.

Johnny had signed the big contract. The team paid him a lot of money to pitch every five games. They also paid him to interact with the fans, to be an ambassador for the game he'd loved for so long. The game that had saved him from a completely different kind of life.

He shared a table with another new player, shortstop Bryce Baxter. They were set up near the home bullpen along the third base line. Several other stations were set up around the park, giving fans a chance to get up close and personal with the players. Some tried to get a little too personal.

"So you're the hot new pitcher." A busty brunette leaned over the autograph table, wearing what appeared to be a toddler-sized tank top. The team logo sparkled in rhinestones and she was obviously well aware of the attention she drew. "I'd be more than happy to show you around."

"No thanks. I'm pretty familiar with the city." He held his pen ready, although she didn't seem to have anything to autograph. Nothing he was willing to sign, anyway.

"I could take you places you've never been." She leaned over even more.

Johnny kept his head down, trying to avoid gazing at what she had to offer. He reached for a stock photo, scrawled his signature across the bottom, and slid the picture forward, hoping she'd take the hint and leave.

"You forgot your number." She pouted.

"Sorry. I don't give that out." Johnny wished he could retreat to the locker room. Get away from her and the crowd that seemed to be growing. He never understood why people would wait in line to make small talk and take his picture. He gripped the black marker, needing something to do with his hands. If he only had a baseball, he could roll it around in his palm. Feel the smoothness of the leather, the rough contrast of the raised stitches. Find comfort in the weight and the symmetry of the one thing he could always control.

His teammate inserted himself into the conversation. "Do you know who this is? The one and only Johnny 'The Monk' Scottsdale."

"The Monk?" She drew her gaze over Bryce, then glanced at Johnny before settling on Bryce once more.

"He's a god." He flashed a grin indicating he was more than willing to play her game. "Me? I'm a mere mortal." Bryce leaned toward her, clearly enjoying the interaction.

"You're new, too." She scooted over to his side of the table, dismissing Johnny's rejection as strike one. She must think she had a better chance of scoring with Bryce.

"I am. I think I left my heart somewhere in the city. Could you help me find it?" He slid one of his photos across the table to her.

"I can help you find whatever you're looking for." She took the pen from him and wrote something on the inside of his forearm. Her number, most likely.

Bryce grinned as if he enjoyed having a stranger tattoo him with a permanent marker.

"Bring your friend, too. If he's up for a challenge."

"I'll see what I can do, sweetheart." Bryce tipped his cap and winked at the woman.

Johnny exhaled, realizing he'd been holding his breath during the entire conversation.

"Thanks man, I owe you one." Johnny shook his head, as relieved as if Bryce had just snagged a line drive with two outs and the bases loaded.

"So it really isn't an act." Baxter eyed him carefully. "You really do walk the walk."

"What walk?"

"The celibacy thing. It's for real." A lot of guys thought he was full of it. That it was just for show. A way to get attention, and women. But once they realized he was genuine, most of the other players accepted him. Some even respected him. "You really don't mess around."

"No. I don't. I'm not perfect, but I try to stay out of trouble." Johnny removed his cap and ran his fingers through his hair. Since they were both new to the team, their booth wasn't as crowded as some of the others. They had a chance to catch their breath. He was able to finally sit back and enjoy the perfect weather. It was one of those glorious Northern California days when the sun came out to tease, dropping hints of spring and the fever that came with it.

"You looked like you were a little uncomfortable there." Bryce, on the other hand, seemed to relish the attention.

"I know it's part of the job, but it's not the part I'm good at."

"You let your game speak for itself. That's cool." Bryce reclined in his chair, looking as relaxed as if he was sitting in his own back yard. "Some of us have to use our charm to make up for lack of talent."

Johnny laughed. Baxter had plenty of talent. And more than enough charm to go around.

"She was pretty fine, though." Bryce continued to check her out as she walked away, collecting ballplayer's numbers like kids collected baseball cards. "Exactly what I need to get me in shape for spring training."

"Is that so?" Johnny managed to avoid the whole groupie scene. His entire career had been about control, both on and off the field. The Monk kept his cool. The Monk never got rattled. And The Monk maintained a spotless reputation. He had to, considering where he'd come from.

"There he is. Come on, Mom." A kid, about twelve or thirteen, rushed up to the booth, practically dragging his mother by the arm.

Johnny slipped on his best fan-friendly smile.

"We're, like, your number one fans." The boy was practically bursting at the seams. "Right, Mom?"

The boy's mother stepped forward, taking Johnny's breath away.

He'd had several reasons to come to San Francisco. Eleven million obvious ones, and several others that he'd done his best to articulate to the fans. There was only one reason he should have stayed away.

"Alice." Just saying her name sent a line drive straight to his heart. Even fourteen years later.

"Congratulations on your new contract. I know you're going to have a great year." She sounded like any other fan, wishing him well. She just marched right up to his table to ask for an autograph. A freaking autograph? Like he meant nothing to her.

A slight breeze blew her hair around her face. She tried to smile as she tucked a loose strand behind her ear. Blond, straight, silky—and if he remembered correctly—oh-so-soft. She wore modestly cut jeans and a soft blue sweater that on anyone else would have looked plain and proper. He didn't need to glance at her left hand to know she was off limits. Yet, she still moved him like no other woman ever could. Made him long for what he'd had. What he'd lost. What he'd tried for years to forget.

"Wait." The boy gaped at her. "You guys know each other? For real?"

"Yes. Johnny was . . ." She held Johnny's gaze just long enough for him to catch a flicker of regret. She turned to her son, who was about an inch or two taller than her. "He was your dad's college roommate."

"You knew my dad?" The boy seemed more impressed by that than the fact that people waited in line for his autograph.

"Yes. I knew him." Johnny swallowed the lump in his throat. "Before he married your mom."

"Cool." The kid smiled and nodded his head, like it was no big deal. "I mean, I know you played for the Wolf Pack when they went to Nevada, but I had no idea you guys were, like, friends."

Sure. Friends.

"Zach." She placed her hand on his shoulder, ready to steer him away. "I'm sure Mr. Scottsdale is a busy man. Let's leave him alone."

They'd once been as close as two people could be. But now he was Mr. Scottsdale.

The boy shrugged, dismissing her and looking up to Johnny with admiration. "It's totally awesome to meet you."

Johnny nodded, giving his most sincere smile, even though seeing Alice, and her kid, hit him like a 97-mile-an-hour fastball.

They started to walk away.

"Give my best to Mel." As if he hadn't already done that.

Alice turned around.

"Mel died. Eight years ago." A pained expression flashed across her face.

"I'm sorry. For your loss." Johnny said the words. He wanted more than anything to mean them, but he'd carried that resentment around for so long, it had become as much a part of him as his right arm.

"Thank you." Alice gave him a sad little smile. It was forced. Polite. The kind of smile she'd give a stranger. "It was good seeing you. Really good."

"Yeah. Sure." He could say the same, but he'd be lying. Seeing her again only reminded him of everything he'd sacrificed.

* * *

The minute she'd seen Johnny on the stage, Alice's heart had swelled big enough to fill the stadium. There he'd been, larger than life. Damn. The man looked good. Better than on TV. Better than she remembered. He'd gained some muscle. A lot of muscle. Even without the jersey, there'd be no doubt he was an athlete. He moved with the kind of confidence and grace that came with being totally in tune with his body. Like he'd once been totally in tune with hers. She ached at the memory, but shook it off, uncomfortable having such thoughts with her son sitting next to her. Like Johnny had clearly been uncomfortable onstage, addressing the media and the crowds. He never did like to talk about his game. He'd simply let his talent speak for itself.

Just as she'd predicted, women lined up at his booth. They all wanted his autograph. Some of them wanted a little more. She hadn't been able to handle it back then. And now? What he did was his business. Especially since she'd been the one to walk out on him.

"Mom. Are you okay?" Zach was protective of her. And a little too observant.

"I'm fine, Zach." She shook her head to clear the fog of memories that rolled over her. With only the briefest look into his eyes, she couldn't forget the three years they'd spent together, nearly inseparable. Studying. Hanging out. Making love. "I'm surprised to see him, that's all."

"But you knew he'd be here." Zach had that tone, the unspoken *duh*. They'd been coming to Fan Fest every year since Mel's death. She'd known Johnny would be here. She just wasn't prepared for the impact of seeing him again. She'd thought she'd put those feelings behind her. Packed them away with her college sweatshirts and student ID card. "You were so excited when you heard it on the radio. Your favorite player finally becoming a Goliath. Why didn't you tell me you guys were, like, friends?"

"I didn't want you to think it's a big deal." She tried to place her hand on his shoulder, but he squirmed to avoid the contact. That was new. Not unexpected, given his age, but she missed her little boy. The first time they'd come to Fan Fest, he'd held her hand. Until they'd gotten to the miniature version of the ballpark. He'd joined the t-ball game like he was born to play.

"It is a big deal." Zach looked at her like she was hopelessly out of touch. Something he did a lot these days. "Mom, you actually know Johnny Scottsdale."

There it was. The star-struck admiration bordering on worship.

"I *knew* him, Zach." Alice tried to keep her tone neutral. She couldn't betray her emotions. A wave of regret washed over her. The question of what might have been. "But that was a long time ago."

"Wouldn't it be cool if he came to the foundation's minicamp?" Zach couldn't know why it would be such a bad idea.

She'd hoped to avoid him. Avoid digging up the past. And the question that had plagued her more and more as Zach grew. "I already have a pitcher lined up. Nathan Cooper. He's done it for years."

Alice had worked for the Mel Harrison Jr. Foundation since its inception, a little more than a year after her husband's death. The initial donations were privately funded, set up to provide grants to community schools and youth organizations. As the foundation had grown, they were able to provide services for greater numbers of children, but the more successful they'd become, the less contact she had with the kids.

Until a few years ago, when the team had approached her about setting up a minicamp for youth players. It evolved from a Saturday demonstration and meet-and-greet to a weeklong afterschool program where the ballplayers worked directly with the kids, helping them learn fundamentals of the game while boosting their confidence with the attention and mentorship of the pro athletes.

"Cooper's alright." Zach sounded disappointed, bordering on whiny. "But he's not Johnny Scottsdale."

"Zach, we made a commitment to Nathan Cooper."

"And Harrisons always keep their commitments." Zach parroted the family motto. She could tell by the tone of his voice he had to restrain himself from rolling his eyes.

"Yes, Zach, Harrisons keep their commitments." No matter what. She'd made a commitment to Mel, to the Harrison family. She'd hoped her feelings for Johnny would eventually fade. She'd made her choice. A desperate one at the time, but once she'd committed to Mel, she wouldn't look back. She still couldn't. "Cooper's a good player. A good guy. We can't just tell him we don't want him anymore."

"Well, maybe they could both do the pitching clinic," Zach suggested. "Since Cooper's a lefty, maybe it would be better to have a right-handed pitcher too."

"Johnny's a busy man. He doesn't need us bugging him." And she didn't need to be reminded of what she'd given up.

"Yeah, but he probably doesn't know very many people here yet." Zach sounded hopeful. Like they'd be doing Johnny a favor. "It would be good for him to get involved in the community."

"Zach. He doesn't need us." She'd made sure of it.

"But . . ." Zach couldn't let it go.

"I think it's time for some lunch." Lately, food seemed to be the best distraction.

"I could eat." Zach shrugged. "You want to split some garlic fries?"

"You know I do." The ballpark's signature fries had become a tradition. But if she ate a full order herself, she'd be sorry later.

"Can I get two hot dogs, then? Or maybe some nachos?"

"You're that hungry?" Wasn't it only yesterday that she begged him to eat? Playing airplane with the spoon or bribing him with a toy to take three more bites.

"Yeah. I guess meeting Johnny Scottsdale increased my appetite." He grinned at her. For a second there, he reminded her of someone she used to know.

"Oh, Zach . . ." She sighed, her emotions getting the better of her. Seeing Johnny for even a few minutes had her all mixed up.

It had been easier when Johnny was on the other side of the country. When he'd been nothing more than a box score. An image on TV. She'd followed his entire career. From his earliest days in the minor leagues, to his first start in Kansas City, to when he was traded to Tampa Bay. She'd watched him. Cheered for him. Wished him nothing but success.

"Oh please, Mom. Don't go there." She was embarrassing him. As she often did whenever she talked about how quickly he was growing up. Becoming a man. Neither of them was quite ready for it, but that didn't matter.

She put her arm around him but felt him struggling with the idea of pulling away. Reluctantly, she let him go, knowing it was only a matter of time before he wouldn't need her at all.

"Order whatever you want. Just don't complain about a stomach ache later."

"I won't." He ordered a hot dog, nachos and a root beer.

She stepped up behind him and ordered her hot dog, the garlic fries and a Diet Coke. She struck up a conversation with the lady behind the counter while they waited for their order.

"Geez, Mom. Why do you have to talk so much?" He'd waited until they were at the condiment station before complaining.

"I was only being friendly. There's nothing wrong with that." She unwrapped her hot dog and placed it under the mustard spout.

"Yeah, then why weren't you very friendly with Johnny Scottsdale?" He kept his head down, concentrating on his food. She'd learned to pay attention more when he seemed least interested in making conversation. "You actually knew him in college and you barely said a word to him."

She hit the pump on the mustard a little too hard and it splattered all over her sweater. She quickly grabbed a napkin to wipe up the stain.

"Is it . . . Is it because he reminds you of Dad? Does seeing him make you sad?"

"Oh, honey." She put her arm around him, pressing him against her. How could she possibly explain why seeing Johnny again was so painful?

"It seems kind of weird that they didn't keep in touch after college." Zach had no idea how weird it would have been if they had. The three of them had been the best of friends. How many times had they let Mel tag along on their dates? Or how many times had she made herself at home at their place? But Johnny had been at the heart of their little group. And when he'd moved on, she and Mel turned to each other.

"Johnny was trying to make it to the big leagues." She used the same story she'd told herself over the years. "He had to work very hard to get to where he is today. Mel had a job here in the city, and I was busy raising you. We just drifted apart, that's all."

"But, maybe you and Johnny can be friends again." He had a tiny hesitation in his voice. Telling her there was more to the story than he was willing to share.

She waited. Pushing him would never get him to open up.

"Maybe . . ." Zach took a long slurp of his soda. "Maybe he could tell me more about my dad."

Well, that was a mistake. By bringing up his dad, he'd upset his mom. Zach could tell because she got really quiet. They sat in the stands to eat their lunch and watch the next round of interviews. She nibbled on her hot dog and absently picked at the garlic fries. He ended up eating most of them, which was fine. He loved garlic fries. But it was weird with her not talking. Normally she would chatter on and on about the upcoming season and especially all the new players. He'd expected her to be really excited about Johnny Scottsdale. She was probably an even bigger fan than he was.

She'd actually cried when he pitched his perfect game. Cried and hugged Zach like they'd been there. But she barely said a word to him when they met today. And they didn't even get an autograph.

Now, she was all quiet, and he wouldn't be surprised if she said she wanted to leave soon. He'd seen what he wanted to see. Johnny Scottsdale's first interview as one of the Goliaths, and then he'd gotten to meet him. Sort of.

Kip Michaels stepped onstage to introduce the next set of players. He was one of the best. He never had anything bad to say about an opponent, but he was a Goliath to the core. He also managed to throw out a few tips for young players during every game. He'd point out simple things, like keeping balanced in the batter's box or following through on a pitch. Plus, he'd been there. Way before Zach's time, but he'd pitched in the majors for ten years. So he knew what he was talking about.

"Thank you, San Francisco!" Nathan Cooper stepped up to the mic for his turn in the spotlight. "It's going to be a great season. I guarantee it."

Yeah, he was alright. Kind of a showoff, though. Like it was more about him than the team. Cooper played to the crowd, making them laugh and cheer and get pumped up for the season. Even if he was kind of obnoxious, he was a pretty good pitcher. Most of the time.

Zach glanced over at his mother. She was trying to rub the mustard stain out of her sweater. He wondered if that would be her excuse for leaving early. He wouldn't mind. Not really. He just wished he could have talked to Johnny Scottsdale more. He had a lot of questions. Mostly about baseball. Like what it was like to pitch a perfect game.

He had questions about his dad.

He barely even remembered him. Only a few fuzzy memories—mostly good—of a guy in a suit taking off his tie and getting down on the floor to play with the Thomas the Train set. He remembered watching movies and going to the park, but he didn't think he'd ever played catch with his dad.

He'd played catch with a few different major leaguers. As part of the minicamp. He never really felt like he was part of the program though. It was more like he tagged along, just because he could. Because his mom ran the show and his grandparents had started the whole charity thing after his dad died.

Some of the other kids had it real tough, though. Single parents who worked two jobs just to pay their rent. So they didn't have time to play catch with their kids. There were foster kids who never lived in one place long enough to be part of a team. Some of the kids had dads in the military, serving overseas in Afghanistan or places like that.

Zach felt kind of bad, taking up a spot for a kid who needed it more. At least he didn't have to worry about money. Or his mom didn't have to worry, anyways.

"Hey Mom?" He had an idea.

"Don't tell me you're still hungry." She smiled at him, but she was kind of distracted.

"No." Not really. But he would be after dinner. They'd probably have a big salad or vegetable stir-fry—something healthy to make up for all the junk food. "I was just thinking. Maybe I'm getting too old to be in the minicamp."

"You're not too old." She folded up her napkin and wrapped up the last of her unfinished hot dog. "There will be plenty of other kids your age."

"I guess." He wasn't as excited about it as he'd been the last few years.

"You don't have to do the minicamp." She tried to sound like it didn't matter to her, but he knew she'd be disappointed if he wasn't there. "I hope you're not quitting because I haven't asked Johnny Scottsdale to join us."

"That's not it." He grabbed the last garlic fry. Except maybe that was part of it. "I just don't know how much more I can learn from the same guys."

That kind of made him sound like a jerk. Like he thought he was some great baseball player already. That's not what he meant. He just didn't know how to say it without sounding like he was spoiled or something. How many kids got to work with real Major League baseball players every year? Not many. For most of them it was a once-in-a-lifetime kind of thing.

"If you don't want to come, that's okay. You won't hurt my feelings." She said that, but she didn't like when he didn't want to do stuff with her. It was hard for him to tell her he'd rather be with his friends. She always worked so hard at finding fun things to do together. Maybe it was because he didn't have his dad around anymore and she felt like she had to make it up to him. Or maybe it was because she didn't have his dad around and she was lonely.

"I'll come," Zach said. But he didn't really want to.

Johnny plopped down in front of his locker to change out of his jersey and into his street clothes. He was wiped out, but not in a good way like after a game. His muscles were sore from tension, not exertion. He was still reeling after his encounter with Alice. For years he'd pretended they were both dead to him. Come to find out, Mel had died. And even though they hadn't spoken in years, it still came as a big blow. The man had once been Johnny's best friend. Almost a brother. And now he was gone. Was it an accident? A long and painful battle with disease? Whatever the cause, Alice was left to raise their son alone.

Alice was a mother. Not a big surprise. She'd always loved kids. She was going to be a teacher. Until she'd married Mel and didn't have to work. Mel was rich. Came from money and probably couldn't help but make even more money once he graduated and went to work for his father, helping make other rich people richer.

It bothered him more than he wanted to admit. Her having a kid. Not that Johnny had ever really wanted to be a father. But maybe a part of him would have wanted to be the one to give her that gift.

He was wrestling with that thought when his manager, Juan Javier, approached him.

"Just the man I need to see." Javier had been a catcher during his playing days. A pretty good one too, until his knees gave out. But he was still in good shape. Still had a commanding presence.

"Sure, what do you need?" Johnny didn't know the man well enough to determine whether he should address him by his first name, last name or just call him "Skip." His reputation around the league was that of a player's manager. Well respected and well liked, with a thorough knowledge of the game and an uncanny ability to get the most out of his players. Johnny looked forward to working with him.

"I need a hero." Javier parked himself next to Johnny. "Got word this morning that Nathan Cooper didn't pass a drug test. He's out fifty games, unless he appeals."

Did that mean Johnny would be moved to the bullpen? Cooper was a relief pitcher, a left-handed specialist. Johnny was a right-handed starter. At least he had been his entire career.

"Don't worry, you're still a starter." Javier clapped him on the back. "This is a PR nightmare. At least it didn't leak out this morning. That would have put a dark cloud on the Fan Fest."

"So what can I do?"

"Your reputation is spotless. It's one of the reasons the team was so interested in signing you." They didn't call him The Monk for nothing. His composure on the mound was only part of the story. "We had a few years where . . . well, you catch the news. The fans are sick of this stuff. Sick of the cheaters. We need someone like you. Someone the kids can look up to."

"I try to be one of the good guys." Johnny shrugged. It's all he'd ever wanted to be. He wanted his name to be associated with honor, integrity and respect.

"Russ Crawford, from the front office, had Cooper lined up for this charity event." His manager placed a sturdy hand on Johnny's shoulder. "We don't want a guy suspended for drugs representing us to the community."

"No. We don't." Johnny never understood what would drive a guy to take such a risk. Or why there were still guys who felt they could get away with it. He balled his fists, thinking about how much harder the rest of them had to work at proving they were clean.

"We need someone to take his place. I thought you'd be perfect." He gave Johnny a friendly pat on the back.

"I was perfect once in my life." Twenty-seven batters had faced him. Every one of them had walked back to the dugout shaking their heads. None of them had reached first base. No hits, no walks, no errors.

"You and only about twenty-three other guys." Javier gave him a smile of admiration. Of respect. Not only for Johnny, but for all the players who'd come before him. "But you're not just perfect on the field."

That was his reputation. No wild parties, drugs or women. When he went out with his teammates, he stuck with one beer. Just to be one of the guys. Then he would return quietly to his room. Alone. He politely refused advances and room keys from his female fans.

"What kind of charity thing are we looking at?" *Let's get to the point.* What really mattered. As long as it wasn't a speaking engagement. He could pitch in front of a sold-out stadium. Or an empty one where the few fans in attendance tried to make up for the lack of numbers with an abundance of noise. But talking to a room full of people? No thanks. He'd much rather run the bleachers, drag the field, or even cut the grass by hand, one blade at a time.

"It's a minicamp for youth players," Javier explained. "They come to the ballpark after school and we take them through a few drills, demo mechanics and basically share your knowledge of the game."

"That sounds like something I could do." Johnny was just beginning to think about what he might do after his career was over. Coaching was something to consider; it would keep him in the game. But he wasn't sure if he'd be any good at it. He didn't know if he could explain things in a way others would understand. He could show them, though. He could demonstrate what worked for him.

"So you'll do the pitching clinic." It wasn't a question. The new guy on the team had to prove himself, no matter his reputation, and picking up a teammate was a good way to do just that.

Johnny nodded. Why not? Anything to keep his mind off Alice and Mel. And their kid.

"Tell me about the kids." Johnny didn't have a lot of experience with kids. Like, none. Even when he'd been a kid, he didn't really know how to relate to them. He was the quiet boy in school and in the dugout. "How old are they?"

"I think anywhere from about nine to twelve or thirteen."

"Old enough to tie their own shoes, then." In other words, about Zach's age.

"Yet still young enough that they don't think they know everything," Javier added with a slight smile. "About baseball, at least."

"So these kids should be coachable." When he'd been that age, he'd soaked up every tip and tidbit of information about the game. He'd been eager to learn and apply the knowledge to his rapidly growing skills.

Could he be the kind of mentor he'd had back then? Could he pass down his knowledge of the game to the next generation? He hoped so.

"They're good kids. Some of them may have caught a bad break. Single parent homes, families fallen on hard times. Some of these boys might be homeless or in foster care." Javier was starting to make Johnny a little nervous. He'd been one of those kids. He'd known hard times. Lived with a single mother who'd worked too much. Without a father or a man to look up to.

Until his coach had stepped up.

"I guess you've got your man." Johnny hoped he could be the kind of man these kids needed. "Just give me the time and place."

"I knew I could count on you. The camp starts Monday. Here's your contact at the Harrison Foundation." The manager handed him a slick business card. Johnny's heart seized as he read the name.

ALICE HARRISON, DIRECTOR

"She's a great gal. Professional. Knowledgeable." Javier seemed not to notice all the air had been sucked out of the room. "You'll love her."

Oh yeah. Johnny had loved her. He'd once loved her even more than he loved the game.

Chapter 2

Zach was off playing video games, so Alice took the opportunity to work on last minute details for this week's minicamp. She went over the schedule again, making a slight change in the rotation. She cross-checked the participant roster with the t-shirt order, making sure they had the right sizes ordered for each of the players. Tomorrow she and Zach would sort the shirts into groups for easy distribution at the sign-in station. Everything seemed to be in place. It should be—she'd been doing this so long, the program practically ran itself. But for some reason, she had a nagging feeling that this year wasn't going to be as easy as she'd hoped.

She took one last look at her notes, hoping whatever it was would work itself out by Monday, and closed the file. She took a deep breath and opened the other file she'd been working on. The one with the nearly completed application packet to the teacher credential program she planned on enrolling in for next fall. She'd managed to graduate before Zach was born, but her dream of becoming a teacher had been put on hold.

She had the application, résumé, test scores and letters of recommendation. But for some reason, she still wasn't satisfied with her essay. She'd rewritten the darn thing so many times, it might as well be a novel. She knew exactly what the problem was.

Fear.

She wasn't afraid of not being accepted. That was the easy part.

She'd graduated with a near perfect grade point average. She'd taken all the preparatory courses and tests. The only reason she hadn't gone straight from her undergraduate program to the credential program was because she'd gotten married, had a baby and moved out of state.

At the time, it had made the most sense. Mel only wanted to take care of her and the baby. She'd done her best to be a good wife and mother. And daughter-in-law. The Harrisons lived two doors down. Most young brides would have been uncomfortable having their mother-in-law so close, but Alice had been grateful.

When Mel's mother had approached her about starting the Mel Harrison Jr. Memorial Foundation, Alice hadn't hesitated. She knew nothing about running a charitable foundation, but giving something back to the community was a wonderful way to honor Mel's memory. And help them all through the grieving process.

She'd had no idea how successful the foundation would become. They'd started by gathering private donations to support youth programs already in place in the community. But Frannie and Mel Sr. were able to gather a lot of support from his wealthy clients and her social contacts. Soon, they had more money than programs to donate to. By then, Zach had started participating in youth sports and Alice got to see the impact positive male role models could have on a boy without a father.

When the Goliaths had contacted her about doing a community service project, she suggested having the players interact with young athletes. They started small. A one-day thing more about signing autographs and taking pictures than actual player development. But the program evolved from there, growing into a weeklong afterschool clinic.

Doing a summer camp wouldn't work, since the pro athletes were in the middle of the season when the kids were out of school. So they lined up an early February camp. Right before the pros reported to spring training, and just in time to prepare the kids for their Little League tryouts.

It was a good program. A worthy cause. But it wasn't enough anymore.

She read over her essay one more time. Not bad. Not perfect, but it gave a sense of who she was and why she would make a good teacher. She just had to attach the letter and hit Send.

She moved the cursor to just a click away from her future.

The phone rang, shaking her conviction. She saved the file and closed it without sending. She got up to find the cordless, but Zach poked his head into the kitchen.

"Mom. Phone." He handed it to her on his way to the refrigerator. "It's Russ Crawford."

Russ was the Director of Player/Community Relations. He was the liaison between the Goliaths and her program. He lined up the players. She lined up the funding. He helped her communicate with the pros, and she helped them communicate with the kids.

"Bad news." Russ had been working with Alice for the last five years, and he was always a straight shooter. "Cooper won't be available next week."

"What seems to be the problem?" She managed to maintain a professional composure. Even though he'd just told her she would be scrambling the next few days. At least now she knew where the nagging feeling had come from.

"Didn't pass a drug test." The frustration in his voice came through clearly. He'd worked too hard to restore the team's image in the wake of the steroid era. "But don't worry. I have someone lined up to fill in on short notice. You'll love him."

She had a feeling she already did.

"Who do you have in mind?"

"Johnny Scottsdale."

"He'll do." She hoped her voice didn't betray her. The idea of working with Johnny was tantalizing and terrifying at the same time.

"I know how much this program means to you." Russ was a good guy. He knew his job was more about how the players could benefit the community and not how the charity work could further the careers of the players. "Harrison Foundation has done a lot of good for a lot of people."

"That is the goal." Alice rubbed her temples. "I'm proud of what we've accomplished in such a short time."

"Seven years." Russ reminded her.

"Has it been that long?" She'd been a widow for two years longer than she'd been a wife. Yet she remained close with her in-laws. They were still her family, and they would be lost without Zach helping fill the void from losing their only son.

"You'd just started your second year when I came on board." Yes. That was when he'd hit on her. She'd used the excuse that she didn't have time; she was too busy getting the foundation off the ground. Her son needed her.

He'd at least taken the hint. They'd been able to maintain a professional relationship.

She hoped she could be as professional with Johnny.

"Time flies." In many ways it seemed like just yesterday when she'd made that one mistake that changed her life forever. Maybe it was a series of mistakes. Starting with letting Johnny go. Ending up naked in a hotel room with his best friend. And then marrying Mel when she felt she had nowhere else to turn.

"Don't worry about a thing." Russ said. "I'm sure Johnny Scottsdale will come through for you. From what I hear, he's as solid as they come."

You have no idea how solid he is.

Where did that come from? She had no right to think about how strong he was. No right to long for his arms around her. Absolutely no right to wish she could trade the last fourteen years for one more night in his bed.

"Does Johnny know he's going to pinch hit for Cooper?" Alice spent way too much time around the game. She couldn't help but use baseball clichés.

"He's all set. Juan Javier told me he's ready to step up to the plate." Russ was just as bad. Came with the territory, she supposed. "I'd expect a call from him soon."

"Do you happen to have an email for him?" She was a coward. She didn't want to hear it in his voice that Johnny was still angry. Or worse, devoid of any feelings for her. "It would be easier to send him the information than try to go over it over the phone."

"Sure. I'll get it to you right away." Russ must have been in his office, because her inbox popped up with an alert for a new message. All of Johnny's contact information.

They ended the conversation with a bit of small talk before hanging up.

She opened her email program. Attached the necessary files and got no further than *Dear Johnny* in the body of the email before she noticed Zach standing there with an empty milk glass and the container of leftovers she'd planned on saving for lunch at least two days this week.

"So, I guess Johnny Scottsdale is going to do the camp after all."

Zach tried to act like he didn't care one way or another, but he couldn't contain the grin that spread across his face when she nodded. "Cool."

He set the glass on the counter and opened the fridge again.

"Zach, you can't possibly be hungry."

"I guess not." He flopped down on the bench seat of their little breakfast nook. "Do you think Johnny would teach me how to throw a curveball?"

"I'm pretty sure he'll stick to the basics." Alice had done the research on protecting young pitchers. There was some dissention, but most of the experts were all about protecting younger players. "As part of the program, he'll focus on proper mechanics of the fastball, and for those kids who are ready, I'm sure he'll work with them on the changeup."

"Yeah, but some of the guys . . ."

"Zach, even if he wanted to show you how to throw a curveball, I'm not going to let you work on it until you're in high school."

"I know." His shoulders slumped. "Not until I have hair under my arms. So lame."

"You do want to play in high school, right?" They'd been over this. He wanted to push his limits and she wanted to protect him. "Maybe even beyond?"

"Yeah. But what if I'm not good enough?"

"You are. You don't need a curveball. Your fastball is solid and your changeup is coming right along."

"You have to say that, you're my mom."

"I'm your mom, but I don't lie to you." Unless she'd been lying to him about who his father was.

Zach couldn't be more thrilled to have Johnny Scottsdale working at the minicamp. But nervous, too. What if he thought Zach was some annoying little kid who just tagged along because his mom ran the camp? He was *Johnny Scottsdale*. The best of the best. Perfect, even. "I was thinking maybe instead of participating in the camp, I could, like, help. Be your assistant or something." He hoped she wouldn't think it was a lame idea. "I mean, I know a lot about baseball already. And maybe I could work with some of the younger kids."

"Really? You want to do that?" She sounded kind of surprised, but not in a bad way.

"Yeah. I mean, you're always talking about giving back and stuff."

"Good to know you've been listening." She ruffled his hair. Kind of embarrassing, but he didn't mind all that much. As least not when none of his friends were around.

"I just think that maybe it might be easier for kids to see someone more their age, you know."

"I think that's a splendid idea." She gave him one of those smiles. Like she was so proud of him she might cry any second now.

"Yeah, okay. And if you want me to especially help Johnny Scottsdale, that would be cool." Yeah, like he was fooling her with his pretending that he didn't care one way or another.

"You want to help Johnny." She had that weird thing in her voice. Like it had gotten caught on something sharp. "I think it's a great idea for you to want to help out. But let's not get too excited about working with a particular player."

"He's new to the team." Zach tried to keep it cool. "It might help for him to have someone around who knows how we do things."

"We'll see." Why did moms always have to say that? Why didn't she come right out and tell him no? "But Johnny might be more comfortable working alone."

"I just want to help." It was true. But he also wanted to get to know Johnny. He'd always felt a connection to him that he couldn't explain. Johnny Scottsdale had always played in the eastern part of the country, so Zach had never seen him play in person. But he'd seen him on TV. He was exactly the kind of pitcher Zach hoped to be someday. Johnny never got flustered. He never got upset when he'd pitched well, only to lose 1-0 because his offense couldn't score any runs. He never blamed his teammates if they made an error behind him. He just shook it off and went out and pitched even better the next time.

"It's great that you want to help." His mom got that funny kind of look. "I'm sure we can find plenty for you to do. But don't plan on following Johnny Scottsdale the whole time."

"Yeah, I'm not a stalker."

"I know. But if you get too excited about meeting him, it might make him uncomfortable." She sounded like she couldn't quite find the right words. "You know how you get embarrassed when people talk about you too much. Like when Nannie or Grandpa start bragging to their friends about you and you're there in the room?"

"Yeah. Totally embarrassing." Zach didn't like having too many people look at him. And when he was playing sports he had to tune out the crowd. At least his mom wasn't too loud. She'd just yell *Go Zach!* or something like that. Some kids' parents got a little obnoxious. Trying to coach from the bleachers. Usually shouting the opposite of what coach told them to do.

"Well, Johnny's the same way. He doesn't play baseball because it makes him famous."

"He plays because he loves it." Zach could totally relate. "And because he's awesome."

"Just don't tell him that." She was probably joking, but it didn't sound like it.

"So are you saying I blew it when I told him we we're his number one fans?" Great, now he'd probably think Zach was a dork.

"No. You didn't blow it. Just try to act like you don't have his stats memorized and his poster over your bed."

"I get it, Mom. I'll play it cool." He could totally do that. He was in eighth grade. Playing it cool was probably the most important thing they'd learned this year. How many times had he seen his friends make fools of themselves by letting a girl know they liked her? But then if they acted like they didn't like her, her friends would come up and ask why he ignored her.

Zach was so confused, he decided it would be better to stick with baseball. At least the rules were clear.

Sunday morning brought Alice's father-in-law to her door. He came bearing gifts. Or rather, a gift for Zach. A new set of golf clubs.

"He's outgrown his old ones." Mel Sr. made the excuse before she could protest the latest offering. "We'll donate them. Maybe we could start a program to get more kids playing golf."

"You really don't have to buy him so much." Alice placed a daughterly kiss on his cheek. "He enjoys spending time with you."

"Well, an old man can't take any chances." Mel stepped inside the foyer. "I don't know how many more golf games we've got together."

Mel Sr. had taken his son's death hard. Even harder than the rest of them. He often shared his regrets with the two women in his life. He worried he hadn't spent enough time with his son. Hadn't told him how proud he was of him. He'd been too busy providing for the future; he hadn't taken the time to live in the moment. So he tried to make up for it with Zach.

"Zach's not going anywhere." As soon as she said it, she realized she was a liar. If she went back to school, he'd move to Reno with her. She'd already determined which high school she'd enroll him in.

"Maybe not, but I'm no fool. He'll find someone much more interesting to hang out with." He tried to smile, but couldn't quite pull it off. Was he worried about Johnny stepping into Zach's life? He shouldn't be. Unless . . .

"Hey Grandpa, I'm ready for our tee time." Zach's golf shirt looked a little snug. He was already almost as tall as his grandfather. Harrison men weren't known for their height. But they'd certainly made their presence known. Mel Sr. was still a big man in the financial world. Like that old commercial, when Melvin Arnold Harrison spoke, people with money on the line listened.

"Zach, are you sure you want to spend your Sunday morning with the old man?" Mel put his arm around the boy. Another inch and they'd be the same height. But she had a feeling Zach wasn't even close to ending his growth spurt. He was going to be tall. Very tall. Well over the six feet her husband had aspired to in vain.

"Thanks for taking me." Zach hadn't even noticed his new clubs yet. "I like golf. It's, like, my second favorite sport."

"If it wasn't for that one fellow . . . I was this close to converting you when his scandal broke out." Mel shook his head.

Zach looked away, embarrassed. They all knew the famous golfer he refused to mention by name.

"Now almost as many people watch, hoping he'll lose, as used to cheer him on. It's a damn shame."

"That's why I'm glad we've got Johnny Scottsdale working for our camp. He's a real hero." Zach had built his image up so high, Alice hoped for both their sakes, Johnny wouldn't let him down.

"Is that so?" Mel looked at her, surprised by the news. Alice hadn't had a chance to touch base with the Harrisons about the change of players. She was planning on calling Frannie after Zach and Mel left.

"Johnny Scottsdale." Mel turned his attention back to his grandson. "So did you meet him?"

"Yeah. Only for a few minutes, but he was totally cool." Zach exaggerated their interaction. Johnny had barely glanced at him. He'd seemed surprised to see her. "He didn't know my dad died, but then he seemed really sorry. So sorry he forgot to sign an autograph, but that's okay. Getting to work with him is even better."

"Zach's going to be an assistant. What he doesn't know is, that means he gets to be my slave for the duration of the camp." Alice thought about how she was going to use him. "He'll help me check in kids at registration. Run equipment from station to station. And of course, collect any personal belongings left behind to organize a lost and found."

"But I'll also help any of the pro players if they need someone to demonstrate pitching or anything," Zach added hopefully.

"Of course." She hoped Johnny would be willing to have him help. He had no idea how much Zach looked up to him. Of course, he wouldn't. He'd forgotten all about her and Mel, so he certainly wouldn't have thought about their child.

After Zach left with his grandfather, Alice busied herself with pre-camp activities. She sorted the t-shirts into groups, pinning a color-coded and laminated number to the back of each shirt. It would have been nice to be able to provide uniforms, but she had no way of knowing if each family had access to nightly laundry facilities, so it was easier to use the pin-on numbers.

Once all the shirts were numbered, she placed them in a reusable tote bag with the Goliath's team logo, along with a packet of special edition trading cards and a Harrison Foundation Fun Camp water bottle.

She'd just packed the filled tote bags into large plastic bins, ready to be loaded into the back of her compact SUV, when her phone rang. She figured it was probably her mother-in-law, so she didn't bother to check the Caller ID before answering it.

"Alice." A voice from the past caught her off-guard. "It's Johnny. Johnny Scottsdale."

"Hello Johnny." She hoped he didn't catch her sharp intake of breath. "Did you get my email? I sent over everything I could think of to help you prepare for the camp."

"Yes. It was thorough." A shuffling sound told her he was switching the phone from one ear to the other. She'd bet he was walking around his apartment, or wherever he was calling from. He'd never been able to have a phone conversation while sitting in one spot. "I was kind of hoping we could meet sometime today. So you could... walk me through it."

"Sure, I've got a few things to wrap up, but I can meet you this afternoon."

"How about a late lunch?" Johnny suggested. "Is that one place still around? That diner Mel liked to go to?"

"It's still around. Still owned by the same family." She allowed her mind to drift back to happy times. When Mel had been excited to show his friends around the city he grew up in. He'd made an effort not to take them anywhere too fancy. He'd been almost as ashamed of his wealth as Johnny had been of his poverty.

Her mother hadn't understood why she'd chosen to spend that Thanksgiving with her boyfriend's roommate's family rather than coming home. But her mother hadn't offered Johnny an invitation, so where he'd gone, she'd followed.

At the time, she'd thought she would have followed Johnny anywhere. To South America, Japan or even Australia if that's what it took for him to make a career in baseball.

She would have followed him so she wouldn't have to worry about all the other women. He acted like he didn't notice the number of female fans who seemed to increase with each win. But she'd noticed. She couldn't help but notice how popular he'd become. Some even hit on him when she was standing right next to him.

She hadn't wanted to drag him down with her jealousy. Her insecurity. And she'd never survive any kind of infidelity. So she let him go. Let him leave for the Minor League camp as a free man. To focus on baseball. To become the pitcher he was today.

They agreed on a time and Alice knew she didn't have nearly enough work to keep her occupied until they'd meet. She wondered if it had been worth the sacrifice. If he'd been happy. If she'd be able to work with him without her heart breaking all over again.

Chapter 3

Johnny went for a run down the Embarcadero, dodging seagulls and skaters and street performers. He was really dodging his feelings. His past. And the realization that he needed to start thinking about his future. He usually started his preseason workout sooner, but with the cross-country move he was behind schedule. He finished his run but failed to clear his head.

Long drives, cold showers and intense workouts had been his go-to distractions. Had he really believed he could brush away the memories like an umpire dusted off home plate? He'd spent the last fourteen years shutting down his emotions like he'd shut down his opponents' lineups. Not quite—his career Earned Run Average was 3.28. His emotional response averaged more like zero.

Johnny headed over to the training room at the ballpark. When all else failed, he would do what he did best—focus on his game. His best friend was gone. He'd lost him fourteen years ago. But now it was final. First Mel had taken Johnny's girl. Then he'd mailed that announcement, making sure he knew it. So Johnny had closed the book on their friendship. And Alice? He'd tried to forget her. But he had a better shot at the American League batting title. Even though they used a designated hitter and he only got to hit when playing interleague games at a National League park.

He sat down at the weight machine and tried to work out the stiffness in his shoulders. Stress had begun to settle into his muscles. Not good for someone who made a living with his body. Signing autographs wasn't much of a workout, and while just thinking about Alice got his heart rate up, it wasn't exactly cardio.

Bryce Baxter sauntered into the weight room about a half an hour after Johnny started lifting weights. He wore dark sunglasses and had the slow movements of someone who'd spent a late night out on the town.

"Mornin'." Bryce eased himself onto the machine next to Johnny. "How's it going?"

"Good. Trying to keep busy these last couple of weeks before spring training." Johnny glanced at the clock. Morning was pretty much over; it was almost noon.

"I could have used you last night, man." Bryce stretched his arms overhead and rolled his neck side to side. "That brunette had a friend."

Johnny took a swig of his water. "You took on both of them?"

"Nah. I'm not that talented." He laughed like they were old friends, sharing an old joke. "Maybe when I was a rookie five—okay, eight years ago. Of course, back then I was excited to have even one chick into me, you know what I mean? No. I guess you don't know what I mean."

"I'm not really a monk." Johnny had spent half his career explaining himself. "I've been known to swear, have a beer. I've even had relationships with women before."

"No, man. I didn't mean anything." Bryce rubbed his temples. "Except you seem to be smarter than the rest of us."

"I doubt that."

"You'd think I'd learn. She wasn't interested in me. The real me. She was just looking for another jock to add to her collection." He laughed again, mostly at himself. "I came out of the bathroom and she was typing into her phone. Couldn't even wait for me to get dressed before updating her blog with her latest conquest."

"How'd you find this out?"

"She sent me the link." Bryce uncapped his water bottle and drained it. "I did get a 'Homerun' rating. So that's good. I guess."

"She's got a rating system?"

"Sure. Single, Double, Triple, Homerun and Strikeout." Bryce rested his forearms on his knees, not ready to work out anytime soon. "So I guess I should be proud of hitting one out."

Johnny didn't exactly know what to say about that.

"She's coming to Arizona." Bryce stretched. Rolled his neck from side to side. Then he exhaled loudly.

"You going to meet up with her again?"

"Hell, no." Bryce laughed as if Johnny had told a dirty joke. "I've got a *one and done* rule. Besides, she's got her sights set on you, big guy."

"I'm not interested."

"Exactly. That's the challenge."

"She'll have to find someone else. I don't play that game."

"She was pretty hot, though . . ." Bryce leaned back on the weight bench. "But I guess you're more into blondes."

"I'm only interested in getting ready for the season." Johnny pulled down on the machine he'd been working on, thinking the conversation was over.

"I don't know about that." Bryce started his reps. "There was that one woman, in the blue sweater. She was there with her kid."

Johnny concentrated on lifting and lowering the weights. Maybe if he ignored Bryce, he would do the same.

"She was married to your roommate, huh?" Not working. Bryce was a chatty fellow. Oblivious to the fact Johnny didn't want to talk about it. "I get it, now. It's not a religious thing. Or a . . . gay thing. You've got a thing for your college buddy's wife. That's the secret behind The Monk."

Johnny's weights slipped, crashing down with a bang.

Bryce sat up.

"So, you are in love with her."

"No. I'm not." Damn.

"Hey, she's not married anymore." Bryce grinned.

If he'd had a ball in his hand, Johnny would have thrown it at him. Wiped that smug look off his face

"I got a vibe . . . she was just as into you."

"She's not interested in me. Not anymore."

"Oh, so she knew you were hot for her?"

"We dated three years in college." Why did Johnny share that?

"And she married your roommate? Harsh."

"You have no idea."

"Most guys in your situation would have gone the opposite route." Bryce leaned in, fully engaged in the conversation now. "Banged anything that moved. Hell, most guys would do that anyway."

Johnny had always known he wasn't like most guys.

"When my wife left me..." Bryce let out a low chuckle. "I took advantage of every opportunity that came my way. She didn't want me anymore. There were plenty of women who did."

"Must be the uniform." Johnny was only half joking.

"Yeah. Sometimes I feel like a baseball card with batteries." Bryce started lifting again.

Johnny took that to mean the conversation was finished, so he got back to work. He couldn't remember how many reps he'd done, so he started over.

They worked out in comfortable silence for the next hour, only the sound of the clanging machines and grunts as the two men pushed their bodies through the exercises.

"You work with kids much?" Johnny asked, feeling the need to talk to someone. Anyone. Even bad boy Bryce Baxter.

"A little. Why?" Bryce rolled his neck and shoulders.

"Javier asked me to fill in for this charity thing. A minicamp."

"Yeah? You'll be fine. Just teach 'em what you know." Bryce stretched his arms overhead and leaned forward. "Clinics are easy. Hospital visits are tough. Visiting kids you know probably won't be around next season, that sucks."

"Yeah. I hate those, too. I feel so helpless." And insignificant.

"So when is this camp? It's gotta be soon, since we have less than two weeks before we head down to Arizona for spring training."

"Tomorrow."

"Doesn't give you much time to prepare. But you'll do fine." Johnny wished he had Bryce's confidence.

"My ex is running it." Johnny had no idea how much time he'd be forced to spend with her. She'd emailed a bunch of information to him last night. Along with a very impersonal message about how she was looking forward to working with him and his teammates. She'd agreed to meet with him this afternoon, so that was something.

"Awkward." Bryce seemed to think the situation was amusing. But then he was the kind of guy who found most things amusing. Baxter's reputation was pretty much the opposite of Johnny's. Enthusiastic. Fun-loving. Charismatic. Always happy to be the center of attention, especially when the attention came from attractive and willing females.

"You have no idea." Johnny was starting to like him, in spite of their differences. As much as Bryce liked to goof around off the field, he was all business once he stepped onto the diamond. He seemed like a happy-go-lucky kind of guy, but he was serious about his game. Johnny was looking forward to having him behind him on the field.

"Who knows? This could be your chance to rekindle the old flame." Bryce gave him a wink.

"Not going to happen." He'd given her his heart once. She hadn't wanted it. He wasn't good enough for her. "I'm going to be there for the kids. That's all."

"Sure. The kids." Bryce chuckled as if he knew something Johnny didn't.

Alice arrived to find Johnny already seated at the restaurant. He stood to meet her and she needed to remind herself to breathe. His bio listed him at six-five, two-twenty, but he seemed so much bigger. Stronger. More *there*. He'd been a little thinner in college. Lankier. Not yet sure of his power as a man.

He pulled out her chair and his arm brushed her shoulder. She became all too aware of Johnny's power. He was a fully grown man, now. One who made his living with his body. He returned to the other side of the table, and she was able to draw a breath. To draw her attention back to why they were there.

She pulled a thick folder from her tote bag. "Most of the information in here is a hard copy of what I already sent you." She slid the folder across the table. "But I added a brochure detailing the foundation's mission statement, program offerings and a list of major donors. There's also a booklet on coaching youth sports, focusing on positive player progression. I've included some icebreaker games for getting the kids' attention. And of course, a copy of the schedule for the week."

"Thanks. I did take a look at the website links you sent me." Johnny's voice was warm, almost friendly. It would be so easy to believe they could slip into that easy companionship she'd taken for granted. A unique combination of passion and camaraderie that she now knew was one-of-a-kind. "I like that you keep the focus on skills development and teamwork."

"I'm pretty proud of this program. It's more than just a game for some of these kids." Alice felt a small surge of pride. She'd seen what baseball had done for Johnny. What it was doing for Zach, although thankfully, Zach had plenty of other opportunities. For Johnny, baseball was all he'd had. "We're developing skills they can use on or off the field. Teamwork being one of them."

"So, are we a team?" To anyone who didn't know their history, the question would have sounded perfectly innocent.

"I hope we can work together. For the kids." She missed him. Missed them. They'd been quite the team. And Johnny's skills went well beyond the baseball diamond.

"Sure. The kids." Johnny flipped through the folder. If he was overwhelmed by the amount of information she'd provided, he didn't show it. "Wow, you went to a lot of trouble."

"I remembered how much you liked to prepare before a game." Maybe she'd gone a little overboard. But she wanted it to be perfect. "And you always did pretty well cramming before a big exam."

"I got lucky a lot." He glanced down at the information in front of him. But not before she saw the barest trace of a smile that hinted he was referring to more than his grades. She'd been a big part of the reason he'd needed to cram in the first place.

He hesitated when he got to the back page of the brochure. He stared at the photo of Mel and Zach, taken not long before the accident.

"Were you happy?"

It was a simple question. But she didn't have a simple answer.

"Hi, I'm Tiffany and I'll be taking care of you today." The waitress's appearance gave her a minute to compose her response. "Can I start you off with something to drink?"

"I'll have an iced tea." Alice could answer that one easily enough.

"The same." Johnny took his gaze off Alice just long enough to be polite to their server.

"Do you need more time?"

"I know what I want." Johnny stared at Alice. Once upon a time he would have been hinting at something more than a sandwich.

"I'm ready to order." Alice closed her menu and smiled at their waitress. She ordered the French onion soup with a Caesar salad.

Johnny chose the clam chowder and a sourdough turkey melt.

"So, you didn't answer my question." Johnny watched her pour three-quarters of a sugar packet into her tea. He took his plain. Some things hadn't changed. But so many things had. "Were you happy with Mel?"

She stirred her tea long after the sugar had dissolved.

"He was good to me." For the most part. "He was a good man."

"I used to think so." Johnny balled up the straw wrapper, rolling it between his fingers. "I never thought he was the kind of guy to fool around with my girlfriend behind my back."

"We weren't fooling around behind your back." She played with her straw, stirring the ice in her glass. Anything to avoid looking at him. Seeing the hurt that was still there. "We weren't together until after you left."

Timing wasn't the issue. She'd slept with his best friend. She could have slept with his whole team and it wouldn't have hurt him nearly as much.

"So he just swept you off your feet?" There was no mistaking the bitterness in his voice.

"Is this really what you wanted to talk about?" So much for the illusion of a potential friendship.

"No. Not really." The waitress arrived with their meal. "I don't think I'd ever seen him that happy."

He pointed to the picture. It had been a difficult decision, choosing the photograph that would represent Mel in all their promotional materials. Their wedding photo seemed a little too formal. Too staged. There were a few family photos taken at holidays and such, but she never liked the way either of them looked. As if one of them was trying too hard. Or not hard enough.

In the end she'd selected the candid photo of a trip to Golden Gate Park. She'd snapped the picture when they took a break from the aquarium to grab a bite to eat and let Zach run around on the grass. He'd come up behind Mel to surprise him, and put his skinny little arms around Mel's neck. At that moment, Mel had been truly happy.

"He was good with Zach." Alice smiled, remembering how hard he'd worked at fatherhood. How much effort he'd made to be a good husband to her. "He really wanted to be a good dad. When he was around."

Johnny nodded, taking a bite of his sandwich.

She hadn't meant to imply Mel was too busy working to spend much time with her and Zach. But that had been the case. And in some ways, she'd preferred it that way. She'd been happy raising Zach. Making a home. Trying to be a good wife. But when they were alone, just the two of them, Alice couldn't deny something was missing from their marriage.

A connection. A passion. A spark she'd only felt with one man.

"Do you miss him?"

She nodded, unable to put it all into words. "Do you?"

"Yeah. Yeah, I do. I hadn't realized it until I found out he's gone." Johnny wiped his mouth with his napkin. "I was too busy being pissed off at him."

"And you can't stay mad at a dead man." She should know. At least, it was impossible to admit it. Even to your oldest, and once upon a time, dearest, friend.

"No. I can't."

"Are you still pissed at me?"

"A little." He looked up at her. Gave her an honest half-smile. Broke her heart just a little.

"And yet, you're here." She swallowed, even though she hadn't been able to eat very much.

"My boss asked me to do this." Johnny shifted in his chair, making the metal groan. Making her all too aware of his size. His strength. His power. "I'm the new guy on the team. I can't very well tell him no."

"So that's the only reason you're here? Sucking up to your new boss?" She knew better. Johnny didn't suck up to anyone. He might deflect attention away from himself, but he didn't suck up. He stood up for his teammates. Gave them more credit than they might deserve. But it wasn't because he wanted something for himself.

"I think you've got a good program." Johnny lifted his gaze to meet hers. "You can make a big difference for some of these kids. It's important. And I'd like to be a part of that."

"Thank you." For the praise of her program. For wanting to help. For not letting their history get in the way of doing a good thing.

The conversation was getting a little too personal, so she was grateful when the waitress came by to refill their iced tea. They finished their meals, while Johnny looked over the packet she'd created for him. He asked a few questions about the camp, and she did her best to fill him in on the details that would help him feel as confident teaching his game as he was playing it.

"Thanks for going over this with me. It helps to have a game plan." Johnny reached for the bill.

"I've got it. It's foundation business. Let me take care of it."

"No. I can actually afford to pay for lunch." Johnny gave her a teasing grin. They'd both struggled financially in college. It led to some very creative dates. Or letting Mel tag along, more often than not, since he'd been the only one of the three of them who could afford luxuries such as pizza and hot wings.

"I'm sure you can."

"Oh, yeah. I'm loaded. You should have held out for my millions." Johnny leaned forward, a teasing glint in his eyes. "Do you know what they're paying me?"

Yeah. She knew. And she also knew it was less than he'd have been offered almost anywhere else. Just for the chance at chasing a World Series title. Or did he have other reasons to come to San Francisco?

No. Of course not. He'd thought she and Mel were still married when he'd signed the contract. He'd given up probably a few million dollars to come here. And long-term security. It had nothing to do with his feelings for her.

"Do you think I married Mel for his money?"

"I gave up a long time ago trying to figure out why you chose him over me." He said it casually, as if it didn't matter to him. But it did. She didn't miss the underlying hurt. The bewilderment. And the barely contained anger.

"I didn't choose him over you." She leaned back into her chair. As if the extra few feet could lessen the blow. "It just happened. We were both missing you. And..."

He looked at her. Searching her face for some part of it to make sense.

"I got pregnant."

She waited for him to ask for more details. To ask the one question she hadn't been able to answer. Hadn't wanted to know for sure. Not when she'd needed to make a quick decision. One that would change her life forever, but hopefully wouldn't ruin Johnny's.

"Look, Ali, I'm sorry..." He tossed a couple of bills on the table.

"Don't worry about it." She folded her wallet and put it back in her purse. "But I'm not your Ali. Not anymore."

"I guess you'd prefer Mrs. Harrison." His words were neutral. His tone was not. He was pissed at her. Extremely pissed.

"Excuse me." She shoved her chair back and headed for the ladies' room. She'd hurt him. And neither one of them had forgiven her for it.

Johnny followed Alice to the ladies' room. Why couldn't he be the calm, cool, always-in-control guy he was on the mound?

Because this was Ali. She'd always made him a little crazy. She had a way of lighting him up like post-game fireworks on opening night. She still did. Even though she'd moved on. Had a life without him. She even had a kid.

But that didn't stop him from wanting her. From missing her. Even more now that he knew she was no longer married.

She emerged with her head down and she nearly bumped into him.

"Oh, Johnny. I didn't see you there." She looked up.

Her mascara was smeared. Her eyes were red and shimmery. He'd made her cry.

Damn.

"Ali." He wiped away the smudge with his thumb.

She leaned into his palm and it would have been the most natural thing in the world to kiss her. To lean down and press his lips against hers like he'd wanted to do since that day at the ballpark. Like he'd wanted to do since she walked out on him. Since the first time he'd seen her.

He took a step back. As far as he could go in the narrow hallway.

"Ali . . ." He cleared his throat, since he sounded like the oxygen in the air had been replaced by helium. "Alice, I'm sorry. I was out of line. It won't happen again."

"It's okay." She tried to sound brave. But the mascara streaks gave her away.

"No. It's not." He stepped closer. He couldn't help himself. "I hurt you."

"I hurt you first." She glanced up at him, her eyes shimmering with regret. And maybe a little bit of longing.

Yeah. She'd hurt him. More than he could ever admit.

"It was a long time ago." He should get over it already.

"Johnny, I never meant to hurt you." She sounded almost convincing. "I was just . . . scared."

"Afraid I'd sleep with other women." They'd had that argument enough times. She'd worried about the women who hung around trying to score with a ballplayer. Groupies. Oh, how he hated that word. And everything it stood for.

"A little." She smoothed her hair back, twisting one strand before tucking it behind her ear. "But mostly, I was afraid of holding you back. Of being too much of a distraction."

Johnny didn't know what to say. He shoved his hands in his pockets, so he could control his urge to touch her.

"I knew you had what it takes to make it to the majors." She leaned closer, placing her hand on his chest. Sending his heart rate up. "I had to love you enough to let you go."

"Look at me now." Johnny tried to smile. Did she expect him to be grateful? He was no expert, but he didn't think love meant abandoning someone when he needed her the most. When he was sent clear across the country, scared and alone, competing with guys from bigger schools. Guys with private coaching, fancy summer camps, and all the advantages Johnny never had.

"I am so proud of you." She hugged him, nearly knocking him into the wall before releasing him. "And I know you're going to be great with these kids."

"Yeah. Sure." The kids. That's why they were here. "Thanks again for meeting with me. For preparing the folder."

Which he'd left on the table.

"Well, thank you for lunch." She smoothed her hair back again. "I should get going."

He let her go. Watched her walk away. Again.

Retrieving the folder, he flipped to the page with the brochure of the Harrison Foundation. He stared at the picture of the man who used to joke about being jealous of Johnny. Johnny had the height, the athleticism, the good looks.

But Mel, at five-eight with bad skin and a slightly receding hairline, had ended up with the girl. He'd been the one to offer her security, financially and otherwise. She never had to worry about Mel hooking up with some stranger on the road. She didn't have to wait to see if he'd be successful. He had a job at his father's investment firm waiting for him upon graduation. And Mel had given her a son.

Johnny looked closely at the picture of a younger Zach. He didn't look anything like his father. He didn't look very much like his mother either. But there was something familiar about him. Maybe he took after his grandparents. Most likely his grandmother, since Mel was a junior in every way.

He needed to keep his focus. Get through the minicamp. Then get his head in the game. He had a season to prepare for. It might even be his last. He didn't need the distraction of Alice. Or her kid.

Maybe she'd been right all along. He was better off without her. He'd just need a World Series ring to prove it.

Chapter 4

About sixty boys lined up with their parents at the front gates of the ballpark. Most of them brought their gloves—some quite tattered—but each wore an expression of nervous excitement. Johnny recognized the look. First-day-of-camp jitters. He'd be sporting the same expression in less than two weeks, when he reported to spring training with the other pitchers and catchers. He wasn't nearly as anxious to get started as he normally was. He was... distracted. Alice had been right about that.

He looked out at the group of boys and knew he'd do whatever it took to get through this week. He understood why it was important for him to be there. Baseball had been the best thing in his life growing up. The only thing he could count on. The only thing he could control. He owed these kids a chance to find out if baseball could do the same for them.

Zach worked at the check-in station, helping each participant sign in to get their t-shirt, water bottle and a color-coded number breaking them into groups of about twenty kids each. Once they were checked in and several of the boys changed into their camp t-shirts, Alice led the parents to the stands. She introduced herself and thanked the parents for enrolling their sons in the program.

Johnny couldn't help but admire the way her dark gray pantsuit hugged her curves, and destroyed his focus. She'd probably chosen the outfit thinking she looked modest and professional. She looked professional alright, but sexy as hell. Maybe because he knew what she had hidden underneath.

"Today's focus is on teamwork, working together toward a common goal." Alice spoke into the microphone, her voice clear and confident. She turned to face Johnny and the two other players she'd recruited for this event. "And now, I'd like to introduce my teammates, men who have taken the time out of their busy schedules to work with your kids. Goliaths' catcher Roberto Luis, right fielder Trent Wilson and pitcher Johnny Scottsdale."

The kids and their parents applauded, while each player tipped their cap. Had anyone else noticed the way his name rolled off her tongue? Memories, as thick as the marine layer, settled around him. Chilling him to the bone. He recalled with a pang the way she used to whisper his name when they snuggled together watching a movie with Mel on the other side of the room. Or the way she cheered his name louder than anyone else at all his home games. And the way she'd cried out his name when they made love.

Focus. Breathe. Let her go already.

He felt like he was nineteen again, having only been with one other girl before Alice. He was thirty-five years old. A professional athlete. He could have any woman he wanted. Too bad he'd never wanted anyone else the way he wanted the woman standing in front of him.

He'd tried. Gone out with other women. Beautiful, intelligent, confident women. But when it got to the point where they expected more of him, when they wanted to "take it to the next level," he couldn't do it. He was capable—physically—but couldn't quite give it his all. Couldn't give himself completely to another woman. Not when he knew she expected his heart to follow.

Alice continued addressing the crowd, but he'd stopped listening. He simply watched her in her element. She was good. No, great at what she did. She held the attention of everyone in the crowd. The kids and their parents, and most of all him. People had always been drawn to her. She had a way of making everyone around her feel special. Johnny had learned the hard way special didn't mean exclusive.

When she'd told him she thought they should see other people, he'd come to the sad conclusion she already had. He still couldn't believe Mel had been the other person. Mel had everything—money, family, a name he could be proud of—but it wasn't enough. He had to take the one thing Johnny had that he didn't: Alice.

Finally, she put down the microphone, and everyone's attention turned to the kids and the ballplayers. Thankfully, they weren't expected to speak. She'd let them off the hook. Told the crowd that the players didn't want to waste any more time with speeches. They were here to work with the kids. To break a sweat with the young athletes. After splitting into their groups, Johnny took the boys assigned to him over to the left-field section of the ballpark.

Zach followed, holding a clipboard. "I get to be your assistant." He seemed more than eager to help. "Since I've been through the camp and you're new, we thought it would be a good idea for us to team up and work together."

"Sounds great. If I have any questions, I'll know who to ask." Johnny wasn't sure if he could spend the whole day with Mel's kid following him around. But he didn't want to hold it against the boy. It wasn't his fault who his parents were.

"Okay boys, get your gloves and make two lines." Johnny hoped they couldn't tell how nervous he was.

"Um, what if you don't have a glove?" One boy spoke up, but then dropped his gaze to the ground, kicking the grass with a worn cleat, when Johnny looked at him.

"No problem. We have extras you can use." Fortunately, Johnny had been given a heads-up about this exact situation. "Zach, why don't you check my equipment bag and grab a glove for anyone who needs one."

"Sure, Coach Scottsdale." Zach jumped at the chance to help. He dug through Johnny's bag, which contained a selection of new or gently used gloves donated by community members. No one should have to sit on the sidelines because their parents couldn't afford the gear.

Once each player was properly equipped, they paired up to toss the ball back and forth for warm-ups. Zach carried his clipboard and trailed behind Johnny as he went up and down the line offering praise and suggestions for each pair of players. The kid dutifully jotted down notes, taking his job very seriously. He was like his mother that way.

One of the boys overthrew his partner and Johnny bent down to pick up the ball and toss it back.

"Thanks." It was the boy without a glove. His shoes were worn and his jeans were a little too short and his hair a little too long. Instinctively, Johnny knew this kid had it rough. The boy served as a sharp reminder of why he was there. His job was to teach these boys about the game he loved. The game that had saved him from a life of who-knew-what.

"Hold the ball like this." Johnny demonstrated and then handed the ball over for the kid to try. "Now throw through your target, not at him."

"Okay. Through him." The boy tried again, firing one off almost perfectly. Maybe Johnny had a shot at this mentoring thing. It felt pretty good to make a difference. Sure, it was only one throw, but the smile on the boy's face after he made it was worth more than Johnny's last contract.

After warming up for about fifteen minutes, the players started their rotations. Johnny's group started with infield practice, taking grounders and covering bases. Next they would rotate to the outfield to work on fly balls and hitting the cutoff. Lastly, they would practice base running. Sliding, leading off and tagging up were some of the more subtle skills needed to have success at the higher levels of the game.

At the end of the rotations, Alice blew a whistle. She congratulated the kids on a job well done, and explained the details for the base running game. Each of the pro players demonstrated the rules, while the kids watched with rapt attention. Then it was their turn. She'd created a drill that was fun, fast-paced and cooperative. Every member of the team had a role and they'd need to work together in order to win. Each team won at least one round.

Johnny headed to the locker room at the end of the day feeling exhausted, exhilarated and a little bit in awe of Alice. She'd worked hard to put together a program that encouraged and supported the youth players. She made it fun, while reinforcing the fundamentals. Her passion for teaching shone through in the attention she paid to setting up the activities, recruiting the experts, and following up on each player. She made a point to stop by each station, and comment on what she observed. She asked questions of the kids, and actually listened to their responses.

If he wasn't careful, he would end up falling for her all over again. He had a feeling it was already too late.

Zach came in while Johnny was changing out of his jersey. Alice was right behind him. He couldn't help but notice her reaction to his bare chest. If Zach hadn't been there, he would have been tempted to show her a little more of what she'd been missing all these years.

"So, I asked my mom if you could come over for dinner." Thankfully, Zach was oblivious to the undercurrent of attraction between his mother and Johnny. "We could go over the plans for tomorrow and I was kind of hoping you could help me, like, with my pitching. I haven't pitched since last summer and I'm moving up to the bigger field and—"

"Zach, take a breath. Let Johnny think about the first question before you bombard him with twenty other things." Alice placed her hand on her son's shoulder. It wouldn't be long before she'd have to reach up to do so.

"Dinner sounds good." Johnny wasn't quite ready to come down from his high yet. He wasn't ready to return to his apartment. Alone. "Do you want me to pick up some take-out?"

"No. I'll cook. I owe you, anyways, for stepping in on such short notice."

"You'll cook?" Johnny couldn't help but tease her a little bit. Back in the day, she could barely make ramen. But mostly because she'd been busy with other things. Like him. If it hadn't been for Mel, they might have all starved to death.

"Yes. I cook. I'm pretty good, actually." She seemed a little offended. Or maybe a little embarrassed about the reminder from their shared past. "Right, Zach?"

"Oh yeah. My mom makes the best pot roast, and meat loaf, and pasta primavera and pie." Zach was either in on the charade or he was actually fond of his mother's cooking skills. "Even better than Nannie Frannie."

"Is that so?" He smiled at the boy and then turned his gaze to Alice. "I seem to remember one Thanksgiving when the three of us came to their house and the food was almost the best thing about the whole trip."

Johnny didn't mention the part about sneaking into her room at night, thankful that he'd been able to give her seconds . . . and thirds, if he remembered correctly.

"Yes. Well, I learned a lot from her." She looked away, possibly because she, too, recalled the details of that trip. There weren't many corners of San Francisco they hadn't turned into their personal playground.

"So, you pitch?" Johnny turned his attention to where he needed to keep it focused. On the kid. "That's great. I'd like to see what you've got."

"Really?" Zach beamed. "I've only got a fastball and a changeup. Mom won't let me try a curveball yet. She says it will ruin my arm."

"Well, it can. If you don't learn how to throw it properly." Johnny remembered being his age, and wanting nothing more than to learn the specialty pitches that looked so impressive on TV. But his coach took the cautious approach. Made sure he had command of his fastball and could throw an off-speed pitch to keep hitters on their toes. It took him years to understand his coach's reasoning. He'd also seen his fair share of promising young pitchers leave the game too early due to injury. Most of them had been pushed too far too fast.

"Thanks," Alice mouthed, and gave him a grateful smile.

"So when do you want to see me pitch?" Zach asked. He was trying to sound like he wasn't at all excited about the one-on-one lesson.

"Whenever you want." Johnny pulled a t-shirt over his head and couldn't help but notice Alice looked relieved. And maybe a little disappointed.

"Like, now?" Zach asked.

"Sure. Unless you have homework or something."

"No. I mean, not much." Zach's face lit up. "And I can finish it after dinner."

"Do you have your glove?"

"Yeah. Of course." His tone suggested that it was a silly question. Didn't everyone carry their glove with them at all times?

"Okay, let's head over to the practice mound." He had to give the kid points for enthusiasm.

Besides, Johnny could use a game of catch.

"Do you mind if I tag along?" Alice asked, even though she had no intention of missing out on this.

"If you want." Johnny grabbed his glove, a well-worn model that was almost an exact copy of the one he'd used in college. It was the same one she'd bought for Zach, because he'd begged for a glove just like Johnny Scottsdale's.

She followed them to the indoor practice field. They started slowly, getting a feel for each other. They tossed the ball back and forth in the timeless ritual played out by fathers and sons for generations.

Alice couldn't breathe. And she couldn't deny the possibility that she was watching a father-son game of catch. Only, neither of them knew it.

She'd kept the two of them apart. She had her reasons. Denial being the biggest one. Looking at them now and realizing how many games of catch they'd missed, she wondered if she could have done it differently.

She'd seen firsthand what happened to a man who sacrificed his dream for a family he wasn't ready for. She'd lived her whole life knowing that, if not for her existence, her father might have made something of himself. He might have been a star of something bigger than a small town varsity football team.

It didn't matter. Johnny had made it. He was a star. If he put himself in the limelight, he could be a superstar. He didn't date supermodels or movie stars, and he didn't appear on reality shows or celebrity competitions. Just played his game and played it well. And he kept his private life private. While he might be one of the best pitchers to ever take the mound, he wasn't generally recognized out of uniform.

She imagined he liked it that way. Never one to play for fame, he just wanted to win. To do his job to the best of his ability and come back and do it again five days later. She'd read the articles about him. He'd been called a workhorse. A solid player. A quiet champion.

His nickname was "The Monk." He was well known for his calm composure on the field. His almost Zen-like control. The tighter the game, the more focused he seemed. The higher the stakes, the calmer he appeared. He never got rattled. Something to be praised in an All-Star pitcher. But it had driven her crazy in their relationship.

Maybe she'd expected too much of him. She'd wanted romance and flowers and pretty words. He'd been able to give her friendship and passion, but not poetry. Or promises. Whenever she'd pressed for assurances about their future together, he'd become restless and withdrawn. She'd thought it meant he wasn't serious about their relationship. But maybe she'd been asking too much. He'd always been a little insecure about his place in the world. Outside of baseball, he thought he had nothing to offer.

So, she'd made sure he had baseball.

Just like she'd made sure Zach had baseball. Maybe it was her subconscious way of connecting him to his real father. Or maybe it was her way of staying connected to the man she'd never stopped loving.

Oh, she'd made a huge error. She never should have let Johnny go. She'd been so afraid of losing him, that she'd pushed him away. She hadn't known she might be pregnant. She'd thought it happened the night she and Mel went out to celebrate Johnny's success. They'd had a little too much to drink and instead of getting behind the wheel, they'd gotten a hotel room. One thing led to another and when she missed her period a few weeks later, Mel proposed.

Neither of them wanted to acknowledge the possibility that the baby could have been Johnny's. They both knew Johnny was headed for the big leagues. He deserved a chance to follow his dream. She couldn't take that away from him. Not when there was a chance he'd be giving it up for a kid who wasn't even his.

But now, seeing the two of them together, she wondered if she'd done the right thing. If Zach was Johnny's son, they'd both missed so much.

Alice sent Zach in to shower before dinner. She took the opportunity to take a good look around his room. He still kept a few Lego creations gathering dust on a shelf, but she was seeing fewer and fewer signs of the little boy he used to be. The Thomas the Train set had been replaced by baseball card collections, and *Sports Illustrated* magazines were piled up where his picture books used to be. His elementary school drawings had been taken down to make room for Goliaths pennants and posters of his favorite baseball players. Including the one of Johnny Scottsdale tacked up over his bed.

She'd never really looked too closely at the poster. She didn't need a reminder of what she'd given up. But now, she couldn't help but notice how much he looked like Zach. The eyes mostly, but also the curve of the lips, the set of the jaw that was becoming more apparent in Zach as he grew older. Did he look up at the picture and feel like he was looking into a mirror?

"Mom! What are you doing in here?" Zach stood in the doorway, with a towel wrapped around his waist and his hair still dripping from the shower. She remembered with a pang when he would run down the hall naked, not caring who saw him in his birthday suit.

"I was just making sure your room was company clean." She

picked up his glove off the end of his bed and set it on the dresser. "In case you want to show Johnny your trophies, or something."

"Do you think he'd want to see stupid Little League trophies?" Zach tried to sound like he couldn't care less, but she knew him. He was trying not to get his hopes up.

"I think he would be impressed by your accomplishments." She swallowed, trying not to let her voice betray her emotions. He couldn't know that Johnny might be more than just a guest. At least not until she knew what to do about it.

"Yeah, right. Like my t-ball participation trophy is going to mean anything to a guy with two Cy Young Awards." Zach rolled his eyes, not understanding how his award could measure up to the one given to the best pitcher in the league.

"You never know." Alice slipped out of the room so Zach could get dressed. And so she could regain her composure. That t-ball trophy would mean something to Johnny if he was Zach's father. But it would also serve as a reminder of the things he'd missed. Would Johnny have traded his All-Star appearances, his Cy Young Awards and his perfect game for the thirteen years of memories he hadn't been there for?

Or would he have resented them for taking away his dream? She never wanted Zach to feel the burden of knowing he was the reason his father had given up on his shot at making it as a professional athlete. She knew what that felt like. Knew all too well. Her father had passed up a football scholarship to work at the mines and support the family he'd never planned on. She couldn't do that to Johnny or Zach.

Johnny arrived right on time. He even brought a bottle of wine. A California zinfandel that would go perfectly with the pot roast she'd put in the Crockpot that morning.

"Thank you for coming." She took the bottle and led Johnny into the dining room. She and Zach usually took their meals at the breakfast nook, but she needed to put more space between her and Johnny. Although having an entire continent between them hadn't done much to cool off her feelings for him.

"Would you open the wine?" She handed him a corkscrew. "I have a few more things to get from the kitchen."

"Sure." Johnny made quick work of uncorking the bottle. "Is there anything else I can do to help?"

"No. I've got everything under control." Except her heart rate. Her emotions. Her longing to touch him again.

Zach came into the kitchen, wearing his nice clothes. He wore a button up shirt tucked into dress slacks. All that was missing was a tie. Wow. This was important to him. Did he suspect that Johnny was more than just a friend? Or was he simply trying to impress the man who'd been his hero for so long?

"Will you take the salad to the table?" She tried to sound normal. To keep the pride from sneaking into her voice. "Johnny's already here."

"He is?" Zach smoothed his hair back. Yes. He was hoping to impress. "Cool."

Alice picked up the platter of pot roast, potatoes and vegetables. She carried it into the dining room as if she were serving any other meal.

"Everything looks delicious." Johnny was talking about the food, but he looked at her with a different kind of hunger.

"Thank you. It's Zach's favorite." She glanced at her son, hoping he wouldn't notice the color in her cheeks. The warmth that spread all the way down to her toes from the sound of Johnny's voice.

They sat, and Zach loaded his plate before she even had the chance to unfold her napkin.

"My mom makes a killer pot roast," Zach said through a mouthful of food.

"Zach." Alice shot him a look meant to remind him of his manners.

"Well, you do." He swallowed before speaking, but wiped his mouth with his sleeve. His napkin was still folded beside his plate. She glared at him and he got the message, slinking down in his chair a little as he spread the cloth over his lap.

"I have to agree." Johnny gave her a warm smile as he dug into the meal. "This is very good."

Alice watched Johnny and Zach mirror each other's movements. They were so much alike it was as if they were related. Neither of them liked to talk much while they were eating. The quieter they were, the more they enjoyed the food. They were both quiet tonight. She could tell Zach must have a zillion questions for Johnny, but he didn't know where to start.

Johnny, too, seemed to have unanswered questions. He wasn't all that talkative in the best of situations. When he was uncomfortable, or unsure of himself, he became even more withdrawn. It had driven her crazy when they were dating. Tonight, though, it gave her a chance to observe the two of them.

Zach looked so much like Johnny, she couldn't believe she hadn't seen it before. Denial was a powerful hallucinogen. Zach's hair was lighter and a little longer, but she was seeing signs that it would someday darken to Johnny's deep golden brown. Their expressions were similar, too. The crooked smile, the crinkle of the eyes when they were amused. Even their scowls were identical. But the eyes really stood out. Zach's eyes were an exact copy of Johnny's. A deep, dark, chocolate brown. The kind to make a girl go all gooey inside.

"You guys up for dessert?" Alice asked when they were getting close to the end of the meal. They'd talked a little bit about baseball. Johnny kept his humility. Didn't do a lot of name dropping or making it seem too cool to have been on the same All-Star team as guys like Derek Jeter. He actually made it sound like any other job.

"No, thank you." Johnny never had much of a sweet tooth.

"Um, maybe?" Zach cleaned his plate, having seconds of everything. "Do we have any ice cream?"

"You can help yourself." Alice was starting to wonder if she could afford to go back to school. Zach was going to bankrupt her with his never-ending appetite.

"You sure you don't want any, Johnny?" Zach asked, knowing she wouldn't have any. She was more of the bite-sized dark chocolate kind of girl.

"No, thanks. I'm good." Johnny reached for the glass of wine he'd barely touched.

"Yeah. The best." Zach's voice held a bit of awe. He smiled at Johnny before heading off to the kitchen.

"He's really impressed." Alice kept her voice low; she didn't want to embarrass either of them. "He's always looked up to you, you know."

"Why is that?" Johnny asked. "Since I've always played on the other side of the country, how did he even know about me?"

"I've followed your career. Every step of the way." Alice barely had time to explain before Zach returned with his ice cream. Three scoops. Covered with chocolate syrup. And sprinkles.

"Zach, that's a little much."

"I'm sure he'll burn through those calories before he even finishes eating it." Johnny laughed. "He's built like I was at that age. It drove my mother crazy when I'd eat a whole week's worth of groceries in one day."

His mother. That was the first time she'd heard him mention her without a note of bitterness in his voice. Maybe he'd finally been able to forgive her for what she'd had to do just to get by.

"I don't eat that much." Zach shoveled ice cream into his mouth like he hadn't eaten in days. "Just when I'm hungry."

"Which seems to be all the time these days." Alice shook her head, but couldn't help but smile.

"So tell me something no one knows about you." Zach gulped down another bite. "Something about your family or when you were a kid."

"There's not much to tell." Johnny never did like being put on the spot. He especially didn't like talking about his past. But then, why would he? His mother had been a prostitute in one of Nevada's legal brothels and he'd never known who his father was.

"Did you have any brothers or sisters?"

"Nope. I'm an only child. Like you."

"Pets?"

"No. Just my ball and my glove."

"Did you ever name your glove?"

"No. I never did name my glove." Johnny smiled and gave her a look that showed amusement and hope the questions would get less personal.

"I read somewhere that you lived with your coach in high school. Is that true?"

"Yes. I did."

"Why?" Zach didn't seem to notice he was being a pest.

"Coach Ryan was like a father to me. He was a huge influence on my game. And my life. I don't think I would have made it to college or the majors if not for him."

"Cool." Zach seemed satisfied for the moment.

"It's getting late, young man. And we have a busy day ahead of us tomorrow." She took the opportunity to change the subject before Zach could ask any more questions. Questions she knew Johnny wouldn't want to answer. About his mother's profession. About her roommates who'd offered their services to Johnny, on the house. About why he couldn't finish high school under the same roof as the woman who'd given birth to him.

"Yeah, I know. It's just..." Zach glanced over at Johnny, like maybe he could help a fellow out. "There's so much I want to ask Johnny and I know he's not going to be around for very long."

"I'll be around." Johnny gave him a quick smile. "You'll see. Maybe we can play catch again tomorrow."

"That would be awesome." Zach jumped up, clearly excited about the prospect. "Maybe you could help me some more with my pitching."

"I'd be more than happy to work with you." He put a fatherly hand on his shoulder. "I think you've already got pretty good stuff."

"Really?" Zach looked up at him with such admiration. No, awe.

"Really." Johnny nodded. He meant it.

"I'll see you tomorrow." Zach's excitement was evident in the way he practically skipped up the stairs.

"You have no idea how much this means to him." Alice stood, suddenly aware that they were alone in the room. "He's nervous about moving up to the big field this year. Some of the kids are so much bigger than him. He's tall, but thin."

"He's got a good head for the game. His body will catch up. You'll see." Johnny was the voice of experience. "And I'll be around."

"Not for long. You've got six weeks of spring training. Then you'll be on the road half the time."

"But I'll be here half the time too." He moved closer, the heat from his body radiating in waves. "Look, if I'd known about Mel... No kid should have to grow up without a man in his life. I'd like to be there for Zach. If that's okay with you."

"Johnny, that's..." She swallowed the lump in her throat. "That would be wonderful."

"I know my schedule won't make it easy, but I want to be a part of his life." He actually sounded excited. "It's not the same as having his father here, but I'd like to think Mel would have stepped up if I'd had a son and couldn't be there for him."

He had no idea how Mel had stepped up.

Damn. He liked the kid. A lot. It surprised him. But it also made it possible for him to accept their dinner invitation. It hadn't been that bad. Considering the torture of sitting in the same room as Alice. In the house Mel had given her. With the child he'd given her.

But Mel wasn't here anymore. Johnny was. Did that mean he could just forget what they'd done to him? He wasn't sure. He wasn't sure if he'd be able to forgive them. But knew he had to try.

For the kid's sake.

"Can I help you with the dishes?" Johnny stood with his plate. Feeling awkward that he needed to even ask. There'd been a time when they worked as a team. They could read each other's body language to find out what the other needed. He'd never had that kind of connection with anyone else.

"Thanks." Alice gathered her dishes and Johnny helped with the rest. "I usually have Zach clear the table, but he really does need to get cracking on his homework."

"He's a great kid." Johnny followed her into the kitchen.

"I don't know what I did to deserve him." She sighed. A dreamy, proud, awestruck kind of sigh. Stopping him from blurting out something about her having slept with his best friend.

"You've done a hell of a job with him."

"I had a lot of help. Frannie was amazing, especially in those early years." Alice let out another sigh. "And Mel Senior has been wonderful, too. He takes Zach golfing. And sailing. They both take him to museums and art galleries. Expose him to all that San Francisco has to offer."

"That's great." Johnny helped her load the dishwasher. "How about your family? Do they spend a lot of time with Zach?"

"We spend some time up there every summer." Alice rinsed the plate she'd already cleared off. "They're not real close with him, like they are with my brother's kids. But you know?"

Yeah. He knew. Alice had never been close with her parents. She'd been the reason they had to get married. They hadn't exactly neglected her, but it seemed like they never fully appreciated her either.

"It's a good thing he has one set of grandparents he's close to." Johnny didn't have any. His family had consisted of him and his mother. And he hadn't had much of a relationship with her growing up. She tried, but Johnny couldn't get past the shame of her profession to feel especially close to her. It was out of guilt more than love that he bought her a house in Vegas as soon as he was able. He sent her money, made sure she was well taken care of, but he didn't visit very often.

"Yes. It is a good thing." Her hand shook a little, and the plate nearly slipped as she reached for the dishwasher.

Johnny rescued the dish, placing it carefully in the lower rack.

"Thank you." She rested her hands on the counter, steadying herself.

"Do I make you nervous?" Johnny slid his hands around her waist. He couldn't help himself. It felt so natural. Like old times.

"A little." But she leaned back against him. Sighing.

"Ali." He breathed her in. Her hair smelled good. Familiar. Was it possible she still used the same shampoo she'd used in college? He nuzzled her neck before spinning her around and lowering his mouth for a kiss. A long, slow, deep kiss that almost transported them back in time.

Almost.

"Johnny. I can't . . ." She pushed him away. "I can't do this."

"I can finish the dishes. No problem." Johnny had said the first thing to come to mind. Damn. He was a fool. To think she could want him. "Still not over your husband?" He backed up, putting much needed space between them.

"No. Not that. I . . ." She looked up at him, her eyes stormy. A deep, dark blue.

"How did it happen?" Johnny had spent the last few days wondering. He could have done the research, but he needed to hear it from her. "How did Mel die?"

"A car accident." She held her head high and steady. But she didn't look at him; she gazed off in the distance. Into the past. "It was raining. And we'd had a fight."

He willed his feet to stay still. As much as he wanted to pull her back into his arms, he knew that wasn't going to make everything okay. "What was the fight about?"

She folded her arms across her chest. Shutting him out. Maybe trying to shut out the memories. "Mel wanted to have another baby. But Zach was starting school, and while I enjoyed helping in his class, it wasn't enough."

"You had dreams of your own." She'd wanted to be a teacher almost as much as Johnny wanted to play baseball. Maybe even more. "And you didn't want to put them on hold any longer."

"Yes, but that's exactly what I've done." She picked up a dishcloth, but didn't return to the sink. "I jumped right into the foundation and never looked back. Until recently."

"You're not happy with your work?" Johnny inched closer. His lips were still humming from their kiss. "You need something more?"

"I thought about going back to school. I miss Nevada." She closed her eyes and inhaled as if she was trying to catch a whiff of the sagebrush they'd grown up around. The smell of home. "I want to go back and finish my credential. I've even filled out the application, ready to send . . . But I can't take Zach from everything he knows. I can't take him from his grandparents."

"He's almost in high school. He's going to move on in, what . . . five years?" Johnny wasn't sure exactly how old he was. Only that Alice told him she married Mel because she was pregnant. They got married the day after graduation. Imagine his surprise when he'd opened a wedding announcement instead of news of the commencement ceremony he'd missed.

"I know. And that's even more reason for me to move forward, but . . ." She blinked hard. She'd never been one of those weepy females. She'd cried when he was drafted, but not when she'd said goodbye. "I don't know if they can take another loss."

"You really care about them, don't you?" Johnny admired her loyalty. He just wished she'd directed some of it toward him.

"They need me." She turned her attention back to the dishes. "Maybe it's just not meant to be. It seems like every time I try to take that final step, something comes up. Getting pregnant, then Mel's accident."

"What's stopping you now?" Johnny moved closer. He couldn't help himself.

"You." She flashed him a weak smile, stopping him in his tracks.

Chapter 5

He was the one holding her back? Sure, she'd tried to backtrack. To stutter out a weak "you wouldn't understand," and a bunch of nonsense about how the Harrisons were good to her and Zach and she owed it to them to stick around and how rewarding working for the foundation was. But he'd seen it in her eyes. She was afraid to move forward. Because of him.

He'd helped with the last of the dishes and left with some lame excuse about an early morning appointment. But his morning run hadn't done a damn thing to get her out of his head.

They weren't over. She'd married Mel, but eight years after his death, she hadn't moved on. Not out of loyalty to her husband. But because of him.

And Johnny?

He'd known for a long time that he wasn't ever going to get over her. So he'd stopped trying. He could spout all kinds of nonsense about commitment to his team. To his game. But the real reason he hadn't moved on was because he didn't want to.

He'd found a refuge in baseball as a child. He'd returned to that refuge when Alice left him. He wasn't going to be able to hide behind his glove much longer. His arm was slowing down. He still had control—most of the time—but it would only be a matter of time before much younger hitters would catch up to his fastball.

He needed to start thinking about his future. But first he had to face his past.

It was time for him to pay his respects to Mel's parents. He drove across town to their house, fully expecting them to slam the door in his face. Sure, they could forgive him for not coming to the wedding. They were probably relieved he hadn't shown up. He might have tried to stop it.

But he should have gone to Mel's funeral. They'd treated Johnny like part of the family. He should have been there for them.

"Hello, Mrs. Harrison." Johnny took a deep breath to slow his heartbeat as Frannie opened the door. "I don't know if you remember me."

"Johnny Scottsdale." Frannie pulled him into a quick hug. "Of course we remember you. Come in. I heard you were coming to San Francisco. Mel would be so thrilled."

Which Mel? Her husband or son?

"Thank you." Johnny felt as out of place as the first time he'd come here. The Harrisons were one of San Francisco's oldest, most respected families. Generations sunk their roots into the community. And Johnny? For all he knew, he'd been named after his own father. Some nameless john who'd left his mother with more than just an evening's pay.

"I'm sorry I haven't been around." No words felt quite right. No excuse seemed good enough. "I let Mel down."

Frannie turned around. He almost expected her to ask him to leave. Instead she pulled him into a tight embrace.

"He missed you. He really did." She let go before he could start to feel smothered.

He felt awkward standing in the foyer of their elegant home. As always, there were fresh flowers artfully arranged on the front table. An antique, no doubt. The house was full of very stylish, classic furniture. It was like walking into a museum. Except for the warmth that Frannie and Mel Sr. shared with everyone who entered their home. Even him.

"Come on back to the kitchen. I have pie." Frannie had that mom thing down. The one he'd seen on TV, read about in books. The need to comfort and protect and feed.

"Of course you do." Surprised by the catch in his voice, he took a calming breath. "I'd love some."

"Great. It's good to have you home." She led the way to the kitchen, past the formal dining room with seating for twelve, the living room with grand piano and antique furniture and into the bright, warm kitchen that smelled as if she'd been baking just this morning. "I hear our Alice roped you into working the baseball camp."

"I was a last minute replacement." Johnny found it interesting that she claimed Alice as her own. "My manager asked and it seemed like a good way to fill my afternoons. I can only take so many cable car rides or tours of Alcatraz."

"I hear you're doing a fabulous job." Frannie gave him a generous slice of pie, with a large glass of milk to wash it down. "Zach is over the moon at finally getting to meet you."

"I guess I should have stayed in touch." Johnny wasn't sure what he could have done to impress the kid so much. He followed Alice's game plan, and played catch with the boy afterward.

"It's understandable why you didn't." She patted him on the shoulder before sitting down next to him, with a cup of coffee but no pie. "I'm not sure what kind of magic my son worked on Alice, but we are forever grateful she came into our lives. And brought that dear child of ours with her."

"He's a great kid. I can see why you're proud of him." Johnny took a bite of apple pie, hoping it would settle the churning in his stomach. He'd also like to know what kind of magic Mel had worked on Ali, but it didn't matter. The past was over and done with. Time to put yesterday's failures behind him.

"We couldn't be more proud of our boy." Frannie smiled warmly. "And Alice, too. She's a fine woman. A good mother. She's been... I don't know how we could have survived without her."

Johnny mumbled something about how sorry he was, but it seemed too little, too late.

"But enough about that. Tell me, how have you been?" She patted his hand. "Is it as exciting as it seems, being a superstar baseball player?"

"I don't know about being a superstar." Johnny felt his cheeks warm. "But yeah, baseball has been very good to me."

"You always were such a modest boy." She smiled affectionately. "We've followed your career very closely, you know. We couldn't have been prouder if... if you were Mel's true brother."

"Well, thank you. That's..." Damn. His throat tightened, the realization that he'd lost more than just his girl hitting him hard. "That's quite an honor."

She rose, to pour herself another cup of coffee. Her hands shook a little as she stirred cream and sugar before returning to the table.

"You know, Mel thought the world of you." Frannie sat down next to him. "He didn't have a lot of close friends growing up. He certainly never hung out with the jocks."

"No. I don't suppose he did." Johnny remembered the skinny kid who he'd been stuck rooming with that first year of college. Somehow, despite their vastly different upbringings, they had become fast friends. "But he didn't hold that against me."

"And you didn't hold it against him that he was a rich city kid." Frannie had been close with her son. Something Johnny envied more than he could ever admit. "The two of you managed to see past your differences and form a meaningful friendship."

"I should have been a bigger man," Johnny admitted. "I shouldn't have let Alice come between us."

"He shouldn't have . . ." She stared down at her coffee. "Can I get you more pie?"

"No. Thank you." Johnny had eaten more than his fill. "I should get going. Kids are counting on me."

"Alice has done a great job with that program, hasn't she?" Frannie stood. She took his empty plate and waited for him to drain his glass of milk. "We're awfully proud of her, too."

"Yeah. I can see that." He wasn't sure what he'd expected from this meeting. But this love fest wasn't it.

"I hope we'll see more of you now that you're here in the city." Frannie's smile was genuine. He wasn't sure why.

A light rap sounded on the back door.

"That would be our Alice now," Frannie said as the door swung open.

"Well, I really should be going now." Johnny stood. This time he was leaving. "Thank you for the pie."

He'd almost made it without seeing Alice again. Without his heart thudding in his chest. Without his head spinning when all the blood rushed below his waist as he recalled their kiss.

"Johnny, how nice to see you here." She said the polite thing, but she didn't sound all that pleased.

He'd reappeared in her life, and she was afraid. Afraid of the physical attraction still burning between them. They were adults. They could spend a week together and be able to control their hormones. Especially if the kid was around to chaperone. It was one thing to not care about being interrupted by a twenty-year-old roommate. But the chance of being caught by a thirteen-year-old kid was enough to keep them under control.

He hoped.

"I was just on my way out." He wiped his hands on his jeans. His palms were sweaty. His mouth dry. His heart thudded erratically. "I'll see you at the ballpark this afternoon."

"Yes. Of course. We'll see you there. It's going to be a great session." She tried to smile, but didn't quite pull it off.

"I'm looking forward to it." He then turned his attention to Mrs. Harrison. "Please give my regards to Mr. Harrison. I'll be in touch."

He nodded goodbye to the two Mrs. Harrisons, but it wasn't enough for Frannie.

"We'll see you soon." She gave him a quick peck on the cheek and a pat on the shoulder as he slipped out the back door. The door reserved for family. And friends.

"What was Johnny doing here?" Alice felt like she couldn't escape Johnny or a constant reminder of what she'd done to him.

"Having a slice of pie." Frannie put the teakettle on the stove and placed a cup on the table for Alice.

She stopped by most mornings after taking Zach to school. It was their daily bonding session. They usually ended up talking about foundation business, but in an informal way. Bouncing ideas off each other, sharing visionary goals, having the kind of discussions they couldn't at a formal board meeting.

"Johnny doesn't eat sweets." At least, he hadn't. But it'd been a long time since she'd known him. Since she'd been able to anticipate his wants, his needs, his desires.

"I guess he didn't want to hurt my feelings." Frannie motioned for Alice to sit. The space was still warm. Still carried Johnny's scent.

"No. He wouldn't." Alice went ahead and took a deep breath. She wasn't going to escape him. Or the feelings that lingered like his aftershave.

"You two aren't finished." Frannie had her back to her, busy with the teakettle. The whistle sounded and she poured Alice a cup of Earl Grey, her favorite. "He still cares for you."

"I doubt that." Alice accepted the tea, holding it in front of her. "He tolerates me only enough to do his job for the camp."

"No. He regrets leaving you. I can see it in his eyes. In the way his heart stopped when you walked in that door."

"He may have regrets." Alice stirred a scant teaspoon of honey into her tea. "But he wasn't the one who left."

"He wasn't?" Frannie held her coffee mug in both hands, eyeing her suspiciously. "I was under the impression he chose his career over you."

"I made that choice. Not Johnny."

"Really? Why?"

That was a question she'd been unable to answer for the last fourteen years. She'd tried to convince herself she was only doing what was best for Johnny. Giving him a chance to be the star he'd become. She'd regretted her decision, but couldn't look back. She couldn't afford to. Not when she had a child to look after.

"I knew Mel caught you on the rebound." Frannie was a realist. She knew Alice and Mel's marriage had been more about friendship than passion. "I assumed Johnny had been the one to leave. That Mel was there to pick up the pieces."

"No. I left Johnny. And I chose Mel." He'd been there to pick up the pieces, but she'd been the one to shatter her own heart. She'd been the one to bring Mel along, eventually breaking him in the process.

"Oh honey, you don't have to lie to me." Frannie reached across the table and patted her hand. "And you don't have to lie to yourself."

Alice didn't know what to say. She tried to pull her hand away, but Frannie held on.

"Is Johnny Zach's father?" Frannie squeezed her hand.

"I don't know." Alice squeezed back. "It could have been either of them."

"I see." Her tone held just enough reproach to make Alice feel like a slut. She'd only been with two men in her life, but it didn't matter. She had slept with them within the same month. She would need a DNA test to determine who the father was.

"Well. It doesn't matter to me." Frannie let go of her hand. "Zach is my grandson, biologically or otherwise. He will always have a place in my heart. In my family."

"Of course." She didn't want to hurt the woman who'd been so good to her. Didn't want to take away the only family she had left.

"But it's not my family you need to worry about. It's yours." Frannie stood, gathering the cups. "You need to do what is best for Zach. And for Johnny."

She'd thought she'd done that. Marrying Mel had seemed like the only choice at the time. If she'd gone to Johnny with the news of her pregnancy, he would have quit baseball. They would have struggled and he would have ended up resenting her. Especially if it turned out that Mel was the father of her child.

Mel knew the child could have been Johnny's. He was no fool. But he didn't want to find out. He proposed, with the understanding that if she took his name, the child would be his. But Mel wasn't here anymore. And Johnny needed to know the truth.

They all did.

Zach had done most of his homework in class and during his lunch period. He hoped Johnny still wanted to throw with him, and he didn't want to let something as boring as schoolwork get in the way.

They drove straight to the ballpark after school. Johnny was already there. Ready for the day's activities.

"Hey there, champ." Johnny gave him an encouraging smile. "How's it going?"

"Good. Can I tag along with you again?" He hoped like crazy that Johnny would say yes.

"Sure. We made a pretty good team yesterday." Johnny clapped him on the back and for a minute there, Zach wished he could have Johnny around all the time. "Unless your mom needs you somewhere else."

Johnny and Mom looked at each other. It was kind of weird. Like they liked each other, but didn't. Mom looked away and shook her head.

"No. You can have Zach again today. I think that would be great." Her voice was kind of thick. Like she was happy and sad at the same time.

"Great," Zach and Johnny said in unison.

"You two have fun." Mom smiled at Zach and then at Johnny. She seemed to smile at Johnny a little longer, but maybe Zach was imagining things.

They gathered the equipment and set up their station before the other kids got there. Today they were going to work some more on throwing and catching. Basic stuff, but really important. Nothing worse than making a perfect throw only to have your teammate drop the ball.

They wouldn't get to pitching until Thursday. By that time they would know which kids had a strong enough arm to be good pitchers. They'd still give everyone a chance to try. Because that's the kind of camp this was. It wasn't like some coaches who'd decided before the first practice who would be their pitchers and who would be stuck in right field. Zach didn't mind playing right field. He liked making catches at the fence or getting a ball on one hop and throwing the runner out at the plate.

But he really wanted to be a pitcher. He wanted to be like Johnny Scottsdale. To control the game. To get strikeouts or weak ground balls. He liked snagging come-backers to the mound without even thinking about it. He liked hearing the umpire yell "Strike!" He liked the tension of the battle between batter and pitcher.

But he wasn't sure if he was good enough anymore. As his opponents got bigger and stronger and knew more about how to hit, he needed more than being able to get the ball over the plate.

Johnny could help. Maybe. He could teach him how to be a better pitcher. Help him be the kind of player that people other than his mom and grandparents would want to watch.

The camp was fun, and it went by quick enough. Johnny was great with the kids, no surprise there. Zach couldn't wait to get his glove and learn as much as he possibly could from Johnny while he was here.

"Hey Johnny, you still want to warm up with me?" No, that didn't sound lame or too eager.

"Sure. Let me get my glove." Johnny smiled like he wasn't annoyed at all to have some kid bugging him after a long day. "Is your mom going to join us?"

"No." His mom was still acting weird. Maybe she was nervous

about the camp going well. She'd told him one time that putting on the camp was kind of like playing in a big game for her. "She has some stuff to do, paperwork or something."

"Well, let's get to it, then." Johnny patted him on the shoulder and led him down to the practice mound.

They started with a slow warm-up, tossing the ball back and forth. Like a kid playing catch with his dad. Stupid for even thinking something like that could happen. His mom was kind of avoiding Johnny. It's not like she'd start dating him all of a sudden. It was starting to look like she'd never date anyone. Ever. For all he knew, she'd follow him when he went off to college. Wouldn't that be lame?

"Okay, let me get some catcher's gear on," Johnny said once they were warm. "You throw too hard for me to try to catch you unprotected."

"Really?" Zach didn't think Johnny was the kind of guy to say stuff just to make him feel good. But he didn't really know him. Just the image of him he had from watching him his whole life. But so far, the real guy was even better. He was cool. Not like a famous person, but just a regular guy. He didn't show off or act like he was too good for anyone.

"Yeah, you've got good stuff. A natural."

"You're just saying that." Zach felt his face get kind of warm.

"No. You're good. Maybe you could be really good." Johnny sounded like he meant it. "Are you planning on playing in high school?"

"I hope so." But in high school, not everyone made the team. And he didn't know if he was going to get much bigger. His dad hadn't been very tall. In some pictures, it looked like he and his mom were almost the same height.

Johnny was, like, six-five. Zach wished he could be at least six feet tall. But since no one in his family was that tall, he figured he didn't have much of a shot.

"I don't know if I can throw hard enough." Zach knew a kid who threw really hard. He threw a no-hitter twice in Little League. "I'm moving up to a bigger field. The same size the pros use."

"You'll get used to it real quick," Johnny assured him. "Trust me, you'll be ready."

"Thanks." Zach still couldn't believe he was playing catch with *the* Johnny Scottsdale. "I know you're only working with me because you knew my dad, but thanks."

"Your dad was one of my best friends ever." Johnny turned and looked right at him. "Your mom, too. But that's not the only reason I'm helping you." He smiled then. A real and encouraging smile. "You have something here." Johnny grabbed his right arm. His pitching arm. "You remind me a little of myself."

Wow. He couldn't think of a bigger compliment.

"I guess I try to copy you." Zach was a little embarrassed by the comparison. "I mean, we DVR every one of your starts."

"Really?" Johnny seemed surprised.

"Yeah. My mom's always been kind of crazy about you."

Now Johnny looked like he was embarrassed. He looked down at his feet.

"Well, it seems like you've picked up some good habits." Johnny grabbed a ball. "Let's fine tune your mechanics and if you keep working at it, I think you'll be great."

"Cool."

Johnny put on the mask and crouched behind the plate.

Zach tried to remember everything Johnny told him. But he was all jittery. Johnny Scottsdale thought he was good. Thought he could be great, even.

Johnny stood up.

"Sorry. I'm taking too long." Zach tried to refocus. But Johnny walked toward him and put his hands on his shoulders.

"You're in control. You decide when to make the throw. I'm just here to catch it."

"I know, I'm just . . ."

"Focus. Breathe. Let it go." Johnny closed his eyes, like he did when he pitched. "That's what I tell myself when I'm on the mound. Sort of my mantra."

"Focus. Breathe. Let it go." Zach had always wondered what Johnny's secret was. Now he knew.

Johnny returned to his spot behind the plate. He got ready and Zach felt like he was ready now, too.

Focus.

Zach looked in at his target. Didn't even think about who was holding the glove.

Breathe.

He took a deep breath. Held it.

Then he let it go.

He fired the pitch and hit the target. It made a loud pop in Johnny's glove.

"Great. Just like that." Johnny tossed the ball back to him and got ready for the next pitch.

Zach repeated the whole routine. Again. And again. Each throw better than the last. Louder. Stronger. Maybe even faster.

They were getting into a good rhythm when Zach's mom came up to them.

Johnny stood, tucking the catcher's mask and glove under his left arm. He and Mom stared at each other, like they were surprised to see the other one here. Johnny didn't even seem to notice that a reporter was there, too. The friendly one who did all the dugout interviews.

"Johnny. This is Rachel Parker." His mom finally shook out of her trance. "With Bay Area Sports Network. She's here to do a feature on you."

"Sure." Johnny put on his interview smile. The one that was a little fake, but not too phony. "Zach's got a few more pitches to throw. Maybe Alice could catch him."

He turned back to his mom and smiled for real.

"He looked like he was throwing pretty hard." She didn't like catching him lately; she flinched too easily.

"You used to catch me." Johnny's voice sounded different. Like he was sharing some secret between the two of them. "And I was pretty wild back then. Zach has good control. You'll be fine."

"He is pretty good, isn't he?" She tore her eyes away from Johnny and smiled at Zach, totally embarrassing him.

"Yes. He is. If you can finish up here, I'll be ready for that interview." He looked at Rachel Parker, who was just standing there, probably taking mental notes. Zach really hoped she didn't say anything about him in the interview.

"My cameraman is set up in the press room." Rachel flashed her reporter smile at Johnny. "Maybe you could throw on a jersey and we'll get started."

"Sure. Give me ten minutes?"

"Sounds perfect." She glanced briefly at Zach and then his mom before turning and walking toward the press room.

"I gotta go." Johnny patted Zach on the back. "But your mom will finish you up. Say about ten, fifteen more throws."

"Okay. And I'll put everything away when we're done."

"I can take care of it," Johnny offered.

"No. I don't mind." Zach was used to helping out, putting stuff away. He didn't always remember at home, but his mom had him pretty well trained. Most of the time.

Johnny nodded at him and walked off for his interview.

Chapter 6

"This is Rachel Parker, with Bay Area Sports Net." The auburn haired reporter sat across from Johnny in the press room. She'd set up a couple of chairs to make it look like they were two friends, having a chat. "Today our guest is Johnny 'The Monk' Scottsdale, a right-handed pitcher for the San Francisco Goliaths."

"Thank you, Rachel. I'm happy to be here." He hoped he sounded sincere. He really would rather be working with Zach, though. He didn't have a lot of time to get the kid ready for the season. He was close, but there were a few little things he could do to tweak his delivery.

"You've had quite a career so far. Two Cy Young Awards, numerous All-Star appearances and one perfect game." The reporter let him know she'd done her homework. "What brings you here to San Francisco?"

"I think you probably know the answer to that." Johnny gave his aw-shucks grin. "I'm looking for the same thing all athletes want. A chance to play in the biggest game of our lives. To leave a lasting mark on our sport. To earn a ring. I think I'll be a good fit with this team, this group of players. I hope that together we can bring home a championship."

"The Goliaths have one of the strongest rotations in the league. It's almost not fair to add a starter with your credentials." She leaned forward. "Some fans would say the team would be better off going after a big bat."

Johnny took a deep breath. He'd heard that argument enough times, he should have a clever answer by now.

"But we've all seen how dominant pitching can be more than enough to quiet even the loudest bats." She smiled at him almost flirtatiously.

"I do believe that winning at any level requires teamwork. No one man can make or break a season," Johnny said. "When I'm not as sharp as I need to be, I have guys behind me who will pick me up. When I threw my perfect game, my defense was spectacular. They made plays that weren't human. It was like we fed off each other."

"I've seen the replays of that catch in centerfield." She nodded in agreement. "It was like Andrews sprouted wings."

"He didn't want to let me down." Johnny would miss his old teammates. But most of them were gone, too. After making it to the American League Championship two years ago, they didn't make the playoffs last year. The team wanted to move in a new direction. They let go or traded most of their stars. He wouldn't be surprised if the team itself wasn't up for sale in the next year or two.

"She glanced down at her notes. "According to my sources, you turned down a long-term contract offer from Chicago."

"Who wouldn't want to come to San Francisco?" He smiled for the camera. "The Goliaths organization is one of the finest in all of baseball. The ballpark is beautiful. The fans are amazing. And there's a lot of talent on this team."

"You'll only add to that talent. And at a bargain price." She leaned forward, making Johnny a tad uncomfortable. "I'm sure we'll all be very pleased with the acquisition."

"Thank you." Johnny found that a simple response to praise was the easiest. He didn't want to talk about his contract. His agent wasn't very happy with him for accepting a lower offer, a one-year deal, but Johnny had his reasons for coming here. Getting a ring was only one of them.

"You're already making your presence known here in San Francisco." She tapped her pen against her thigh. "You're participating in the Mel Harrison Jr. Foundation's annual minicamp for youth players."

"Yes. Actually, Mel Harrison was a friend of mine in college. I think it's a . . ." Johnny swallowed, the sting of losing his friend causing an unexpected lump in his throat. "It's a nice way to honor his memory."

"I wasn't aware of the connection." Rachel sounded flustered for an instant. Like a straight-A student getting an answer wrong for the first time. "But I'm sure he'd be proud of the work you're doing to help young ballplayers."

"Yes. Kids are the future. Without them, there would be no reason to play." Did that sound corny or what?

She laughed, a throaty, seductive laugh that made him feel more than a little uncomfortable. He wondered if she would ask him about his work with Zach. He hoped not. He wasn't sure if he could explain why it was so important for him to take the boy under his wing. Why he felt like he owed it to Mel to help his son.

"The Harrison Foundation has made a difference in the lives of so many kids in our area." She dialed down the charm enough to make Johnny relax. "They must have been pleased to have you step in at the last minute when Nathan Cooper was suspended."

"I'm more than happy to help. I've met some terrific kids this week." Johnny wanted to deflect the conversation away from steroids. The focus should be on the kids. On the game. "Real hard-workers. Eager to learn. Ready to play."

"And they're lucky to have such a stellar role model." She got a certain glint in her eye. The conversation was about to get personal. "They call you 'The Monk.' Can you share the origins of that nickname?"

"I think it has something to do with the way I'm able to shut down all outside distractions." Johnny breathed in, trying to bring that sense of calm to this interview, without going through his whole routine. "I keep my focus on the next pitch. I don't think about the last one that didn't fall right where I wanted it. I don't think about the last time I faced this batter and whether or not he took me deep. And I don't think about anything other than my game."

"I have heard that theory." She tilted her head just enough to signal she had something else in mind. "But something tells me it's only part of the story."

"Oh really?" Did she honestly have nothing better to talk about?

"Your reputation around the league is somewhat unique." She smiled in a way that made him think she was almost embarrassed to take the questions in this direction. Almost. "Or is your celibacy exaggerated?"

"I prefer to keep my personal life private."

"Is it because of a religious conviction?" Genuine curiosity in her tone was the only thing that made him willing to continue this conversation. That and the fact he was on camera.

"For some, baseball is like a religion. But no, it's not because of any particular religious beliefs." Johnny wondered if Alice would catch the broadcast. Now that he knew she'd been watching his entire career, he thought it was likely. "It's more of a personal choice. If I'm not in a serious relationship, I choose to remain celibate. End of story."

"You do have a lot of self-control." Her gaze dropped to take in the whole package. "You're a young, healthy, vibrant man."

"Sure, and when I need a physical release, I go for a run, lift weights or play catch."

"Well, that seems to be working. As your stats show."

"Yes, I've been fortunate that I'm able to put all my energy into my game." At least that's what he'd been telling himself.

"Don't you ever get lonely?" Was her curiosity professional or personal?

"Sure. But spending the night with a stranger doesn't cure that." He'd tried that. Once. He couldn't get his mind off knowing Ali was spending her wedding night with someone else. With Mel.

"So, Johnny Scottsdale, you're a romantic." Her voice took on a wistful tone.

"No. Just practical." He shrugged, hoping what he said next wouldn't paint him as some kind of jerk. "I know that there's an element of fantasy some women have about being with an athlete. Any athlete. Some guys are okay with that. I'm not."

Great, now he sounded like he thought he was too good for any woman. "Besides, I'm afraid of lawyers."

He punctuated that last remark with a sappy smile.

She laughed and then turned to the camera, wrapping up their interview. As soon as the camera stopped rolling, she turned back to Johnny.

"My boyfriend is a lawyer." She unclipped her microphone, but kept talking.

"Then I'm sure he'd appreciate guys like me who understand that your friendliness and professional interest don't mean anything more." Johnny wished since the interview was officially over, he'd be free to leave.

"He would." She gave him a smoldering look. "If my *ex*-boyfriend was the jealous type. Or the faithful type."

Johnny shook his head and laughed. An awkward, uncomfortable laugh.

"Oh, come on, you're a very attractive man, Johnny Scottsdale." She leaned forward enough to provide a glimpse of her lace bra. It was turquoise. Not that he wanted to know.

"I'm sure you say that to all the celibate Cy Young Award winning ballplayers you interview." Oh, hell that sounded an awful lot like flirting.

"I do." She laughed, flipping her hair back over her shoulder. "I interview dozens of good-looking ballplayers. Most of them think they're the greatest thing since free agency. You're different. You've got that untouchable thing going."

"I'm sort of seeing someone." He felt heat creep up the back of his neck. He had no idea where that statement had come from. Wishful thinking?

"Oh, you don't have to let me down that easy." There was more than a hint of disappointment in her voice.

The heat spread across his cheeks, like razor burn. Even worse, his mind strayed to thoughts of Alice. Did he really want to start things up with her again? His body was ready. Like a rookie just called up late in the season. *Put me in, coach.* But his heart had doubts. She'd taken him deep last time. Real deep.

"So, who is she?"

Johnny shook his head, forgetting where he was for a moment. "Like I said before, my personal life is, uh, personal."

"Don't worry, I'm not that kind of journalist." She smiled, a you-can-trust-me kind of smile.

"No, I'm sure you're a professional. And since our interview is officially over, I think I should stop talking." He returned his most sincere fake smile.

"Johnny Scottsdale, you really are more than what meets the eye." She dropped her gaze to his lap. "Not that what meets the eye is anything to complain about."

"I don't know what you mean." He tried to choose his words carefully. He didn't need to get on a reporter's bad side.

"Wow, do I really need to spell it out?" She shook her head, tossing her hair so it fell over one shoulder. "You're completely unaware of the power you have over women."

"It's not me. It's the uniform." Johnny wished she'd just let it go. Let him go.

"It's much more than that." She leaned forward and rested her hand on his knee. "Yes, you're an athlete. That means you've got an incredible body. But I see athletes every day. You're different. You're a challenge."

"I've been told I'm emotionally challenged." Why was he still talking to this woman?

"You just need the right woman to help you get in touch with your emotions."

"I don't think so." Johnny shifted his leg, letting her hand fall. "I should get going. I've taken enough of your time."

"I'm sure we'll be spending plenty of time together over the course of the season." She sounded very sure of herself. "I'm the dugout reporter. I'll be interviewing you after your wins. Who knows? Maybe I'll have the honor of catching you after your next perfect game."

"I think that was a once-in-a-lifetime experience." There were times when his perfection was more curse than blessing. It only made his less stellar performances stand out even more. Each failure loomed larger than before.

Maybe that was the explanation this reporter, and a few others, had been searching for. He'd had the perfect woman. He would never find another who could live up to her. So he'd quit looking.

He put everything he had into his game. Let it fill the empty spot in his life losing Alice had created. But he would be leaving the game behind someday. He needed to make sure he had something to take its place in his life. Or someone. And that someone could only be Alice.

Alice grabbed the remote and switched off the TV. She didn't need to watch anymore. It was painfully obvious the reporter was interested in Johnny. And he seemed to respond to her questions with an ease he didn't often have during interviews.

She wondered how long it would take for the woman to jump him. Would she at least wait until the camera stopped rolling?

Jealousy was a stupid emotion. Alice wiped hot tears from her eyes. She had no right. No right at all to feel this way. She'd given him up. So the Rachel Parkers of the world could have a shot at loving the great Johnny Scottsdale.

For the past fourteen years, she'd managed to compartmentalize her feelings for Johnny. He was a baseball player. Nothing more. An image on TV. A statistic on the back of a baseball card. Not a man. A living, breathing, feeling man. She could be proud of him when he earned successes on the field. She could feel bad for him when he had a rough night on the mound. She could even pretend his personal life meant nothing. That she wasn't secretly pleased he'd never married. That his love life never made headlines.

All that had gone away the minute he'd stepped back into her life. He wasn't just a ballplayer anymore. He was a man. *The man*. The man who made her heart quake. Who turned her legs to jelly. The man who made her want to remember what it meant to be a woman.

And he might be the father of her son.

The weight of everything came crashing down on her. She'd given him up. Married Mel and raised Zach as his son. She'd tried to put Johnny out of her mind. Out of her heart. But she'd failed. Miserably. Now it was all catching up to her. With a vengeance.

"Hey Mom, guess who's here . . ." Zach took one look at her face and concern overtook his usually cheerful features. "Are you okay? Have you been crying?"

"Oh, it's nothing." She wiped her eyes and tried to force a laugh. "Something I saw on TV. You know how I get."

She hoped he'd think she'd seen one of those sappy commercials for baby shampoo or greeting cards or something sentimental like that.

"Alice." Johnny stood behind Zach. She'd been so wrapped up in her misery, she hadn't even heard the door. "Did I come at a bad time?"

"No." She stood and smoothed her blouse, suddenly very aware of Johnny's presence. "I was watching one of those reality shows. They really suck you in."

Zach shoved his hands in his pockets. "You sure you're okay?"

He knew she didn't watch those types of shows. She preferred more educational programs. Like *History Detectives* or even *Mythbusters*. But watching the guys blow stuff up just across the bay wouldn't bring tears to her eyes.

"Yeah. I'm fine." She didn't need either of these two knowing why she was upset.

"Well, I've got to finish my homework." Zach was reluctant to leave, but he was a responsible kid. He knew if he got behind, she wouldn't let him attend the minicamp. "So I better get going."

"I hope you get all your homework done." Johnny beamed at Zach. Kind of like he was proud of him, too. "I'll need your help tomorrow."

"Yeah? Cool." Zach skipped up the stairs to his room.

"What are you doing here?" Since he'd told Zach he'd see him tomorrow, she didn't need to worry he was going to back out of the minicamp.

"I, uh . . ." He turned to watch Zach as he disappeared from sight. "He's a great kid. And he has the potential to be a good pitcher."

"Thank you for working with him. You have no idea how much it means." And she had no idea how to tell him.

"I'd like to talk to his coaches." Johnny was all business now. Shutting off his emotion like the flip of a switch. "He has a slight flaw in his delivery. A bad habit he's picked up. Totally correctable, but it will take time."

"Time you don't have." Her heart constricted at the idea of him leaving in less than two weeks. Not to mention, all the women who would be flocking toward him in Arizona.

"Right. Spring training is right around the corner." Johnny looked over her shoulder, studying the bookcase. The framed photos scattered amongst the books and knick-knacks. Baby pictures of Zach. She wondered if he had similar snapshots of his own youth. And if he could see the resemblance for himself.

"Unfortunately, I don't know who his coach will be. Tryouts aren't until the end of the month. Then it will be at least another week or two after that before we know who he'll end up with."

"Well, maybe you could send me his email address when you find out." Johnny met her gaze. "I'd like to keep track of his progress."

"Really?" She felt her throat tighten. Her heart constrict.

"Yeah, the kid's kind of growing on me." Johnny sounded surprised. But pleased. "I thought it would be hard to be around him. Since he's... Mel's. But, he's such a great kid."

The lump in her throat grew. She should tell him. Now. Before she lost her nerve.

He stepped toward her. "You have mascara, here."

He reached out and wiped the smudge under her left eye. Her lashes automatically fluttered closed at his touch. A sigh escaped her lips, an instant before he captured her mouth with his.

He pulled her closer. Closer. Kissing her like they'd been apart for merely a two-week road trip, not fourteen years. His hands wove through her hair. Moved down her back. She leaned against him. She could feel him, his need pressing against her belly. Her insides dissolved. Longing filled her. Powerful. Uncontrolled.

He slipped his hands underneath her blouse. Her breath caught at his touch. He groaned as he deepened the kiss. Sliding his hands higher, sending them both closer to the edge. His fingers slipped beneath her bra.

"Ali..." His breath was ragged, heavy with desire. "Oh, Ali."

She was about to surrender completely, when she heard the toilet flush upstairs.

Zach.

"Johnny. Wait." She pushed him away. Smoothed her blouse. Her hair. "Zach's upstairs. He could come down any minute."

"Right. Zach." Johnny stepped back and her heart gave a small whimper. "I should go."

"Johnny, please... Stay." They needed to talk. She needed to tell him the truth. Or what could be the truth about Zach.

"I really need to go." He retreated toward the front door. "I came here tonight to find out if there could be anything between us."

"I think the answer is pretty obvious." She didn't mean to gaze at his crotch, but the evidence was still there.

"The problem is..." He shoved his hands in his pockets, which only stretched his jeans tighter. "It's not only about us. You've got a kid. A great kid. But I'm not sure if I'm up for all this."

His eyes rested on the formal family portrait. He didn't need to tell her any more. He wasn't ready for a family.

* * *

Johnny got in his Jeep, wanting more than anything to get out of the city. He headed toward the Golden Gate Bridge, hoping he could get his thoughts clear by the time he got to the other side.

He shouldn't have kissed her. He shouldn't have started something he wasn't sure he could finish. She was a mother. He needed to think long and hard about that.

Having a relationship with Alice would mean having a relationship with Zach. He was still getting used to the idea of being a mentor. Could he step into the role of father figure? The toughest years were right around the corner. High school. And everything that came with it. Girls. Sports. College and Major League scouts.

Johnny wouldn't have been able to deal with all of that if it hadn't been for his coach and mentor. Coach Ryan had taken an interest in him. Helped him not only with baseball, but with life. He'd eventually moved in with Ryan and his wife. They'd kept him focused on school and helped him with his college applications and scholarships.

Johnny never would have managed to go to college without his help. Never would have met Alice.

She felt so good in his arms. Too good. He'd come pretty damn close to losing control with her tonight. If she hadn't pulled away, he might have put them both in a compromising position.

That was something no thirteen-year-old boy wanted to even think about his mother doing, let alone witness.

No. Johnny needed to make a game plan where Alice was concerned. He'd have until the end of the week to work with her and Zach at the minicamp. That didn't give him much time to figure things out.

He pulled onto the bridge. Traffic was fairly light this time of night, but nowhere near the open road he longed for. He needed space and time to think. Two things that were just out of his reach.

Damn. What had he been thinking, coming to San Francisco? It wasn't just about taking a shot at the postseason. There were plenty of teams with as much of a chance as the Goliaths. Some with an even better chance. So yeah, he could stop pretending he didn't have a personal reason for coming here.

Alice.

He could admit that now. He hadn't been able to let her go. He'd jumped at the chance to play here because he needed to get on with his life. Baseball wouldn't be there for him forever. And he needed closure with her before he could even think of moving forward.

He'd thought if he saw her again—saw she was happy with Mel—he could finally let her go. He didn't know what he would have done if she'd been married and miserable. If he'd found out Mel had been unfaithful to her, or if he'd hurt her in any way.

At least he didn't have to worry about that.

He just needed to worry about whether or not he could make her happy. He'd sure as hell try a lot harder to give her what she needed outside of the bedroom. Especially now that there was so much more at stake. She had a son who wouldn't take too kindly to Johnny coming in and messing with her heart. Johnny got the feeling Zach's admiration of him would disappear if he ever hurt Alice.

He'd have to make sure he didn't hurt her.

Chapter 7

"Hey, Johnny, can I ask you something?" Zach helped gather up the balls and toss them into the equipment bucket.

"Yeah, sure, what's on your mind?"

"Um... do you have a girlfriend?" He glanced up but quickly busied himself in his task. "What I mean is, how come you're not married?"

"I guess I'm sort of married to my job." Lame excuse, he knew, but it was better than the truth.

"But you've had girlfriends, and stuff."

"Yeah. Not many, but I've had girlfriends before." He wasn't going to mention that one of them was the boy's mother.

"See... there's this thing... it's, uh..." The boy was blushing. Embarrassed to bring up the subject.

"Look, kid, are you sure you want dating advice from a guy called 'The Monk?'"

"No." His blush deepened. "I mean, they call you that because you're so calm and in control on the mound."

"That's one reason the name stuck." Johnny tried not to laugh. The kid sounded like he was seriously in need of advice. "But originally it was a joke. Because I didn't... oh... how do I put this?"

"You didn't hook up with a lot of girls?" Zach turned a ball over and over in his hands. A habit Johnny also had when he was uncomfortable talking about something. "Groupies and stuff?"

"Yeah. That's exactly why I got the nickname. I never hooked up with groupies." Yet they'd still managed to cost him his relationship with Alice.

"Cool." Zach studied the stitches on the baseball as if he'd find the meaning of life in the raised red threads. "I mean, I think groupies are kind of lame."

Couldn't agree with the kid more.

"But you do like girls?" He looked up, almost afraid to ask the question.

"Yeah. I like girls." One girl in particular, but this was hardly the time or place to discuss that.

"Cool. Because there's this thing Saturday night. A fundraiser for the foundation." Zach took a deep breath. And looked Johnny straight in the eye. "I think you should take my mom."

"Really?" He was trying to set them up. Interesting.

"Yeah. I mean, she has to go anyway, but it would be nice if she had a date." Zach's ears were a little pink. But his brown eyes looked so sincere and full of genuine concern for his mother. "She never goes on dates. It's . . . not . . . normal."

"Well, maybe she doesn't have time to date." Johnny didn't want to get too excited about this revelation. Maybe she was just discreet. "She's busy raising you, and working for the foundation."

"Yeah, but she needs to get a life." Zach looked up at Johnny, almost shocked at the boldness of his statement. "I mean, I can't be the only man in her life forever, you know."

"No. I guess not." Johnny barely contained a smirk. "Do you think she'd want to go with me?"

"Yeah. I think she totally would." Zach now sounded pretty sure of himself. "She likes you. I mean, she thinks you're totally awesome."

"Liking what I do on the field is one thing." Johnny needed to make sure neither of them got their hopes up too high. "Liking me for me is something else."

"Yeah. I guess that's the downside of being a famous athlete." Zach tossed the last ball into the bucket. "But that's what's cool about my mom. She knew you before you were famous. Besides, she doesn't need your money. So, you don't have to worry about that."

"No. I guess not." Mel would have made sure she and Zach were well taken care of.

"I know she likes you. I see the way she looks at you." Zach stuck his hands in his pockets. Another habit Johnny shared when he was nervous. "I see the way you look at her, too. But I think maybe you're worried that it would be weird. Because she was married before. To your friend."

The lump in Johnny's throat made it impossible to acknowledge the weirdness.

"But I think my dad would be okay with it." Zach continued his persuasion. "I mean, I don't remember him much, but I think he would want her to be happy. And he could trust you."

The kid looked down at his feet, and then lifted his head to look Johnny in the eye. "I trust you."

"Thanks. That means a lot." Johnny found his voice. Somehow. "But the important thing is whether or not your mom trusts me."

"She should." Zach had total faith in him. "You would never cheat on her or anything. I know you wouldn't."

"No. I wouldn't." If only it was that simple. "But I couldn't quite convince her of that years ago."

"Huh?" Zach shook his head, like he couldn't have heard him correctly.

"I dated your mom in college." Maybe he shouldn't have said that.

"Before she married my dad?" Zach's wide-eyed expression showed his surprise.

"Yeah. For three years. But . . ." How did it still hurt this much?

"You guys broke up." Zach nodded, as if he understood.

Yeah. They broke up.

"But now you have a second chance," Zach added hopefully. "You can start by taking her to the Golden Gate Gala."

"The Golden Gate Gala?" Sounded like quite the party.

"Yeah, that thing I was telling you about." Zach shuffled his feet.

"Is it a dressy event?" Johnny asked. "Will I need to wear a tux?"

"Yeah. I guess." Zach shrugged. Pretending it didn't matter one way or the other. Which told Johnny it was pretty important. "It's kind of fancy."

"I'll want to get a limo." A game plan was starting to fall into place.

"So, you'll take her?" Zach looked at him with such hope in his eyes, Johnny knew he didn't want to let the kid down. Ever.

"If she'll go with me." He wasn't about to tell the kid that she'd been the one to pull away fourteen years ago. And again last night. She'd pushed him out the door. But this time, he wasn't going willingly. This time, he'd fight for her.

"Just ask her," Zach pleaded.

If only it were that simple.

"She has to go. She might as well go with you."

"You think that'll work?" Johnny hoped she'd be more enthusiastic at the prospect.

"She'd be crazy to say no."

"I hope you're right." Johnny was starting to like this kid even more. "You got any tips to make sure she says yes?"

"How did you get her to go out with you the first time?" Zach's curiosity seemed sincere.

"I asked her to dance."

"Really?"

"Yeah. Your dad dragged me to this back-to-school dance on campus." Johnny smiled at the memory. It had been one of the best days of his life. Right up there with getting drafted. His Major League debut. Pitching a perfect game. "Mel saw this girl hanging off to the side behind the tall speakers by the stage. He thought she was pretty. She was pretty. But Mel was too shy to talk to her. So he talked me into breaking the ice."

"That wasn't too smart." Zach grinned, anticipating the rest of the story. "I can only guess what happened."

"I walked up to her, to tell her my friend wanted to meet her." Johnny could see her face even now. "But she looked so perfect. So content. She was dancing. All by herself. But she didn't look lonely. Not at all. More like she belonged there. So I walked up to her and started dancing with her. Like it was . . . meant to be."

"Cool." If Zach thought he sounded like a lovesick fool, he didn't show it.

"I guess she thought so." They'd been inseparable after that. Until he was drafted. And her fear came between them.

"They have dancing at the Golden Gate Gala." Zach encouraged him. "Maybe you could dance with her again."

Maybe.

"Hey what are you two conspiring about?" Alice appeared and for a minute, Johnny saw her as she'd been that first night. So beautiful. And completely unaware of her effect on him.

"The Golden Gate Gala." Johnny stepped forward. It was time for him to make his move. "Zach tells me it's a fancy party."

"Oh, yeah. It's our major fundraiser. I guess I forgot to mention it." She twisted a strand of her hair. "I don't expect you to feel obligated or anything."

"Does that mean you don't want me to attend?" The old fear that he wasn't quite good enough lingered.

"Oh, no. I just know it's not your kind of thing." She glanced at Zach, as if she wasn't too happy about him telling Johnny about the event.

"It could be." Johnny moved closer, close enough to reach out and touch her.

"I forgot something out on the field." Zach made an excuse to leave the two of them alone. Smart kid.

"You don't have to make an appearance." She lowered her gaze. "It's no big deal."

"Do you already have a date?" Johnny placed his hand on her shoulder. "Is that why you don't want me there?"

"A date?" She flinched. At his touch, or the suggestion that she had a date? "Of course not."

"Would you like one?" He slid his finger under her chin, tilting her head so he could see the surprise in her eyes. "Would you like to go to the Golden Gate Gala with me?"

She was speechless. Stunned by his offer? Or trying to figure out a way to politely decline?

"Please, Ali?" His heart stopped, waiting for her answer. "I really want to take you out in style. I'll wear a tux. Rent a limo. I'll even spring for some fancy champagne."

"I'll be working." She hadn't said yes, but she hadn't said no, either. "I should skip the champagne."

"What about the limo?" There'd been a time when he wouldn't have had to beg.

"Are you sure?" She tilted her face toward his, something like hope shining in her blue eyes. "There will be a bunch of stuffy rich people there."

"In case you forgot, I'm pretty rich now, too." She was trying to protect him. He was touched by her concern. "I'll bring my checkbook. I'd like to contribute to the cause."

"That's wonderful, Johnny." Her voice softened. It was obvious she cared a lot about her foundation.

"Does that mean you'll go with me?" His heart hammered in expectation. And hope.

She nodded.

"Great. I'll pick you up on Saturday." He sealed the deal with a quick kiss. A slight brush of his lips on hers. But it was enough for him to feel her tremble. "Who knows, I might get used to the lifestyle of the rich and famous. It could be fun."

"There will be reporters," she warned.

"I can handle a few reporters."

"Like Rachel Parker?" She had the slightest hint of contempt in her voice. Or was it jealousy?

"You saw the interview?" He tried not to chuckle. It probably looked as uncomfortable as it felt.

"Yes. I did." She folded her arms across her chest. "She seemed to really like you."

"I'm sure it's an act." He hoped. "Besides, I told her I was seeing someone."

"Oh?" He saw a flicker of suspicion in her eyes.

"And that was before I even knew about the Golden Gate Gala."

"You have no idea what you're getting into." She uncrossed her arms, her posture relaxed, and her features broke into a teasing grin.

"I think I can use my imagination." Not to mention his memory. He could recall exactly what he was getting into.

"So are you going to the Gala with Johnny?" Zach had waited until they got into the car before bringing up the subject. He didn't want to sound too eager. But he hoped they would get together.

"Is that what you two were up to? A little matchmaking?"

"Why didn't you tell me you used to go out with Johnny?" Was he actually having this conversation with his mom?

"Well, that was a long time ago." Her grip tightened on the steering wheel.

"Did you, like, love him?"

"Yes." She kept staring straight ahead. Like she was concentrating on the road, but she almost ran a red light. "Yes, I did."

"Did he love you?"

"Yes. I'm pretty sure he did."

"Why did you break up, then?" Zach wasn't sure he wanted to know the answer. He had a feeling it had something to do with his dad.

"Johnny was drafted by Kansas City. And we thought..." She pulled up to the next light, stopping in plenty of time. "I thought Johnny would be better off only having to worry about making the team."

"So you didn't cheat on him?" Zach had to ask. He had to know. "You didn't break up because you were with my dad?"

"No." She turned toward him, a strange look on her face.

"Good. Because I'd hate to think you could have been with Johnny Scottsdale if it wasn't for me."

The light changed and she pulled into the intersection.

"Why on Earth would you even ask that?"

"Look, Mom. I'm not stupid." She'd made sure he knew all about where babies come from. "I know when my birthday is. And I know when you got married. There were a lot less than nine months in between."

"Oh, Zach." She braked to let a bus pull into the street.

"I always knew you only married Dad because of me." It wasn't that big of a deal. Half his friends were in a similar situation.

"That's not..." She almost lied to him.

"It is true. Don't even try to tell me it's not." He knew he shouldn't talk back to her, but he couldn't help it. This whole situation was too weird.

"Zach." Her tone was stern. But also kind of sad.

"Sorry. I just wonder if you would have been happier if you'd married Johnny instead."

"That's not something I even think about." She was lying now. He could tell. She didn't lie very often. Just when she thought it was the only way she could protect him. "I am happy. I wouldn't trade the life I've made for..."

She couldn't do it. She couldn't tell him she hadn't wished she'd been Mrs. Johnny Scottsdale instead of Mrs. Mel Harrison.

"Well, maybe you'll get a second chance." He really hoped so. Johnny was cool. So much cooler in real life than he'd ever imagined. "Don't blow it, okay?"

"Don't you have homework, young man?" She pulled the car into their driveway. Shut off the engine. Conversation officially over.

He was glad. He had a lot to think about. Like what if she and

Johnny did get back together? Would they be happy? Would they want to start a new family?

He thought about what it would be like to have a baby brother or sister. Then he'd be the odd one out. The mistake that they'd be reminded of every time they looked at him. He tossed his backpack on his bed and looked up at the poster of Johnny Scottsdale. The guy who just might become his stepfather.

Did he want Johnny and his mom to get back together because he wanted them to be happy or because he wanted Johnny to be his dad?

He studied the picture closely. He'd never really noticed much more than the uniform. But now he looked at his face. The intense stare. Johnny had really dark brown eyes. Just like his. He had the slightest dimple on the left side. So did he. Johnny had stubble on his chin. He didn't even have peach fuzz yet.

He looked in the mirror. Was there really a resemblance between him and Johnny? Or did he just want there to be?

Could Johnny Scottsdale be his dad?

No. It was too crazy. His mom wouldn't lie to him. Not about something important like who his father was.

Would she?

The next day, Alice tried to keep her focus on work, but really, there wasn't much for her to do. By this point, all the kids knew where to go and what to do, and the pro players were comfortable with their roles as mentors. They were working on skills today. Johnny shared his expertise with the pitchers and she wasn't surprised to find out he was a natural teacher. She'd always known he'd be great with kids. Would make a wonderful father. He'd never thought so. He had too many insecurities caused by his upbringing to feel like he had anything to offer.

She'd always known better.

So why, exactly, had she kept him from proving what a terrific father he could be?

Her insecurities had kept her from fully believing in him. She'd believed he'd make it to the Major Leagues. That he'd be the star he'd become. She just hadn't believed he would have been satisfied with a small-town girl once he'd hit the big leagues.

Since she couldn't go back in time and undo her mistakes, she had to be content to be in the present and enjoy watching him work. He gave his complete attention to each boy as if he were the only kid there. While Johnny's focus was on the player on the mound, he kept the full attention of all the other boys. They knew instinctively that Johnny was something special. His calm, controlled demeanor was contagious. There was no horsing around at Johnny Scottsdale's station.

She watched him quietly and effectively guide each prospect through the motions. Outwardly, he was focused on mechanics, teaching them proper throwing techniques. But she saw the true lessons he imparted on each young player. Composure. Confidence. The importance of controlling one's pitches and emotions.

If only she could control hers.

Johnny had asked her to go with him to the Golden Gate Gala. A real date. With a limo and everything. Zach would be at a sleepover with a friend. So she and Johnny would have the whole night. Just the two of them.

If he was willing to take the risk, then why was she so terrified?

Because it had been her experience that if something seemed too good to be true, it usually was.

Mel had been there when she was falling apart. When she was freaking out about Johnny being drafted. He'd understood her fears about him being unable to resist temptation; he'd even encouraged her to be proactive in cutting him loose before he had the chance to disappoint her.

He'd been there for her when she was missing Johnny so much she couldn't leave her room. He'd dragged her out of her sweatpants and out on the town. Then he proceeded to pour ideas into her head about how Johnny had moved on and so should she. All while he poured glass after glass of champagne.

And Mel had been far too good to be true when she'd first suspected she was pregnant. She didn't even have the money to pay for a home pregnancy test. He'd not only loaned her the cash, he'd offered to save her from crawling back home to face her mother's disappointment and her father's bitterness. He saved her from having to ask Johnny to give up his dreams. He convinced her that it was more loving to let him go than to trap him with a baby that might not even be his.

In other words, Mel had used her. For some reason Mel, with all the wealth and privileges growing up, was jealous of the bastard son of a whore. He couldn't understand why Johnny attracted people simply by being himself. Why his ability to throw a ball really hard and with precision meant more to a lot of people than Mel's money and connections. He'd been jealous that Alice had fallen for Johnny almost instantly, while Mel had trouble getting any girl to notice him.

Once he'd gotten Alice to marry him, he seemed to lose interest in her. Like many spoiled children, obtaining the prize was more important than actually having it. She'd meant no more to him than one of his paintings or cars or vintage baseball cards he obsessed over until he actually acquired them. At least he was able to turn around and sell the cards or cars or artwork. He'd been stuck with her.

And she'd been stuck in a marriage that never should have happened.

Chapter 8

After dropping Zach off at his friend Tyler's for a sleepover, Alice treated herself to a manicure, pedicure and new lingerie. She slipped into the expensive gown she'd purchased for the event and did one last pass at her hair. She touched up her lipstick with a flutter of anticipation. Knowing Johnny would be her date for the Golden Gate Gala made her quiver at the likelihood of ending up in his bed later tonight. Or he'd end up in hers. Either way, they would be together. Naked.

She hoped she wouldn't be a huge disappointment. It had been a long time. A really long time. A really, really, really long time. It wasn't just anyone, either. She would be making love to Johnny Scottsdale.

The doorbell rang and her heart leapt. He was here. She opened the door to find a tuxedo-clad Johnny on her doorstep. Wow. He was stunning. Gorgeous. Drop dead sexy. She couldn't let him out in public like that. There would be a riot.

"Wow. You look . . . absolutely beautiful." He looked at her as if he'd never seen her before. He'd never seen her dressed up like this. Back in college, they never went anywhere that required anything fancier than her good jeans. Most of the time it was shorts and a sweatshirt or if she was working in the schools, she wore easy-care dresses that could handle tempera paint spatters.

"Thank you." She couldn't remember why she'd considered canceling on him. She'd spent half the night wondering if she was making a huge mistake getting close to him again. It was probably still a bad idea, but she knew she couldn't turn him away.

"Your chariot awaits." He swept his hand in a wide arc, drawing her attention to the sleek black limousine that somehow managed to pull up to the curb right in front of her house. He was pulling out all the stops in his effort to impress. The thing was, he had her before he'd even said hello.

She shivered as he draped her shawl around her shoulders. The possibility of them ending up naked now seemed like a sure bet.

"We'd better get going." Alice did have to make an appearance. She was the director of the foundation and there were a lot of people counting on her to make sure everything went according to plan. "I need to touch base with the caterers to be sure they have everything they need. And the band will need to do a sound check before everyone gets there."

"I almost forgot, you're working tonight." Johnny sounded a little disappointed.

"Yes... Well... I'm sure there will be plenty of people who'll want to meet you. I'll make sure we sit at the same table, though." She was starting to chatter, a nervous habit she couldn't quite shake despite being able to run this party in her sleep. "Sometimes I even manage to eat at the same time as the rest of the guests. The first year or two, I was so nervous, I ate in the kitchen, grabbing a bite here or there as the evening went on."

"Ali. When was the last time you went out, just for fun?"

Since she couldn't quite consider that first night out with Mel fun, she'd have to say when she and Johnny were dating. So she shrugged her shoulders and gave him a pathetic smile.

"I'm going to show you a good time, tonight," Johnny promised. "I might even dance with you."

"Oh really?" Her heart melted at the memory of how they'd met.

"You won't even have to hide behind the speakers."

Johnny was referring to back-to-school dance where they'd met. Alice's roommate had bailed on her at the last minute, but she'd gone without her. Once she got there, she'd been too self-conscious to mingle, so she'd ducked behind the stage. Off to the side, where no one could see her. Or so she'd thought.

"You were dancing. All by yourself." Johnny caught her eye, holding her gaze for what felt like a long time. "But you didn't look lonely. You looked like the band was playing just for you. That the night and the music were yours alone."

"I didn't realize anyone was watching me." She blushed from the warmth of the memory. "I thought I was hidden from the crowd."

"Mel saw you," Johnny said. "And he wanted to ask you to dance. But I beat him to it."

"Yes. You did." She'd been intimidated by his height, his broad shoulders, and the fact that he'd been spying on her. But there had been a softness in his eyes, a vulnerability that made her trust him. Instead of leading her to the dance floor, he'd joined her behind the speakers and the instant his hand rested on her shoulder, she was gone.

"So Mel saw me first?" That was news to her.

"But I saw you last." Johnny opened the door to the limo and waited while she slid inside. "I'm sorry. I shouldn't have said that."

"No. It's okay." And it was. He was the injured party here, not her. She'd made choices. Johnny never had the chance.

"So what would it take to convince you to skip this party and ride around the city, just the two of us?" Johnny asked once she got settled.

"Considering this is our main fundraiser, I'd say I should be there." She crossed her legs, and the slit of her skirt exposed more leg than she meant to.

"I could write a check." Johnny's voice was low and incredibly sexy.

"I can't be bought." She uncrossed her legs, and smoothed the fabric of her dress down as much as possible. *Not again*.

Johnny leaned back against the seat. She wasn't sure if she'd said that last part aloud. She hoped not. She didn't want him to know that she'd married Mel for financial reasons as much as anything else. He'd promised to take care of her and the baby. And while they'd never lacked for food or shelter or clothing, she'd lacked the one thing she wanted most—love.

The limo pulled up to the front of the hotel. Johnny tipped the driver and led Alice to the ballroom. Fortunately they'd arrived early enough that she was able to check in with the caterer. She made her rounds, assured that everything was in place. Nothing could mar this night. Not when she knew she'd be going home with Johnny Scottsdale at the end of the evening.

She found him over by the bar. He'd been chatting with the bartender. He always did have a way of connecting with everyday people. While Mel would seek out those with power and connections, Johnny tended to gravitate to the people who did the real labor. Alice was in the position of needing to connect with both.

Johnny sipped champagne while he watched Ali work the room. She was amazing; one minute she was dazzling wealthy socialites with her charm and grace, the next she was chatting causally with the worker bees, encouraging and directing them to keep the event running with a cool perfection.

He wasn't the only one watching her. She drew the attention of most of the men in the room. In her ridiculously sexy gown. Instead of basic black, it was blue. A little darker than Dodger blue, but not quite as dark as Yankee pinstripes. He supposed the women in the room had a name for that particular color, but he just knew it made her skin glow and eyes sparkle.

He also knew that at the end of the evening, he'd be the one unzipping that dress. Sliding it down her body, tasting her skin along the way. He sipped his champagne to avoid looking at his watch and wondering if they'd been here long enough to slip out unnoticed.

They'd probably have to stay through dinner, at least. And he did promise her dancing. That is, if he could tear her away from her job.

Johnny looked around, to see if he knew anyone. There were a few people he recognized from the Goliaths' front office. Marvin Dempsey and his wife Helen were there. Clayton Barry escorted his former supermodel wife Annabelle. He didn't see Henry Collins, the man who'd purchased the team back in the nineties and kept them from moving to Florida. There were rumors circulating about his health, some sort of cancer. But his daughter Hunter was there, chatting with the Dempseys.

"I thought you didn't do the whole glamour and fame thing." Rachel Parker approached Johnny as if they were actually friends. "But look at you, all dressed up and ready for the limelight."

"I'm not here to get noticed." Johnny took a sip of champagne, hoping she'd get the hint he wasn't interested in her or this conversation.

"But it's hard not to notice you." She had a throaty, flirty tone to her voice.

"I'm here to support a worthy cause." Johnny continued to stare out over the crowd, hoping to catch a glimpse of Alice.

"It's funny, you never seemed interested in youth charities before."

"What are you, the IRS? Poking around into my charitable contributions?"

"No. I am a little curious about why you've suddenly take such an interest in helping young boys when you seemed to avoid that kind of thing in the past." She had the air of someone making small talk, but the reporter in her was hard to hide. She was searching for an angle. A way she could dig into some dirt. He didn't like the way she'd said the words *young boys*. "You seem to have taken a particular interest in Zach Harrison."

"I told you, his father was an old friend." Johnny was still trying to determine if she was insinuating that he was doing more than work on a few pitches.

"And the fact that his mother—his very single mother—has been eyeing you all night has nothing to do with it."

Johnny let out the breath he'd been holding. So, she wasn't accusing him of anything other than using the kid to get to the mother.

"I'll have you know, I don't need a thirteen-year-old to help me get dates." Johnny tossed back the last swallow of his champagne and set the glass on the bar. Grabbing two fresh glasses, Johnny searched the crowd for Alice. "If you'll excuse me, there's my date now."

He walked away, leaving the reporter behind.

"Ali, relax. Everything is perfect." He handed her the crystal flute and she smiled her thanks, saying goodbye to the couple she'd been talking to.

"I know. I just need to make sure everyone is having a good time." She took a dainty sip, barely even letting the bubbles touch her lips.

"Does that include me?" Johnny tilted his head, daring her with a look that said his idea of a good time had nothing to do with flowers and lighting and passed appetizers.

"You get to have your good time later." She looked out over the crowd, as if looking for a distraction.

"Promise?" Johnny stepped closer to her, close enough that he could smell her expensive perfume, or maybe it was her natural scent that was so intoxicating. "Because we have a lot of catching up to do."

"Yes, but first I need to make sure..." She started to pull away from him.

"No. Stay. Everything is perfect." He whispered in her ear, purposely letting his breath tickle her neck. "You're perfect."

"Johnny, I—"

"Don't look for excuses to get away from me." He blew across her skin, delighting in making her shiver. "Or I'll drag you out of here right now."

"You wouldn't." She protested, but didn't pull away.

"I guess I can wait." He shifted his body away from hers. "But don't make me wait too long."

"Thanks." She reached out and squeezed his hand. "I don't know why this event has me more nervous than any other. I mean, I've done this every year for the past seven years. I should have it down by now."

"It's because this could be your last. You want to go out on top." Johnny traced his thumb along her wrist. "I know exactly how you feel. No one's going to remember what I did last year if I don't pitch well this year. No one's going to care about my awards if I don't win it all this season."

"That's not true." She tensed up again, after finally relaxing a bit. "You've had a terrific career. So many things to be proud of."

"Yeah? My statistics only count in negotiations." Johnny said. "If I start the season one and four with an ERA over five, they'll be calling for a trade long before the deadline. No matter how many games and awards I've won. Especially since I didn't win them here."

"I'm sure you'll be great." She sounded kind of wistful. She took a long sip of her champagne before asking, "Was it worth it?"

"My career?" He asked. "Yeah. I guess. Besides, I've never had any other job."

"Ever?"

"Not that wasn't related to baseball. I worked part time as an umpire when I was in high school. The one day a week I didn't have games or practice."

"So what will you do after?" She didn't need to add *after your arm gives out and you're a has-been.*

"I have no idea." Johnny wasn't kidding.

"Ever consider coaching?"

The question took him by surprise. Even though he'd thoroughly enjoyed working the minicamp. "I don't know." For some reason, he still felt like he wasn't good enough. That no one would want him working with their kids once they found out his background.

"You should. You did a great job with the kids this week. Especially with Zach." She handed him her half-full glass and walked away.

He watched her thread her way through the crowd. It wasn't until she stepped up to the podium at the front of the room he understood she wasn't blowing him off. She had an announcement to make, now that most of the guests had arrived.

"Good evening, ladies and gentlemen." She spoke clearly into the microphone and the room grew silent. "Welcome, and thank you for coming tonight. This is my seventh . . . my seventh year chairing this event and I'm amazed at how each year has grown to be more successful than the last."

For a minute there, Johnny thought she was going to announce this would be her last year. But she didn't. Instead she went on to thank the major donors, including the Harrison family, the Goliaths organization and several other big name contributors. She also made a point to thank the caterers, the hotel staff and other behind-the-scenes people who put forth more time than money to contribute to the cause.

Alice finished her speech and announced that dinner would be served shortly. She and Johnny were seated at a table with Mel, Frannie and a bunch of their friends and associates who would have had nothing to do with Johnny if it wasn't for his fame. Some of the people at the table even eyed him suspiciously until Mel introduced him as *the* Johnny Scottsdale.

Talk turned to the team and their chances this year. There were several season ticket holders in the group.

"With this pitching staff, I think we'll go all the way this year." The man sitting directly across from Johnny punctuated his statement by pointing with his fork. "All the way."

"We'd better." The fellow to his left sipped his cocktail and stared at Johnny, almost as if he was daring him to argue. "I can't even remember the last time the stadium didn't sell out. With the amount of money we're paying these guys, they owe us a World Series."

It would be nice if a large salary could guarantee success. But Johnny didn't think this was the time or place to point out that all of his opponents made as much, if not more money to try to beat him.

"Fan support does mean a lot." Johnny tried to keep his comments neutral. The last thing he wanted to do was upset a fan who thought he knew more about the game than he did. "But it takes twenty-five guys on the field, plus the manager and coaches and trainers and staff to really pull it off. If it was just because of the fans, San Francisco would never lose a game. We've got the best fans in the world."

"Oh, call the *Chronicle*," Mel joked. "I think they should quote you on that."

"Please, a lot of people feel that way." Johnny wondered why his ability to throw a ball hard and with consistency made his opinions newsworthy.

"Well, I do know a few people down at the paper," Mel said. "If you ever need a favor, some additional coverage, let me know."

"I'm sure Johnny will make headlines all on his own." Frannie smiled when she said it, but it felt like added pressure. They were all counting on him to be the missing piece of the puzzle that would take the Goliaths from being a good team—one in contention—to being a championship team.

"So, Johnny, will you be the first player to pitch a perfect game in the American League and the National League?" the wife of the man across from him asked with a friendly smile.

"With this defense behind me, who knows?" Johnny tried to shrug it off, but he was feeling the heat. It was almost as bad giving a press conference after a particularly disastrous start.

"It's certainly possible. And we'll be able to say we knew him when." Mel made light of the challenge, but it was a challenge all the same. As long as he was a star, he was welcome in their circle. But what about when he was through with baseball?

"It doesn't matter if you win the World Series or the Steve Young award." Frannie was trying to be diplomatic.

"Cy Young, Frannie." Mel corrected. "Steve Young was a football player."

"Yes, dear, that's what I meant." She smiled at Johnny as if her mistake had been intentional. "The point is, we love Johnny because Mel loved Johnny. Not because he can throw a wicked slider."

"Thank you." Johnny wished he could slide right out of there.

"Yes, and if it wasn't for Johnny breaking poor Alice's heart, we wouldn't have our Zach, now would we?" Mel gave him a stare that made him wonder what story Mel and Alice had given them. "We wouldn't trade our Zach for a thousand all-stars, now would we?"

"No." Frannie looked at her husband, with tears forming in her eyes. "Having Zach—and Alice, our dear, sweet Alice—has been the only thing that has made losing our boy bearable. I don't think we could have gotten through it without them."

"Now, Frannie, don't get all mushy on us," Mel commanded. "Everyone here knows what that boy and his mother mean to us. And now that Johnny is here, well, it's like having a bit of Mel back too."

It was all Johnny could do to finish his meal. He hated these kinds of things. Polite dinner conversation with strangers. Even worse, having Mel's parents gush over him. And it wasn't because he was a semi-famous ballplayer. They acted as if they liked him.

Just like Mel had acted as if he'd liked Johnny.

He was about ready to make his excuses when the band started to play.

"Excuse me. It's been lovely to meet all of you. But I promised Alice a dance." He stood and extended his hand.

"Yes. You did." She smiled as she slipped her hand into his and followed him to the dance floor.

"Are you okay?" Somehow she could still tell what he was feeling. That he was overwhelmed by too much attention.

"Yes. I'm fine." He pulled her toward him with a little more force than grace. He tried to relax as he placed one hand on her shoulder and the other at her waist.

"Johnny. Talk to me." They'd had plenty of fights because he'd never been good at expressing himself. But she didn't sound angry. Not this time. "Please. Tell me what's wrong."

"Nothing." He closed his eyes and tried to get into the music.

"I can only imagine how hard it is to listen to guys who think they know what it's like." She swayed to the music and pressed her body against his. "As if they could do their jobs with thirty thousand people watching their every move, every night."

"It's no big deal." He wanted to forget about it. To concentrate on having her in his arms, but sometimes it got to him. The pressure. The feeling that he would never be good enough. Especially when he thought about how much money he made.

Because all the money in the world hadn't made up for what he'd lost.

He pulled her closer to him. Molded his body against hers. And wished he could go back in time. To when he was twenty. When all he needed was his game and his girl. When he played for the love of the game and he loved because he couldn't help it.

But it hadn't been enough.

He hadn't been enough.

And if he didn't come through this season, it would all be for nothing.

"I'd better let you get back to work." The slow song finished and Johnny was itching to get out of there.

"I'm done here." She wrapped her arms around his waist and looked up at him like he was some kind of hero. "We can leave any time you want."

"Are you sure?" He knew how much this night meant to her. To her cause.

"Absolutely." She slipped her hand in his and gave him a comforting squeeze. "I think I've done enough here. I'd say tonight was a huge success."

"You have a lot to be proud of." Johnny was still in awe of what she'd accomplished. He wondered how much money they'd brought in tonight. And how many kids it would help. "You're the real hero."

"Hardly." She blushed. "We've been doing this so long, the event practically runs itself."

"Sure." Johnny waited while she got her coat. "And all these wallets just open up on their own."

"Everyone here knows what they're getting into. If they weren't planning on spending the money, they wouldn't have come."

"I don't know, those crab cakes were worth the price of admission." He helped her into her wrap and led her to the street where the limo would be waiting for them.

"Well, you have to give them something for their money."

"I suppose I should make an additional contribution." Johnny tried not to think about money too much. It had never been important to him. But now, he felt guilty for not doing more with it. Other than taking care of his mother, he pretty much ignored it.

"Don't even think about it." She said. "You already gave so much. Something that none of these people could contribute. You gave your time and expertise."

"It was one week. And I didn't even come close to teaching them everything they need to know." Johnny felt frustrated that he couldn't spend more time with each kid. Especially Zach. The boy had real potential. But he would need a lot of practice. And regular monitoring. "I could do more."

"Okay. So do more." She took his hand as the limo pulled up. "But not tonight. Tonight you're mine."

Chapter 9

Johnny was far too quiet in the limo. Something was on his mind, but Alice knew from experience that he wouldn't share without a little push.

"So, you must get tired of fans who think they own you because they buy a ticket." She certainly did.

"I'm used to it." Johnny sat stiff in the plush leather seat, bothered by more than just the loudmouths at their table.

They rode on through the city. Heading the opposite direction of her house. They must be going to his place. Close to the ballpark.

"Don't you ever get tired of the Harrisons?" Johnny asked after a few minutes of silence. "They act as if they own you."

"Is that what you think?" She was surprised. Then she recalled their conversation at dinner. The way they referred to her as "our Alice."

"I guess it was Mel who brought you home, and stuck you on a shelf like some kind of prize." Johnny's voice sounded strained. As if he worked really hard to control his anger.

"Are you saying I was a trophy wife?" She couldn't help but laugh at that. She couldn't have felt more out of place on Mel's arm.

"Something like that. Only you were mine." The hurt in his voice made her reach for his hand. "He had everything. Money. Family. A name he could be proud of. He took the one thing in this world I had besides baseball. He took you."

"Johnny, I'm sorry we hurt you. Neither of us meant for it to happen. It just did." This was hardly the conversation to get them in the mood. But maybe it was for the best. They really should hash it all out. Get to the truth before they even had a chance to make love.

If they had a chance at all.

"So how did it happen? How did you and Mel end up together?"

"I was missing you." She let go of his hand. "We both were. So we turned to each other."

"I see." He leaned forward, resting his forearms on his knees.

"One night we went out to one of the casinos. Had a little too much to drink and instead of driving..." She couldn't do it. Couldn't tell Johnny about how she'd woken up in that hotel room, naked and full of regret.

"You don't need to tell me any more." Johnny let out a huge sigh. "I think we need to put the past behind us."

Yes, but before they could do that, she needed to tell him everything.

"Johnny, the thing is..."

The car lurched to a stop.

"I promised you a romantic evening." Johnny placed his fingers over her lips. "I need to deliver. Let's go up to my place, shall we?"

One simple touch and Alice forgot about everything but getting this man into bed. It had been so long, yet her body remembered exactly what he could do to her.

Johnny paid the driver and led her to his apartment building. Once in the elevator, he took her hand. He seemed nervous, almost shy all of a sudden, so she squeezed his hand reassuringly.

"Don't worry, you're going to get lucky." She smiled up at him flirtatiously, but he didn't smile back. He simply unlocked the door and led her inside.

"I haven't had time to really decorate." He apologized for his apartment's sparse décor. His lack of clutter. "I've barely even unpacked."

She glanced around the room. It was a newer place, spacious and open. An efficient, state-of-the-art kitchen on one side, the living area on the other. A large picture window offered a gorgeous view of the ballpark. The walls were bare. He had a leather sofa, matching chair, stereo equipment and a large flat screen TV. A couple of barstools lined the kitchen counter and that was about it.

It felt very temporary. Like he wasn't planning on sticking around.

But then, Johnny had never been big on possessions. Back in college, he'd been happy with his ball and his glove. His beat-up Jeep to get him to practice and to take a drive when the pressure got to him. Or when they needed a change of scenery. As much as she'd loved hanging out at his and Mel's apartment, sometimes they needed space. And a person couldn't find more space than the Northern Nevada desert.

"Can I get you a drink, or something?" Johnny smoothed his hands down the front of his tuxedo jacket. "I have some wine. Or a beer."

"Sure." She'd had maybe four sips of champagne all evening, so the buzzed feeling had nothing to do with alcohol. "I'll have whatever you'd prefer."

Johnny had never been a big drinker. He didn't like to give up control. But Mel had been a microbrew aficionado. He'd even experimented with home brewing back in college. That made for some interesting concoctions.

Johnny pulled a couple of Anchor Steams from his refrigerator. A local craft beer that Mel introduced to them back when most of their classmates were downing cheap light beer by the case.

"Glass?" he asked, prying the off the caps and tossing the opener back in the drawer.

"No. The bottle's fine." No use dirtying any dishes. It almost appeared as if his kitchen hadn't even been used. It seemed so lonely.

"Cheers." Johnny held his bottle up in a toast.

"Cheers." She took a long drink. The rich amber liquid slid down her throat. But it didn't quench her thirst for him.

The awkwardness continued. Somehow the magic they felt for each other had faded, as if neither remembered how to get started. She had an excuse, having been widowed for so long. Maybe Johnny was used to women throwing themselves at him. She tried not to think about how many he'd caught.

It didn't matter. What he'd done when they were apart was his business. She'd let the mere idea of him being with another woman ruin their relationship years ago. Time to get over it. She wanted him, even if it was only for tonight.

"Can I use your bathroom?" She finished her beer and placed the empty bottle on the sleek granite counter.

"Sure, there's one in the hall and another in my bedroom." He sipped slowly from his bottle. Stalling. But he looked at her with longing. An ache they both felt.

She chose the one in his bedroom.

Johnny didn't quite know what to do with himself. He hadn't had a woman up to his apartment in recent memory. The last woman he'd dated had complained that he never had her over to his place. That he didn't *let her in*, whatever that meant. As if seeing someone's choice of furnishings somehow made a deeper connection. What did it say about him that he didn't hang pictures on the wall? That he spent his money on exercise equipment instead of throw pillows and knick-knacks?

Other than in college, he'd never spent much time at home. As a kid, he stayed away as much as possible. He preferred to be at the ballpark, or even an empty field, instead of stuck inside watching soap operas or talk shows with his mother or her roommates. He never brought friends over, that was for sure. So, entertaining wasn't something that came naturally.

"Hey Johnny, could you help me with something?" Ali called from the back of the apartment. Oh no, did he forget to put towels out? Or worse?

He found her in his bedroom. On his bed. Naked.

He swallowed. Hard. "What do you need?"

"You." She stretched out on his bed, giving him the perfect view of what she was offering. "Well?"

"You're beautiful." So beautiful he couldn't move. The last time they'd made love, he'd been twenty-one. And desperate to show her everything he'd been unable to tell her about how he felt.

They'd broken up weeks before. But he'd stopped by her place on his way out of town. One last attempt at changing her mind. He was scared and hurt and a little bewildered by her insistence he go off to the minor leagues unencumbered. He wanted to tell her he needed her. He loved her. But the words wouldn't come. So he'd done the only thing he could.

Nearly out of his mind with the thought of losing her, he'd made love to her in a frantic and fumbling fashion.

He wasn't going to let her get away this time.

"So, come get me." She shifted, turning away from him slightly, like she might be having second thoughts.

That got him moving.

He shrugged out of his tuxedo jacket, grabbing a condom out of the pocket before dropping it on the floor. He kicked off his ridiculously shiny shoes and tugged at his collar.

Ali rose from the bed and helped him with his buttons. His zipper. She snuggled against him, burying her face in his chest.

"Johnny..." She inhaled as she slid his boxer-briefs down his thighs. "I've missed you. I've missed this."

"Me too." He eased her back toward the bed. "You're even more beautiful than I remember."

"Oh, please. I've gained weight. After having Zach." She blushed, covering her stomach with her hands.

He laid her on the bed then slid in next to her. He put his hand on her stomach and stroked her skin, so smooth, so soft, so perfect.

"Beautiful," he said again. Brushing his lips across her exquisite skin, he kissed her on the mouth. The soft spot behind her ear. He flicked his tongue into the hollow of her collarbone. Then blew gently, eliciting a sound that was part whimper, part giggle. He moved down her body, tasting her along the way. He paused between her breasts, deciding which one to savor first, slid his right hand over her left breast and lowered his mouth to her right nipple. A flick, a swirl, and then he pulled her into his mouth.

She moaned, whimpered, begged for more.

He dragged kisses across her chest to take in her other breast, moved his hand down her body, grazing her hip as she thrust forward. Her skin was silky, soft. And sensitive, too, judging by the way she squirmed beneath his touch. He slipped his hand between her thighs, finding her sweet spot. She was so hot. So wet. So *perfect*.

More unintelligible noises escaped her throat as he stroked, dipped and drew out her orgasm. Her sounds became more urgent and he knew he'd be in trouble if he didn't give her what she wanted.

Him. Inside her. Now.

He tore open the condom wrapper and covered himself. Then he plunged deep inside her.

They came together and it was like they'd never been apart. He remembered where and how she liked to be touched. He recalled the taste of her. The soft little noises that quickly turned into insistent moans. Their bodies collided with the present and the past.

She cried out his name. For real this time. Not like the thousands of dreams he'd had over the years. The times he'd woken up in a strange hotel room in a strange city, sweaty with his heart racing and for a moment, in that place between asleep and awake, he'd swear Ali was there with him. Sometimes, he worried her nightmare had come true, and he'd open his eyes to find a nameless stranger in the bed next to him. But it was only Ali. It had always been only Ali. Or rather, the dream of her.

But tonight she was real. She was beneath him, rocking with pleasure. Accepting everything he had to give. The only thing he'd been able to give her way back then.

It was over far too quickly. But they had all night. A fact he planned to take full advantage of as soon as he was able. Until then, he was happy to just hold her. To feel her warm body pressed against him. Her heart beating in her chest, slowly creeping down to a steady pace.

They fell asleep. Woke up and made love again. Then drifted into a peaceful, perfect state of bliss.

This. This was what he'd been missing. What he'd longed for more than anything. This was the real reason he'd come to San Francisco.

"Do you want to watch a movie?" Zach's friend Ty was trying to get him to stop thinking about his mom being out with Johnny Scottsdale, but it wasn't working. Not when he couldn't stop wondering if he was more than just her old boyfriend.

"I don't care." Zach knew he wasn't much fun tonight. But he was tired of playing dumb old video games. He wasn't interested in watching YouTube videos of people doing stupid stuff. And he had absolutely no desire to try to sneak a beer from Ty's mom's fridge out in the garage.

"You're not much fun tonight." Ty was one to talk. It was like he was in some kind of funk, and only wanted to bring Zach down with him.

"Yeah. I guess not." He'd brought his ball and his glove. But Ty hadn't wanted to play catch. Even though the park was right across the street. Ty had stopped playing baseball a few years ago.

"So did Johnny Scottsdale give you that glove?" he asked in a way that sounded like he was kind of making fun of him. Like he thought it was lame to be so excited about meeting the guy who'd been his hero for so long. A guy who might be a whole lot more.

"No. I've had this glove for years." It was exactly like Johnny's. That's why he'd wanted it. So he could be like his hero. Maybe he was like him in a whole lot of ways. Like, genetically.

"I can't believe you're still into that. I mean, it was okay when we were kids, but baseball's kind of boring."

"No it's not." Zach never understood why Ty quit playing. He was good. He could hit the ball a lot farther than Zach could. At least, he could when they were eleven. "I like playing baseball. I hope I can play in high school. Maybe even college."

"You think hanging around Johnny Scottsdale is going to help you catch the eye of college scouts?" Again, his tone made it sound like he didn't like Johnny. Or baseball. Or even Zach.

"He's already helping me. I can tell I've made improvement in only a week." And he had. He could feel it when he threw the ball. He could hear it when it hit the glove. He just needed to face a couple of batters to know for sure.

"Boy, are you blind." Ty picked up a gaming magazine and flipped through it. "Didn't he go out with your mom tonight? You know he was only using you to get into her pants."

"Don't talk about my mom like that." Zach balled his fist. He punched his glove, since he was still holding it. Like some sort of security blanket. "She's not like that."

"Sure, she is." Ty rolled up the magazine. If Zach tossed him the ball, he could have used it as a bat. "All women are. And all men are only after one thing. Then once they get it, they take off."

"Does your mom have a new boyfriend?" Zach knew how much it bothered his friend that his mother couldn't keep a steady boyfriend. She'd dated lots of guys after the divorce and none of them stuck around too long.

"Yeah. This one's a real loser. He tries to be all buddy-buddy with me. Like it makes up for him sleeping with my mom if he takes me to a ballgame or something."

Was that why Johnny was being so nice to him? Because he wanted to sleep with his mom? Or was it because he felt guilty? Before he could dwell on it too much, Ty's mom poked her head in the door.

"Oh, you two are still up." She sounded kind of disappointed, but not really surprised.

"If you want to have Doug come over, don't wait for us to fall asleep." Ty glared at his mom. "I know he comes over after you think I'm in bed. Don't let me get in the way of your booty call."

"Tyler James!" Her face got all red. She was either really embarrassed or really mad. Or both. Then her face twisted like she was sad all of a sudden and she shook her head. "God, you look just like your father right now."

She turned and shut the door.

"Yeah? Maybe I should go live with him full time then. So you won't have to look at me." Ty yelled at the closed door.

"You really want to do that?"

"No. My dad's a prick." Ty grabbed Zach's baseball. Turned it over in his hands. "But at least I wouldn't make her cry every time she looks at me."

Zach didn't know what to say about that.

"If she hates him so much, why did she ever marry him?" Ty wondered out loud. "I mean, why did she get together with him in the first place? I know why she married him. She had to."

"Sorry. My parents got married because of me, too." Zach kind of felt sorry for Ty right now. At least Zach's mom wasn't angry all the time.

"You're lucky your dad died." Ty flopped on his bed. "Sorry. I didn't mean it like that. It's just, you know, better than having two parents who hate each other. But they have to deal with each other. Because of me."

Zach wished he could go home. But he had a feeling his mom wasn't alone. That would be too weird.

"I gotta take a leak." Zach excused himself to the bathroom. He washed his hands and splashed water on his face. He stared into the mirror. He wondered what his mom thought when she saw him. No one ever said he looked like his dad. In fact, they often commented on how different he was. Maybe it was because his dad wasn't really his dad.

He studied himself more closely. Could he be Johnny's son? They both had brown eyes. Big deal. Lots of people had brown eyes. But not his mom. Or his so-called dad. His eyes had been hazel. Like Nannie's. But Grandpa Mel had brown eyes. Only they were much lighter than Zach's.

He used to practice Johnny's on-the-mound scowl. The intense stare-down of the batter. He had it down pretty good. Was it because he worked at it, or did it come naturally?

He wished he could just ask his mom to tell him the truth. But if she'd lied to him, she must have had a good reason. Like maybe Johnny had left them. Maybe he didn't want to get married and end up like Ty's parents, hating each other.

Maybe he should be glad.

But he still needed to know. He was a big kid. Almost grown up in a lot of ways. He could handle the truth.

Johnny woke to find Ali getting dressed. Was she planning on sneaking out?

"I need to get going," she whispered. Like they weren't the only two people in the apartment. "Zach is an early riser. Always has been. He could call and if I'm not home..."

Zach. He'd forgotten all about her son. The reason she'd married Mel after their rebound encounter.

"I'll drive you. Give me a minute." Johnny sat up, rubbed the sleep from his eyes. He was normally an early riser, too. But last night had been incredible.

"I can call a cab." She pulled on those strappy sandals of hers that sparkled and shined and made her legs look amazing.

"Like hell, you will." Johnny dropped his feet to the floor. He knew better than to expect that everything was going to be perfect between them. But he certainly didn't expect this. Her trying to sneak out like some...some groupie. "I'll take you home. Come on, Ali. You can't take a cab from my house in the dress you wore last night. You know there were reporters at the party last night. I'm not that famous, but still..."

He grabbed a pair of jeans, slipped them on and pulled a t-shirt over his head.

Ali leaned against the wall, waiting for him to get dressed so he could take her home.

"I saw you talking to Rachel Parker. She seems quite taken with you." She was teasing him, pretending to be jealous.

"I'm the new guy. Don't worry, I'm sure she'll find someone else to pick on once the season starts."

"I think she already has. I saw her talking to one of your teammates. The guy with the hair. The pretty boy."

"Bryce Baxter." Johnny hoped he would be the kind of guy to distract the reporter. "He's the shortstop."

"Right. He seems like the kind of guy who enjoys attention." She flashed him a teasing smile, knowing how much he hated being in the spotlight.

"He's a good guy, though. We've sort of become friends."

"Good. I'm glad."

She had no idea how hard it was for him to call another man his friend after what Mel had done to him.

"Let's go." He grabbed his keys and led her to the elevators that would take them to the parking garage.

"You don't still have your old Jeep, do you?" she asked as they descended to the underground lot.

"No." A smile tugged at the corner of his lips. A lot of sweet memories had been made in the back of that Jeep. "I've traded it in for a new one. Twice."

"Oh. No Escalade or Hummer?"

"You know me." Johnny led her to a shiny black Wrangler Unlimited.

"Yeah. I do. I did." Her voice contained enough regret to damn near break his heart.

He opened the passenger door to reveal leather interior, a state-of-the-art sound system. A far cry from the old clunker that didn't even have a stereo. Nothing but an AM/FM radio and an old ice chest he'd used for a center console.

"This is nice." She hopped up into the seat, revealing one long, lean thigh. The same thigh she'd had wrapped around his waist not too long ago. "It suits you. Not too fancy, yet quite an improvement over that old rust bucket."

"Except more often than not, you were riding shotgun in that old rust bucket." Johnny let the memories flow over him. He tried to appreciate what he'd had instead of dwelling on what he'd lost.

"That was a long time ago." She had wistfulness in her voice. "But I guess we can't quite move beyond our past."

Johnny pulled out of the parking garage and they made their way through the city to her house. Neither spoke; perhaps they were both considering everything they needed to put behind them.

He couldn't get over the fact she'd chosen another man over him. He understood a little better why she'd married him. But he still felt betrayed. How many times would he have to make love to her to feel like she was truly his?

They pulled up in front of the house. The one Mel bought for her. Just two doors down from his parents. "It's funny, most women barely tolerate their mother-in-laws when they're married. How often do you have lunch with Frannie? Twice a month?"

"Every week." She almost squeaked when she answered him.

Johnny turned off the ignition and turned to her. "And you have dinner with them, what, every week?"

"Twice a month." She folded her arms across her chest. "So I get along with my in-laws. They're nice people. They made me feel right at home during a difficult time."

"Didn't they think it was a little suspicious that you married their son so soon after I left for the minor leagues? I mean, they knew we were together. They knew how long we'd been together."

"I don't know what they thought about it, I only know they accepted me into their family. And they love Zach."

"Why wouldn't they?" Johnny unhooked his seatbelt. "He's a great kid."

"Yes, he is." Her hand shook a little as she reached for the door.

"I'll walk you in." He wasn't quite finished with her.

"Sure. Come on in." She flashed him a smile. The kind that went straight to his heart. "I'll make some coffee."

"Why don't I make the coffee? While you change." Not that he minded what she was wearing right now. That was one fine dress.

"Thanks." She gathered up her skirt as he helped her climb down from his Jeep.

"I'm sorry, Ali. I guess I can't still be mad at Mel." He needed to tell her how he felt. He couldn't keep it inside any longer. "I guess I'm trying to be mad at the Harrisons instead."

"They've been very good to me." She stood on the front porch glancing up the street toward their house.

"I know. And I'm glad you had their support."

"More than I got from my own family." She reached into her purse for her keys.

"They're lucky to have you." Johnny placed his hand on the small of her back. "I hope they realize that. I hope they don't take you for granted."

"They don't." She slid the key into the lock.

"Good. Because you're amazing. The work you've done with the foundation..."

"Last night was a success only because I have so many good people working for me." She deflected the praise. They were two of kind that way.

"Last night was amazing." He dropped his voice so she'd know he wasn't talking about the party. "But you did an even better job with those kids. If you don't go back to school, maybe you should think about expanding the baseball camp."

She blushed. From the tips of her pink ears to the top of her low-cut gown.

"I'll think about it." She turned the key. "If you'll think about coaching when you retire."

Chapter 10

Alice unlocked the front door and stepped inside. Johnny followed close on her heels. She felt like a teenager sneaking in after an all-night date. Not that she'd ever done that sort of thing. "I'm just going to change. Then I'll make some coffee and—"

"Mom? Mom, why didn't you answer the—" Zach had come in through the back door at the same time she'd entered through the front. He stopped when he saw her in her evening gown and Johnny in jeans right behind her. "Oh."

His face turned about fifty shades of red.

"Zach, I . . . uh."

"You spent the night with him." Zach wouldn't look at Johnny. The man he'd practically worshipped for years. The man he'd become even more fond of after they'd worked the minicamp together.

"Yes. I did. I'm sorry if you were worried." Alice regained her composure. She'd worried this very thing would happen, and now it had. So she'd have to deal with it. "It won't happen again."

"So it was, like, a one-nighter?" He glanced up at her. Like he wasn't quite sure what that meant. He turned toward Johnny. "So that's it? You were just using her? Just using me to get into her bed?"

"No." Johnny's jaw held firm. "Not at all."

"I can't believe this." Zach sounded hurt. Crushed. "I mean, I know other people's moms are, like . . . like they don't care how many guys they bring home or how embarrassing it is. But damn it."

"Zachary John Harrison." She'd never heard him swear before. She wasn't naïve enough to believe he'd never done it. Just not in front of her.

"Zach, you shouldn't speak to your mother that way." Johnny stepped in. While she appreciated his intentions, it only made the situation worse.

"You slept with my mother." The venom in Zach's voice was heartbreaking. "That doesn't make you my father."

He stomped past them and dashed up the stairs. His bedroom door slammed.

"Johnny, I'm so sorry." She knew it wasn't going to be easy, but did it have to be this hard so soon? "He's not usually so rude."

"Why don't you go change. I'll talk to him."

"No. I should talk to him. I'm his mother."

"Yes. You are his mother." Johnny's jaw twitched. He was angry. At Zach? At her? Or did this bring up old wounds from his childhood? "But he needs a little man-to-man conversation on what it means to be respectful to a woman. Especially to his mother."

Oh. A man-to-man conversation?

"He also needs to know that I'm not using you. Or anyone else in this house." Johnny's voice softened. Enough for her to think maybe he could smooth things over. "I'd like to talk to him. If that's okay with you. I'd like to let him know my intentions are honorable."

"Do you think that would help?" It felt so natural to ask Johnny for advice on her son. It was like she had an ally. She was no longer alone in this parenting deal.

"I hope so." Johnny shrugged. Then he squared his shoulders, ready to face the challenge.

"Me too." He had no idea how much they all stood to lose if it didn't.

"Come on." Johnny tugged her hand. Led her up the stairs and stopped as they reached the top. He gave her a questioning look. He didn't know which room was Zach's.

She indicated the correct door with a nod. Johnny took a deep breath and poised, ready to knock.

Alice slunk down the hallway toward her room. Slipped out of her dress and hung it over a chair. She'd toss it in with the rest of her dry cleaning later. As she reached for a change of clothes, she realized she could still smell Johnny on her skin.

After pulling her hair into a high ponytail, she stepped into the shower. She scrubbed the makeup off her face and used a generous amount of body wash to soap up her arms and legs. A quick rinse, and she toweled off to dress and face her son. A boy, who until this morning, had thought her biggest sin was her tendency to be somewhat overprotective.

Johnny knocked on Zach's bedroom door. He fully expected to be told to go to hell.

"Come in." Zach sounded more than a little contrite. He really was a good kid.

Johnny gave Alice all the credit for that. He slowly pushed the door open and stepped into Zach's room.

If, by some miracle, he was ever elected to the Hall of Fame, he had a feeling it wouldn't look much different than this kid's room. There were pictures of him, memorabilia, and a huge poster over Zach's bed.

"Oh. It's you." Zach slumped on the bed, where he resumed tossing a ball toward the ceiling. A trick Johnny had performed numerous times as a kid when he'd been hurting.

"Yes. It's me. I wanted to talk to you. Man to man." Johnny stood in the doorway, waiting for an invitation to come into the room. A sincere invitation.

"Yeah. I guess." Zach sat up, still holding the baseball in his hands. He glanced at it, rather than Johnny. Not exactly sincere, but Johnny understood.

"Nice room." He supposed it was something that Zach hadn't torn the poster from the wall. "Are these your Little League trophies?"

Johnny approached the shelf of awards Zach had earned. He picked up the one closest to him. Read the inscription. T-ball. The Tigers.

"Yeah. Everyone gets trophies when they're little. Doesn't mean anything." Zach sounded almost embarrassed. "My mom thinks they're cool, but . . ."

"She's pretty proud of you." Johnny put the trophy back. "Most of the time."

"Yeah. I guess." Zach knew he'd been less than respectful, but at thirteen probably couldn't admit it.

"You should show her more respect than you did just now."

Zach didn't say anything, so Johnny turned around to gauge his reaction.

"I know." Zach looked him square in the eye briefly, before staring down at his shoes. "I just... She's my mom. And she's never brought a guy home before. I guess I freaked out a little."

"Sorry if I made you uncomfortable." Johnny hadn't wanted the kid to find out about them. Not like that. "And I'm sorry if you think I've overstepped my bounds. But I can't stand to see any woman treated with disrespect. Especially not a woman I care about."

"You care about her." Zach didn't ask. Just confirmed what they both needed to know.

"Yes. Very much."

"Good." Zach met his gaze. He didn't need words to tell him that he wanted to protect her, too. "I'm glad. Because... Well, she's my mom."

"Yes. She is. And I respect your concern. I should have thought of that earlier. And planned to get her home sooner. So you wouldn't have to see..." See what? Her in last night's dress? With her makeup smudged and the glow of a long night of lovemaking?

"I'm glad I know." Zach sat taller. Like he was letting Johnny know that no man, no matter how big, was going to mess with his mother. "I'm not a little kid anymore. I can handle the truth."

"Good. Because I plan on seeing your mother." Johnny was glad the kid wanted to hear it straight. "I plan on seeing a lot of her. If that's what she wants."

"Do you think you'll get married?"

"I don't know." The question was a little more than he was prepared for. But he should have had a better answer.

"Do you love her?" Zach crossed his arms. Her own father hadn't been so protective. Once he found out Johnny was an athlete, he decided that was more than enough reason to make him feel like he wasn't good enough for his daughter. Then again, he hadn't made her feel quite good enough either.

"Yes. I always have. Always will." Johnny saw no reason to deny the truth. "But that doesn't necessarily mean things will work out between us."

"Well, you don't have to worry about me." Zach sized him up, and apparently found him acceptable. "I won't act like a spoiled brat anymore."

"Good." Johnny wanted to pull the kid into his arms for a hug, but thought that might be pushing his luck. "Now, what do you say we make some breakfast for your mom?"

"You cook?" Zach gave him a skeptical glance.

"Sure. When you've lived alone as long as I have, you'd better learn how." Johnny had to restrain himself from reaching out and ruffling the kid's hair.

"Yeah, but you can afford to hire someone." Zach popped up, headed for the hallway. "You could buy your own restaurant or eat someplace different every day."

"Nah. I like being able to take care of myself." He liked the idea of taking care of someone else even more.

"Yeah? My mom is always trying to get me to be self-sufficient." Zach skipped down the stairs, toward the kitchen.

"She's a smart lady."

"So why, exactly, did you guys break up?" Zach held the refrigerator door open, staring at the contents like he couldn't really see anything.

"Sometimes I ask myself that very question." Johnny started pulling items from the shelves and set them on the counter. Eggs. Milk. Bacon. "We were both young. Maybe too young to have been able to make things work."

Johnny filled the coffeepot with water and Zach pointed to the cupboard above the coffee maker. Sure enough, he found a bag of ground coffee and unbleached paper filters inside.

"Bread?" Johnny asked, and Zach pointed to the shiny stainless breadbox on the counter. "Thanks."

"Pots and pans in the drawer under the stove." Zach seemed to realize this would be more efficient if Johnny knew where things were. "Mixing bowls and such in here. Dishes up there."

"Appreciate it." Johnny found the equipment and supplies he needed. "You like French Toast?"

"Sure." Zach tried to sound like he couldn't care less, but he couldn't quite pull it off.

"Good. Wash up and help me." Johnny pushed up his sleeves and washed his hands. He waited for Zach to do the same.

Together they cracked the eggs into a shallow dish. Poured a splash of milk and sprinkled a dash of cinnamon into the mixture. He showed Zach how to dip the bread, making it moist, but not too soggy. Then arranged each slice into the hot, but not too hot, pan. He put slices of bacon in a separate pan on the back burner of the stove.

By the time Ali made her way downstairs, breakfast was ready and Zach had set the table in the breakfast nook.

"So? You guys are good?" she asked as Johnny poured her a cup of coffee.

"Yeah. Sorry I was rude." Zach slid into the back of the booth. "It's just that things are kind of weird at Tyler's house. I guess his attitude rubbed off on me."

"Oh?" She looked at Johnny to see if he knew anything about it, but Johnny shrugged. "What happened? Did you two have a fight?"

"No." Zach looked down at his breakfast, shoulders slumping a little as he doused the French Toast in real maple syrup. "It's just that he's still mad at his parents for getting divorced. And his mom's, like, mad at Ty for reminding her of his father. It's not a good vibe over there."

"I see." Ali moved toward Zach, like she wanted to comfort him, but she must have known that she couldn't fix this. Not at his age.

"It's so screwed up." Zach shoved a forkful of food in his mouth. "I'm glad things didn't get like that with you and..."

He glanced up at Johnny. Looked almost guilty about the direction of his conversation.

"I'm glad you never had to get divorced." He mumbled that last part. Like being widowed was somehow better.

"Me, too, Zach. Me, too." She looked down at her plate before taking a bite of her breakfast. "This is really good."

"Zach made it." Johnny hoped a change in topic would get them all on the right track.

"You did?" She looked at her son, beaming with parental pride.

"I helped. But Johnny did most of it." Zach looked equally proud and embarrassed. Johnny knew the feeling. Knew it a little too well.

"That's terrific." She dug into her breakfast with much more enthusiasm.

"At least I know that Tyler isn't mad at me." Zach's mood darkened once again. "I mean, I thought he didn't want to be friends anymore since he quit playing baseball."

So much for changing the subject.

"I guess he quit around the time of the divorce." Zach gulped down half a glass of milk. "I think he should have kept playing. I mean, it would have taken his mind off things at home."

"Yeah. Keeping active is sometimes a good thing." Ali glanced over at Johnny. She knew all about his troubles at home. And how baseball had saved him.

"He's kind of mad at everyone." Zach reached for another slice of bacon. He'd already cleaned his plate. "So I guess I can't take it personally."

"I'm sorry things aren't going so well between you and Tyler. You two have been friends for a long time." Ali sipped her coffee. "Since, what, t-ball?"

"Yeah. But we won't even go to the same school next year." Zach's tone was drifting toward sullen. "I don't see why I have to go to private school. Again."

"Zach. Can we talk about this later?" She stabbed at the remains of her breakfast.

"Maybe I should get going?" Johnny was starting to feel like he'd overstayed his welcome. At least Zach's hostility had faded. Or rather, shifted.

"Sure. You're just trying to get out of doing the dishes," Alice teased him, knowing full well, he was man enough to stick his hands in a sinkful of soapy water.

"I'll get the dishes, Mom," Zach offered. He got up and carried his plate to the sink. "Johnny did most of the cooking. I was just his assistant."

"Thanks, Zach. I appreciate it." Ali sounded a little choked up. Zach really was a good kid. Almost too good.

"I need to get going." Johnny wasn't sure he was cut out for all this. Between the discussions about other people's family dynamics, the understanding that long-time friendships could change, and the way Zach could be disrespectful and accusing one minute, and offering to help the next had him wondering if he was suddenly way, way out of his league.

Zach was a little bummed when Johnny left. Weird. Especially since, well, the whole thing was weird. He'd come home after an uncomfortable night at his so-called best friend's house. Only to find out his mom had spent the night with Johnny Scottsdale.

And then Johnny got mad at him for getting mad about it.

Well, he was upset at Zach for being disrespectful. He hadn't meant to be; he was kind of shocked. That's all.

But Johnny seemed like he cared about Mom. He even made her breakfast. As far as he knew, none of Ty's mom's boyfriends ever made breakfast. They snuck out in the middle of the night, thinking Ty wouldn't notice they'd even been there.

Zach had to respect Johnny for owning up to what had happened. Even if Zach would rather pretend nothing had happened at all.

"I can get this." Mom started to load the dishwasher.

"No. It's okay." Zach knew she'd want to talk about it. Having something to do would make it easier. Anything was better than sitting down, face to face, to have a discussion.

"Mind if I help?"

"Sure."

"So. Are you okay with all this?"

Couldn't she ease into it? Make small talk like everyone else?

"Yeah. I guess."

"Zach. I know it's a little uncomfortable." She tried to make her voice sound gentle. "I would have preferred you find out about Johnny and me in a different way."

"Look, it's no big deal." Zach really didn't want to talk about it. Not that he had a choice. "You're both consenting adults."

"Where did you even hear a term like that?" She sounded shocked that he wasn't a total baby.

"TV. The Internet. I don't know." Zach wished she'd let it go. Give him a chance to figure out how he felt about all this before making him talk about it.

"Zach, I hope you know that I'd never want to hurt you." She was killing him with the gentle voice. "I don't want you to feel uncomfortable, or worried, or—"

"Look, Mom. I don't really want to talk about you having a boyfriend, okay?" He squirted a big glob of dish soap into the sink and turned the hot water on high. "I don't even want to think about it. Even if it is Johnny Scottsdale. Even if you look like you're really, really happy. It's just weird. Okay?"

"Okay." She stepped back. Like she didn't know she was practically glowing. Eww.

"And no, I don't want to go on a special outing or anything like that to make up for it." He plunged the frying pans into the sudsy water. He scraped the plates, rinsed them and put them in the dishwasher. Like she'd been showing him how to do for years. "I just want..."

Hell. He didn't know what he wanted.

Yeah, it'd be nice if his mom was happy. And if Johnny kept coming around.

He tried not to think about the two of them doing... well, doing what he couldn't stop thinking about the two of them doing. He knew it was normal. And natural. And all that stuff.

But she was his mother.

"Do you want me to stop seeing Johnny?" Her voice got all gentle, like it did when she was trying to make things easier on him.

"No!" He slammed the last dish into the dishwasher. That would be stupid. "I like Johnny. He's great. And I think he really likes you."

Well, duh.

"I know this is a new situation for all of us."

"Can we not talk about this to death?" Because he wasn't sure if he wanted the answer to the question that had been bothering him ever since he found out that the two of them used to date.

"Okay. We'll talk about something else." She sounded part relieved, part disappointed. "Thank you for helping with the dishes."

"And breakfast. I helped with breakfast, too."

"It was wonderful." She had that thing in her voice again. Like she couldn't have been prouder of him. Or maybe she was just happy. "Everything was wonderful."

Man, he hoped things worked out between her and Johnny. Then she'd be happy. And Johnny would be around all the time. Well, all the time when he wasn't on the road. But still. Zach liked hanging out with Johnny. Even making breakfast together was cool. It felt like they were a family already.

So, maybe they were.

If Johnny had left because he didn't want kids, he seemed to have changed his mind. At least, he seemed to like hanging out with him.

But then, maybe Ty was right. Maybe now that Johnny had—okay, he had to stop thinking about what Johnny and his mom had done. At least until he was sure Johnny wasn't going to walk out on them.

"So are you going to see him again?" Zach had to make sure

Johnny didn't forget about her. Forget about them. "Before he leaves for Arizona?"

"I hope so."

"But you don't have any plans?" Zach was growing concerned. "Not even an *I'll call you*?"

"Well, Zach." She laughed. Like this was amusing. "We didn't exactly have a chance to make plans. You came home, and I seem to recall you weren't exactly happy about finding Johnny here."

"I was just ... surprised. That's all." He'd already apologized for his reaction. "But it's totally okay. I mean, I think you guys should, like, be together."

"Well, that's a relief. I'd hate to have to ship you off to boarding school." She ruffled his hair, as if he couldn't tell already she was joking. "But don't get too excited yet. Things may or may not work out between us."

"I know. I just wanted you to know that I'm cool with it working out."

Totally cool with it.

Chapter 11

Five days, seventeen hours and twenty-six minutes. Johnny didn't need the sports talk radio host to tell him how much time he had before he would report to spring training. The clock was ticking. Time to get his head back in the game. He couldn't sit around sipping coffee, eating French Toast and reading the Sunday paper. He had too much to prove. No matter what happened, he would hang up his cleats at the end of the season. If he was lucky, it would be at the end of a championship season.

After changing into his workout clothes, he went for a run through the hills of San Francisco and ended up at the training facilities at the ballpark. A good workout always seemed to make him feel better. But for the first time in a long time, he felt pretty good already. Sure, he knew he had a long way to go in making a relationship with Ali work, but he was ready to commit to the job.

He'd just have to focus, breathe and let go of the past. He'd started by tearing up the announcement from Mel and Alice's wedding. He'd carried that damn thing around to every clubhouse he'd ever been in. Tacked it up in his locker as a motivation. Well, he didn't need it anymore. It was nothing more than a magic feather, anyway. He didn't pitch better because of it; he just believed he pitched better. Well, he'd have to convince himself that he was successful because he'd trained and practiced and worked at it.

Time to work at making sure his shoulder was in perfect shape.

He hit the weight room, grateful to have the place to himself. Not that he minded getting to know some of the other guys, but he was secretly glad Bryce Baxter wasn't there. Bryce would ask questions, wanting to know what was going on with him and Alice, and he wasn't ready to talk about it.

He'd just finished his reps on one of his favorite machines when the door opened. But it wasn't Bryce.

"I had a feeling I'd find you here." Rachel Parker marched right up to him like she belonged here. In his space.

"I wanted to follow up on our conversation from last night. Did you have a good time with your date?" Rachel smiled her camera-ready smile, even though her cameraman was nowhere to be seen. "She's lovely. I can see why you wouldn't be interested in anyone else."

"I'm sorry, but I didn't think my personal life was all that interesting." He wondered if she'd followed the limo. Had she camped outside his apartment, waiting to catch Alice leaving in last night's dress?

"You'd be surprised at the kind of details your fans would find fascinating." She sounded almost ashamed of the fact. Almost. "There's more to your story, and I just couldn't let it go."

"I'd appreciate it if you would." Johnny knew he had to tread carefully. Getting a bad rep with the press was never a smart career move. Even if he was nearing the end of his career.

She hooked her thumb under her chin, and tapped her finger along her jaw. "There was something nagging me after that first interview. I knew there was a secret behind 'The Monk' but I couldn't quite put my finger on it."

"I'd appreciate it if you kept your fingers and everything else out of my business." Johnny reached for a towel to wipe the sweat off his brow. It seemed she hadn't noticed he was busy working out.

"My gut told me I needed to dig a little deeper." She paced up and down between the rows of machines. "I thought maybe there was something about your interaction with the boy. You were spending a lot of extra time with him. Unsupervised. It struck me as odd."

"What are you suggesting?" Johnny didn't like the direction this conversation was heading. Didn't like it one bit. "Do you think I'd have an inappropriate relationship with the boy?"

And here he was worried about getting caught sneaking the widow of his best friend out of his apartment that morning. Forget that she'd been Johnny's lover first. Or he'd been afraid someone would find out about his past. Or rather, his mother's past. It had nothing to do with him. Other than that was how she'd kept him fed and clothed and housed.

"That was one explanation. You spent the last few years of high school living with your baseball coach." She wasn't telling him anything he didn't already know. "So I thought there was the possibility you'd been abused, yourself."

"Don't you dare suggest that Coach Ryan could even consider such a thing." Johnny twisted the towel in his hands. "He's a good man."

"I'm glad." She kept pacing. Like the detective in an old movie who was about to reveal the mystery. "Don't worry. I've come to the conclusion that you're not a pedophile. You have no history of working with kids. Not even when you were a kid. Unfortunately, predators tend to start young. And seek out volunteer work in order to find the intended victims."

Bile rose in his throat. How could anyone be so perverted? And how could she think he could be like that? Just because he didn't sleep around, there must be something wrong with him.

"You're right. This is the first time I've worked with kids." And if he'd known it was going to give people the wrong idea about him . . . well . . . he still didn't regret the week he'd spent coaching those boys.

"And from what I saw, you did a fantastic job." She stopped long enough to give him a smile. "You should consider coaching as the next phase of your career."

"Not if it makes people think I'm some kind of sicko." Johnny assumed his background would make people nervous about having him around kids. It had when he was young. The birthday party invitations that were rescinded at the last minute. The homecoming date who "forgot" she'd already agreed to go with someone else. The mothers who scooted down the bleachers when Johnny's mom sat next to them. As if being a prostitute was somehow contagious.

But this? This was a whole other level of social stigma. A grown man who didn't have sex with tons of women must be some kind of deviant. Rachel Parker probably wasn't the first person to wonder about him. She'd simply been the first to confront him with it.

"See, that's the thing. You're not. So there had to be some other explanation. Some other connection between you and Zach Harrison." She turned toward him, with a knowing look on her face.

"I told you, his father was my roommate in college." Why was that such a big deal? But if she'd seen him with Ali the night before, maybe she'd think that was a big deal.

"Your roommate married your college sweetheart." She was practically twitching with excitement. "Not long after you left for the minor leagues."

"How did you find out all this?" But he knew. There was only one person he'd told.

"I have my sources." She looked away, trying to hide the slight blush that colored her cheeks.

"Bryce Baxter?" He was going to have a little conversation with his new shortstop, and then stop talking to him. Bryce had been at the fundraiser. They'd said a few polite words to each other, but Johnny had been too focused on Ali. Bryce must have found Rachel more than willing to entertain him.

"No. Leave him out of this." She sounded a little too defensive. Did that mean she felt bad for using the information, or for using him? "He may have led me in the right direction, but it wasn't on purpose. He likes you. Respects you a great deal."

How well did she know Bryce? Not that it was any of his business.

"Still, I decided I needed to do a little research on Mrs. Harrison." She resumed pacing. Maybe it was her way of making sure he didn't grab her and escort her firmly out of the building. "She married your roommate only three months after you left for spring training."

"Yeah. I know." He had the announcement to prove it. Or used to. It was crumpled in the garbage can in the locker room. Had she dug through his trash?

"Three months after you left, but only six months before her son was born." Her last words were completely without emotion. She could have been reciting his pitching line from an exhibition game.

"Six?" It didn't add up.

"Is Zach Harrison your son?"

The question slammed down on him like the stack of weights on the machine he'd been working on. Johnny couldn't breathe.

"He couldn't be." He said it with less conviction than he would have liked. If only he had the wedding announcement. And maybe Zach's birth certificate. "No. She wouldn't have..."

"You had no idea?" Rachel's jaw dropped open. "I thought maybe you'd run out on her. I mean, you wouldn't be the first guy to freak out over an unplanned pregnancy. But you didn't know. Oh, I'm so sorry."

She sat on the bench next to him, looking a little deflated. Maybe her big scoop wasn't as satisfying as she'd thought it would be.

"I think you should leave." Johnny was about three seconds from losing his cool. "I think you should leave. Now."

Make that one and a half.

"Johnny, I'm truly sorry. I had no idea you didn't know." She stood up, and backed out of the weight room. "Oh, wow. I guess I should have talked to her first. I really thought you knew. Like maybe that's why you were so careful. Why you stayed away from casual encounters. You didn't want to get burned with another paternity case. That quip about the lawyers."

She wouldn't stop talking.

"Leave. Don't come back." Johnny couldn't breathe. He couldn't focus. And he sure as hell couldn't let this go.

Every other Sunday, Alice and Zach would have dinner with the Harrisons. On the weeks they didn't go over there, they would order a pizza and watch movies. Tonight was a pizza night. It would have been easy to invite Johnny to join them, but Alice needed to spend some quality time with her son.

She also needed to spend some time away from Johnny. Being with him again—being intimate with him again—had short-circuited her system. She needed some time to think. To plan the best approach for bringing up the subject of Zach's paternal uncertainty.

"Can we make popcorn?" Zach asked while she was putting the leftover pizza in the refrigerator. There wasn't much left over; he'd eaten four slices. Now he wanted popcorn. But it would give her an excuse to sit next to him on the couch.

They made a big bowl of popcorn and settled in front of the TV to pick a movie. They had their favorites. Usually this time of year, with spring training right around the corner, they'd load up on baseball movies. But Alice didn't think she'd be able to watch Kevin Costner "have a catch" with his dad. And, well, she wouldn't allow Zach to watch *Bull Durham* until he was married, despite the volumes of baseball wisdom it contained.

When Zach suggested they watch *Star Wars*, she didn't protest.

They'd enjoyed the movie together many times. Part of her even hoped he'd jump up off the couch to grab his toy light saber, to act out the battle scenes, but the toy had long ago broken. Only a few Lego space ships remained from his childhood. She shuddered to think about having to pack those away to make room for an electric razor and body spray.

Zach ate popcorn by the handful. His appetite didn't show any signs of slowing down. He was growing so fast, she was afraid she wouldn't be able to keep up. Just in the last year, his features had changed. He was starting to look more like a man. Like Johnny.

"What?" Zach must have sensed her watching him instead of the movie. "Do I have popcorn on my face or something?"

"No. I was just watching you." She smiled. A bittersweet smile as she realized she was losing her little boy.

"Geez, Mom. It's not like you haven't seen me much the last thirteen years."

"I know. But you're changing so much."

"Please. Let's not start in on that. I'm not your baby anymore. Get over it." But he smiled, enough to let her know that he understood his growing up wasn't easy on her.

"I try. But you'll always be my baby." She patted his shoulder, and then pulled him into a hug.

"Maybe we should have invited Johnny to join us." He wriggled free and settled back into the opposite end of the couch. The look he shot her made her wonder if maybe he wasn't quite on board with them dating.

"Tonight is family night."

"Yeah, but maybe you two will get married." He gave her a glance and then focused on the last kernels of popcorn. "Then we'd all be a family."

"Oh, Zach." Her heart constricted at the idea. "Johnny and I have only recently reconnected. After a very long time apart. It's almost like we have to start over, to get to know each other again."

"So, why didn't you have him come over? So you can get to know each other more?" He had enough sarcasm in his tone to irritate her, but not enough to send him to his room.

"Because." She really didn't have a reason. "Because I didn't want to overwhelm you. You were pretty upset this morning."

"That's because I thought you were just hooking up. But I'm okay with you guys being . . . together. If you're going to be going out and stuff. But if it's just a booty call, then that's just . . . gross."

"A b-b-booty call? Where did you hear a term like that?" She was stunned to hear this kind of frank discussion from her little boy. Even though she'd often encouraged him, and told him that he could tell her anything.

"Ty. That's what he calls it when his mom's boyfriend shows up after they think Ty's asleep." Zach was too young to be having this conversation. Then again, kids his age were engaging in . . . she shuddered to think about what kinds of things.

"Well, you know that's not what's happening between me and Johnny." Was it? They'd been on one date. They'd made love. But that didn't necessarily mean they were going to have a future together.

"No. I know. Johnny told me his intentions are honorable." Right, they'd talked. Man-to-man.

"So are mine."

"Good." Zach said. "I think you guys should get married, then."

"Zach, there's a long way between honorable intentions and getting married."

"Oh, I know. But you already know each other. And it's not like when you were in college. You know, when Johnny was worried about his career and stuff."

"No. His career isn't an issue."

"Good. I know he might not stay here in San Francisco." Zach had obviously given this a lot of thought. "But if he gets traded or signs somewhere else, we can just go with him."

"You'd be okay with moving?" She'd been afraid to bring it up, even when she was considering going back to school. Maybe that was one of the reasons she couldn't quite make the commitment to sending off her application.

"Sure, if there was a good reason to." Zach leaned back against the couch. "And keeping the family together would be a good reason to."

The way he said the word family put her mother's intuition on alert. Did he have suspicions about Johnny? Was it that obvious to everyone but her?

"Well, Johnny's career is only one thing to consider. I have my commitment to the foundation, and your grandparents." Who might not really be his grandparents.

"Yeah, but I'm sure they'd understand." He didn't sound as convinced as he had earlier. "I mean, they'd want you to be happy. Right?"

"I believe they would want us to be happy." For a change, she was the one ready to end the conversation before it got any deeper. "Oh, I love this scene."

She reached for the remote to turn up the volume just in time for Princess Leia to lead them all into the garbage chute.

Fortunately, they wouldn't have time to watch the next movie. The one in which Luke found out who his father was. Would Zach be as devastated to learn the truth?

Would Johnny?

Chapter 12

Johnny picked up the phone. He dialed and took a deep breath to calm himself before he could speak.

"Hey, Johnny, what's up?" Bryce Baxter answered on the second ring.

"Remember when you offered to take me out for a beer?" He needed to have this conversation in person. "I think you owe me one."

"Sure. Whenever." Bryce sounded far too relaxed on his end. Not at all like a guy who'd just betrayed his best friend. Wait, they weren't friends. Not really. Bryce didn't owe him any loyalty. Not off the field. "Name the time and place."

"Fifteen minutes. That sports bar around the corner from the ballpark." He'd walked by it on his way to and from the stadium. It looked like a low-key place during the offseason. They probably made most of their profits before and after games.

"See you there." Bryce hung up. If he knew Johnny was pissed at him, he didn't show it. But then, Bryce wasn't the only one he was pissed with. He was just the only person he could deal with at the moment.

And he was the only person he could talk to.

"Everything alright?" Bryce beat him to the bar. He also lived within walking distance. "You look like hell. And not because you were out late with a certain lovely lady."

"I never should have told you about Alice." Johnny pulled up the barstool next to Bryce. "Then you couldn't have told that reporter about her."

"Oh shit." Bryce caught the attention of the bartender, and indicated Johnny needed a drink. "I didn't mean to spill anything. But she was so damn persuasive."

Bryce made a little sound that told Johnny everything he needed to know about how she'd persuaded him.

"She used you." Johnny almost felt sorry for him. Almost. "For a story."

"Every woman I've ever been with has used me for something." Bryce sounded so matter-of-fact about that admission. "But I was only trying to defend you. She had it in her head there was something not right with you and the kid. I had to set her straight."

"Yeah? Well, you set her straight into my personal life."

"Sorry. All I said was, you were the last person who would hurt a kid." Bryce paid the bartender for Johnny's beer. "I told her you were hanging around him because you used to have a thing for his mother."

"She took that information and ran with it." Johnny took a long pull on the frosty mug in front of him. "She went so far as to check the dates on Alice's marriage license. And Zach's birth certificate."

"What? Why would she do that?" Bryce looked genuinely surprised. And not quite sure he wanted to hear what she'd found.

"I think he might be my kid." Johnny took another long drink. He stared at the bottles lining the wall behind the bar. Not wanting to look at the other man. Not wanting to see his reaction. "All this time I was completely in the dark about it. Then some reporter gets a wild idea to follow up on something you said before, during or after you slept with her."

"It was after." Bryce sounded a little bit remorseful. "Shit, Johnny, I had no idea she'd go after you. I thought she'd drop it once she figured out there was no scandal."

"No, just a different one." Johnny stared at his now empty mug.

"Damn. What are you going to do?" Bryce asked. He sounded truly sorry now. No more bullshit. No more fun and games.

"I don't know." Johnny flagged the bartender. He could use another round and some calamari to go with it. "At least now I know you didn't sell me out entirely."

"Look, maybe I can talk to her." Bryce swallowed the last of his beer. "I'll use some of my persuasive skills to get her to keep this story to herself."

"She's a reporter." Johnny laughed at the absurdity of it all. "She's not going to keep the news that 'The Monk' has a love child to herself."

"She might. If I let her have her way with me." Bryce groaned as he leaned forward to rest his elbows on the bar.

"You like her, don't you?"

Bryce swore under his breath.

Yeah. He liked her. Poor guy.

"So what are you going to do about the kid?"

"I guess I need to start by finding out for sure if he's mine." Johnny didn't have the first clue on how to do that. "They can tell with a blood test?"

"Nah. They just swab your cheek. It's totally painless." Bryce was the voice of experience.

"Except for the part about her keeping him from me all this time." Johnny reached for his second, and what should be his last beer, of the night. "Man, I feel like an idiot."

"Maybe she didn't know." Bryce's cheerfulness made it sound almost plausible.

"Have you seen the kid?" Johnny could picture Zach right now. A younger, blonder version of himself. "He looks exactly like me. How could she look at him every day for the last thirteen years and not know?"

"I don't know. They tend to develop personalities of their own." Bryce stared into his mug. "I mean, my daughter is the spitting image of her mother. But then she'll smile. Or laugh. And she's so different. Not like her at all. And that's a very good thing, let me tell you."

"Sounds like your ex isn't your favorite person?"

"No. Hell, I don't even know how we ended up together in the first place. Other than I was young and stupid and flattered by the attention of a hot chick." Bryce shook his head. "I don't know about you, but I was kind of a late bloomer. Skinny, small, and awkward except on the field."

"I was skinny, tall and awkward." But that didn't mean he hadn't been propositioned. Just the opposite. His mother's friends had felt sorry for him. Offered to relieve him of his virginity. On the house.

"Yeah. And at my school, baseball players were only a step above band geeks." Bryce chuckled to himself. At himself. "It was all about the football players. And basketball. Both sports I didn't have a chance at."

"So once girls started paying attention to you, you let it go to your head." Johnny had seen it enough. The only thing that made him different was, well, he wanted to be different. He didn't want to be like the jerks who used women for sex. Or even paid them.

"Yeah. Both of them." Bryce laughed as if he'd just told the funniest joke. Even if the joke was on him. "Told you I was an idiot."

"You're not the only one." Johnny set his mug on the bar. "Thanks for the beer."

"Thanks for not beating the crap out of me for telling Rachel about you and Alice. I had no idea . . ."

"Hey. It's cool. I'm glad she figured it out. I might have gone on with blinders on. Like I always have where Alice is concerned."

"So are you going to go talk to her?"

"Yeah. I guess I better. Before it becomes public."

"Hey, I'm serious about talking to Rachel for you." Bryce stood up, held out his hand. "If I have to beg. Get down on my knees. Tie her up. Or let her tie me up. Whatever it takes, man."

"Don't hurt yourself." Johnny shook his friend's hand. An hour ago, he hadn't thought it possible to still consider Bryce a friend. But he was, at the moment, his only friend.

"Never." Bryce placed his hand over his heart, as if he was invincible in that area. "And hey, if you need help finding a paternity lawyer, I can ask around for you. It won't come as a shock coming from me. Hell, I'm surprised they haven't started calling me."

"Thanks. I hope it won't come to that, but I appreciate it." Johnny walked the five blocks back to his apartment building. He jumped in his Jeep and drove over to Alice's.

He sat in front of her house for about twenty minutes before he could bring himself to the front door. His talk with Bryce had helped him get his anger under control. But the hurt was still there. She'd married Mel knowing she was pregnant with Johnny's child. How could she? Why did she keep it from him, even after Mel died? The answers could only come from her.

He rang the bell, hoping Alice would answer and not Zach. He wasn't ready to face his son yet. Not until he could get his emotions under control.

"Johnny, what a surprise." Alice opened the door. She was wearing yoga pants and a light blue sweatshirt. Her hair was gathered into a ponytail. She looked so much like the girl he used to know. The girl who'd betrayed him. Even more than he'd ever known.

"What is it? What's wrong?" She stepped toward him.

But he didn't want her to touch him. Not now.

"Can we talk? Just the two of us?" As much as this concerned Zach, he didn't think he needed to hear about it like this.

"Yeah. Okay. Zach and I were watching a movie, but it's almost over." She stepped back to let him in. "He needs to get ready for bed soon, anyway."

"Hey, Johnny." Zach took one look at him and his smile faded. He stepped closer to Alice, ready to get between them if necessary. He might be just a kid, but he wasn't going to let anyone hurt his mother. Not even Johnny Scottsdale. Admiration for the boy swept over him. At thirteen, he was already a bigger man than Johnny had ever been.

"It's okay. I'm . . ." What was Johnny going to say? That he wouldn't hurt her? That the reason he'd come here tonight wasn't going to change all three of their lives? "I'm sorry to drop in on your family time."

"Zach, go get ready for bed. Everything's fine. Right, Johnny?" She plastered a fake smile on her face. "We just need to talk about a few things. Grown-up things that you don't need to worry about."

"Yeah. Sure." Zach's shoulders slumped slightly. Enough for Johnny to recognize that he was giving in. This time.

Zach headed up the stairs but without the carefree enthusiasm Johnny had seen every other time he'd been here.

"So, what's going on?" Alice led him to the kitchen at the back of the house. "Something's bothering you, I can tell."

"Yeah. Something's bothering me." Hell, now he was here, he didn't know how to start.

"What is it? You didn't hurt yourself, did you?" She reached for his right arm. His pitching arm. "You mentioned you were going to work out this afternoon. You didn't pull something?"

"No. I'm fine. My arm is fine." He wished he had something to do. Something to hold while he had this conversation.

"Can I get you a drink? Some wine? A beer? Some iced tea?"

"No. Thanks." He shook his head.

"Okay. Why don't you just come right out and say what's troubling you."

"Zach." His throat closed up on him. He couldn't quite get the words out. "Is he . . ."

Johnny got up, walked to the sink. He opened the cabinet closest to it and grabbed the first glass he found. He filled it with water straight from the tap and gulped it down. His hand shook as he set the empty glass on the stone counter. "Is he my son?" Johnny sank against the counter, bracing himself for her answer.

"I don't know." She crossed to the cabinet and grabbed a wine glass. From a previously opened bottle on the counter, she poured a generous portion. "I honestly don't know."

"You don't know." He repeated her words, as if he hadn't heard her correctly. "How could you not know?"

She took a long, defensive drink. "We'd broken up. And then I was with Mel. So it could have been either one of you."

That made him feel about as special as a hot dog wrapper blowing around the bleachers after the last game of a double-header.

"And you never bothered to find out?" He filled his glass with more water, drank it down and then reached for the wine bottle. He didn't care if he poured it into a juice glass. He just needed something to wash down the rage. The disappointment. And the hurt.

"What was I supposed to do? Call you up out of the blue and say 'Hey Johnny, so glad you're finally living your dream. Guess what? I'm pregnant.' How would that have been?" Before he had a chance to answer, she continued. "'Oh, and by the way, it might not be yours.' How would that have gone over?"

Johnny took a long slug of wine. Yeah. That would have been great. Not much different from the way he felt right now.

"Did you think I would have just left you?" Her lack of faith cut deep.

"No. I know what you would have done." She bit her lower lip in a feeble attempt to keep it from quivering. "You would've quit. You would've made the noble effort to support me and Zach. But you would have resented me. Resented us both for taking you away from the one thing you loved more than anything."

"Baseball?" She'd kept his kid from him so he could play baseball.

"Yes. I couldn't let you give that up. Not when there was a chance you'd be taking responsibility for a child who wasn't even yours."

"But you had no problem letting Mel take responsibility for a child who wasn't his."

"He knew what he was getting into." Alice looked out the window, avoiding his gaze. "He knew it would have wrecked you to find out that I'd been with him too."

"But that didn't stop him from sleeping with you." Johnny tossed back the rest of the wine. "Didn't stop him from marrying you, and raising my child as his own."

"We didn't know for sure whose child he was." She took the empty glass from him. Possibly to keep him from shattering it, he gripped it so tightly. "We didn't want to find out. Once we made the decision to get married, we figured it was best if we just assumed Mel was the father."

"Best for who?"

"All of us." She placed a tentative hand on his arm. "Johnny, I couldn't let you become like my father. Always wondering what could have been if I hadn't trapped you. You would have resented me. Resented Zach."

"I wouldn't." He'd like to think that was the truth. But he couldn't be sure. Not when baseball had been his only shot at making something of himself. If he'd been forced to give that up, yeah, he could see how he could have wound up bitter. "I would have liked the chance to prove you wrong."

"What would you have done if I'd come to you right away?" She asked. "Would you have come back? Given up everything you'd worked so hard for? Maybe you could have gotten a job at a casino, parking cars or making change. That would have been a dream come true."

"I would have figured something out." Like waiting tables or dealing blackjack. Maybe her dad could have pulled some strings and got him on at the mine. Although the one time Johnny had met the man, neither was too impressed with the other. Johnny got the feeling Alice's father was bitter and envious of Johnny's college success.

"We can't go back and undo the past." Alice had a slight quiver in her voice. "But maybe we can move forward. Just tell me what you want to do."

"I don't know what I want." He was still reeling from the news. "I only found out this afternoon that I might be a father. I need a little time to think."

"That's fair." She sighed and leaned against the counter next to him. "So, how did you find out?"

"That reporter. She was suspicious of how much time I was spending with Zach." It still made his stomach turn to think of what she'd initially thought he was capable of. Made it turn even more knowing there were people out there who would do such things. "But then she found out we had a previous relationship and did the math."

"Johnny, I'm sorry. I'm so sorry you had to find out that way."

"Were you planning on telling me? Now that we're . . ." No. They weren't together. Not anymore. "Or were you hoping I wouldn't figure it out eventually?"

"I wanted to tell you. I just didn't know how." There was a catch in her voice. "It's not any easier now than it would have been fourteen years ago."

"No. It's not." He pushed himself away from the counter. "I need to go. I've got a lot of stuff to sort out."

"Are you okay to drive?" She reached out to grab his arm.

He shook her off. Didn't want to touch her. Not right now. Maybe not ever again.

"I'm well under the limit." He certainly didn't feel the effects of the glass of wine he'd drank. Or the two beers he had earlier.

"Mel was under the legal limit, too." She had to bring that up. "But he was upset with me. I can't let you risk your life."

"I'm fine. I'm in complete control." Like always.

"Johnny." She took his hand and this time he let her. "I'm so sorry. I know I messed things up. Terribly. But you have to understand, it was out of love. I didn't want to hurt you. Please, believe me."

"I believe you." He pulled away. Until now, she'd always been the one to pull away. "I just don't know if I can forgive you."

Zach hadn't meant to overhear the conversation between Mom and Johnny. He was going to grab a snack, but there they were, so deep in conversation they didn't even hear him step into the kitchen.

They were talking about him. About how Johnny might be his father. No, the way they were talking, he was his father. Only he'd just found out. And he was pretty steamed about it.

Zach backed up, sneaking upstairs to his room.

In a way, he was relieved Johnny hadn't known. He hadn't just walked away from his mom like it wasn't his problem. Zach was glad Johnny wasn't that kind of guy.

But that meant his mom had been the one to keep them apart all these years. Even after his dad, or make that his stepdad, died. She'd let him go through life without a father, even though he had one. The guy he'd grown up worshipping was, in fact, his real dad. And she'd kept it from him. From Johnny, too.

He didn't care what her excuses were. It was just plain wrong. How could she keep something like that from him? From both of them?

And to marry someone else, letting everyone think Mel was his dad. That his Grandpa Mel and Nannie Frannie were his grandparents.

Would they stop taking him places? Like the golf course and to museums and even those art exhibits he pretended to be bored at, but secretly enjoyed? Would they stop having them over for Sunday dinner?

Would they stop coming to his games? His school events?

Would they stop caring about him?

Did he have a whole other family somewhere?

He had so many questions, but he couldn't go to his mom like he usually did. He was pretty mad at her right now. He knew he wouldn't be very respectful to her if he tried to talk to her. He could think of a lot of things he'd say that would be downright disrespectful. Either she was a liar or she was a slut. If she knew Johnny was his father this whole time, then she was a liar. If she didn't know, then that meant . . . well, he didn't want to think about what that meant but he'd taken *Family Life* in school and knew enough about how things worked.

Maybe he should go down there and tell her he wanted to go live with his dad. That's what Ty always said to his mom when he was really, really mad at her. It always made her cry but she'd give in to whatever Ty wanted, whether it was a new video game or to be able to go somewhere she didn't think he was old enough to go to on his own.

The problem with that was Zach didn't even know if Johnny would want him. He'd been a single guy for a long time. A single, professional athlete. Surely he wouldn't want a kid hanging around, getting in his way. Besides, Johnny would be leaving for Arizona in a few days. He'd be down there for over a month. He couldn't live with him during the season, either. The Goliaths were on the road half the time. Sometimes for up to three weeks at a time.

Man, this sucked. Zach grabbed a baseball and held it in his hand. For some reason that always seemed to calm him. Just feeling the rough texture of the stitches and the scuffed-up leather. He used to pretend he was like his hero. By holding a regulation baseball, he could channel Johnny Scottsdale and he, too, could be calm, cool and completely in control.

He flopped onto his bed, turning the ball over and over in his hand as he turned the problem over in his mind.

Johnny Scottsdale was his dad.

Just this morning, he'd been trying to figure out how he felt about his mom and Johnny dating. He thought about what it would be like if they ended up, like, getting married. Then Johnny would be his stepdad. He kind of thought that would be cool.

But the way they were talking, it didn't seem like they'd be dating anymore. Not when Johnny was mad about not knowing about Zach. Maybe they'd end up fighting. Like Ty's parents. And then Zach would be caught in the middle. Not wanting to live with either of them.

Great. Just great.

Alice found Zach already in bed. His arms were crossed over his chest and he was facing the wall. He had something in his right hand. A baseball.

She sat carefully on the bed, hoping not to wake him. She brushed his hair off his forehead. There was barely enough light for her to make out his features. His dark eyelashes, his determined jaw, the beginnings of fuzz on his upper lip.

Where had her baby boy gone? He'd grown up right before her eyes.

But Johnny had missed it.

"Oh, Zachie." She never called him that anymore. It embarrassed him.

"I love you so much." She kept her voice low, hardly more than a whisper. "I want you to know that no matter what happens—I never, ever regretted having you."

She brushed a feather-light kiss on his forehead.

"I made some difficult choices. Possibly even the wrong ones."

She hoped he wouldn't wake before she finished what she needed to say. "But I made them all out of love. For you. And your father. How am I going to tell you that the man you thought was your father, wasn't? And the man you saw as your hero is really your father."

She didn't know how to break the news to Zach. She'd have to tell him soon, though. Before Rachel Parker went public.

"I do know one thing." She smiled down at her sleeping son. "Johnny will be a good dad. He'll do his best to be there for you."

Johnny would be a part of Zach's life. Of that, she had no doubt. She would just have to get used to seeing him at Zach's school functions. Get used to dropping Zach off for visits. Picking him up when Johnny had to go on the road. Breaking her heart a little bit more each time.

Chapter 13

Alice checked the Internet. She went straight to the Bay Area Sports Network website. Rachel Parker hadn't posted anything. Yet. Next, she went to Twitter to see if Johnny Scottsdale was trending. Nothing notable. She even checked the usual sports insider sites. No buzz there, either. If she couldn't find any rumors when she was actively looking, it was a safe bet none of Zach's friends would stumble across anything before she had a chance to talk to him after school. Hopefully, Johnny would come around and they could tell him together.

Zach didn't have much to say on the ride to school. But that had been the norm lately. He was at that phase of development where his main forms of communications were shrugs, grunts and eye rolls. She used to enjoy their rides to and from school. Now he preferred to walk home, and as much as she missed him, she knew she had to give him more freedom and responsibility. It was just so hard to think of him growing up and not needing her anymore.

After dropping Zach off, Alice stopped by the Harrisons' to make sure the receipts from Saturday's benefit had been deposited. She usually took the responsibility for the cash from the bar, but when Frannie had learned Johnny was going, she'd offered to take care of everything so Alice could relax and enjoy the evening. A blush crept across her cheeks at the thought of how much she'd enjoyed her evening.

Alice rang the bell. She normally let herself in through the kitchen, but now wasn't sure if they were still family and felt like she no longer had the right.

"Alice, dear, what a surprise." Frannie brushed a quick kiss on Alice's cheek. "What can I do for you?"

"I just wanted to make sure the cash receipts from Saturday were deposited. Or if you haven't had time yet, I can run over to the bank." Her job with the foundation had been a blessing in so many ways, but she was ready to move on. Only now she wasn't sure which direction that would be. If Johnny was in San Francisco, then Zach would need to be there too.

"It's been taken care of." Frannie offered a warm smile. "Let me get a copy of the receipt for you. I already emailed it to the accountants."

"Thank you. I appreciate it." With that out of the way, there wasn't any excuse to put off the inevitable.

"I'll make some tea." Frannie didn't give her a chance to decline; she headed straight back to the kitchen. "And you can fill me in on how your date with Johnny went."

"It was lovely, thank you." As much as she considered the other woman a friend, she didn't feel like discussing her date. For some reason it felt like cheating. On a man she'd never loved in the first place. Or at least, she'd never loved Mel in that way.

"My, didn't Johnny look handsome all dressed up?" Frannie put the kettle on, and arranged two teacups and saucers on a tray. She dropped an Earl Grey tea bag into Alice's cup and green tea for herself.

"Yes. Yes, he did." She felt her heart cracking wide open at the memory of their last night together. At least she'd had that. One final goodbye before they settled into their roles as co-parents.

"Zach is becoming more and more handsome." Frannie knew. It still didn't make it easier to have this conversation. "More and more like his father."

"About that." Alice waited for the kettle to finish whistling. And for Frannie to pour the hot water into both teacups. "Johnny knows he may be Zach's father. It could become public. A reporter did some digging around and she connected the dots."

"I see." Frannie's hand shook a little as she stirred honey into her tea. "I guess it's time to find out the truth."

"Yes. I wanted to tell you I've decided to order a DNA test." It was almost like telling the woman she'd decided to take out a hit on her family. What was left of it.

"That's probably for the best."

"What's probably for the best?" Mel Sr. entered the kitchen without either of them noticing. His voice sounded... different. Less commanding than usual. But maybe she was just anticipating how much he'd be hurt by losing Zach.

"Finding out whether Johnny Scottsdale is Zach's father or if..." Frannie couldn't finish the sentence.

"Johnny Scottsdale? Zach's father?" Mel's face drained of color. Sweat formed on his brow. He staggered backward against the kitchen counter.

His face contorted in pain as he slumped to the floor.

"Oh, no you don't." Frannie rushed over to him, reaching him right before he collapsed. She eased him to the floor and slid down next to him. "Don't you dare leave me. You're the only one I have left."

Mel moaned, so at least he was conscious. "Frannie? Frannie, I can't catch my breath."

Alice reached for the kitchen phone. She called emergency dispatch and relayed the scene in front of her, Mel clutching his chest, pale and frightened. Frannie knelt beside him, so calm and strong, assuring him he was going to be fine. No, commanding him to be fine. She loosened his clothing, making him comfortable while they waited for EMTs to arrive. Within minutes, the doorbell rang. Alice slipped out to let the paramedics inside, recounted what she'd witnessed and then stood back to let them work.

Alice felt like an outsider. Outside the family. Even outside her body. Like someone watching the scene in slow motion. She forced herself to breathe while she caught snippets of conversation.

Cardiac arrest.

Questions about medications Mel was currently on.

Stabilized.

Discussion about what hospital Frannie wanted him transported to.

Mel was strapped to a gurney and loaded into the back of an ambulance.

"Alice, would you be a dear and drive my car down to the hospital?" Frannie sounded perfectly calm, as if she was asking her to fetch a gallon of milk from the store.

"Yes, of course." Alice snapped back to reality. "Are you riding with Mel?"

"No. But I think it would be best if I didn't drive." She sounded like she was in better shape than Alice, but she wasn't going to let the other woman down. "I'll just grab a few things in case we need to stay overnight."

"Sure. No problem." Alice had a few minutes to get herself together. She cleaned up the tea and put the kitchen in order. The table had been moved to the side to make room for the paramedics. She pulled the table into place, lined the chairs up and rearranged the flowers in the vase at the center.

"Thank you for putting everything back." Frannie stood in the doorway, with a small overnight bag in her hand and an unsteady smile on her face. "Let's get down there. I'm afraid Mel won't know the name of his doctor or what medication he takes. He relies on me for everything. Of course, that's my fault, you know. I've always taken care of everything for him. Let him worry about nothing more than his work and his golf game."

She was babbling, but Alice didn't think she could handle riding to the hospital in silence.

"I've been after him for some time now to slow down." Frannie let Alice open the passenger door to her Mercedes and she slid into the seat, holding her bag on her lap.

By the time Alice reached the driver's side, Frannie had fastened her seatbelt.

"Maybe now he'll listen to me." Frannie set her bag on the floor at her feet. "The man is too stubborn for his own good. But then, I suppose most men are."

"Yes. They are."

"As much as I want him to slow down," Frannie prattled on, "I don't want him to be one of those old men who have nothing to occupy their time. I want to enjoy our golden years together. Spend time with our grandson . . ."

Alice almost ran a red light. She braked just in time.

"I don't care what the DNA test says." Frannie stared straight ahead. "Zach is our boy. We love him. And we will love him no matter what."

Alice wanted to acknowledge her appreciation of that sentiment, but the words caught in her throat.

"We won't get in the way, of course." Frannie kept her head held high, her shoulders straight. "But it doesn't matter to me—to us—how Zach came to be. We are just grateful that we've had the chance to be there as he grew up."

Alice turned into the parking lot of the hospital. She found a spot right up front. After shutting off the engine, she turned to the woman who'd been so much more than her mother-in-law.

"Frannie. I can never thank you enough for everything you've done for me. And Zach." She swallowed the enormous lump in her throat. "I can't even imagine how I would have done it without you."

"We're happy to have had you both in our lives." Frannie reached across the car and took Alice's hand. "You have always been a blessing to us. And that doesn't change. I don't care what the science says. That boy is family. You are family."

"Frannie, I appreciate the sentiment, but don't you think we have more important things to worry about?"

"That's the thing about a wakeup call like this." Frannie squeezed her hand. "It makes you realize what's really important."

Alice felt incredibly small. Especially compared to the woman sitting next to her.

Zach came home to an empty house. No big deal. In a way he was glad his mom wasn't home. That meant he wouldn't have to have the awkward conversation he knew was coming. But after an hour passed and he still hadn't heard from her, he started to get worried. Her car was in the driveway. She hadn't answered her cell phone. And no one answered at his grandparents' house either.

Something was wrong.

He gathered his courage and picked up the phone. He went into his room, where he usually felt safe. But this time when he looked up at the poster of Johnny Scottsdale, instead of the steadying influence he normally felt, he imagined Johnny saying, "Zach. I am your father." In a Darth Vader accent.

Since he didn't know where else to turn, he dialed his number.

Johnny picked up on the first ring.

"Hey, um, sorry to bother you." Boy, didn't that sound lame? "But I was wondering if my mom was with you."

Hoped she was, anyway.

"Nope. Sorry. I haven't seen her since last night." When they were arguing over him.

"Oh. Okay. Thanks, anyways." Zach wasn't sure if he should tell him that he was worried. He'd hoped they were together and had just lost track of time. Even if it meant they were, you know, *together*.

"Is everything okay?" It was like Johnny could tell something was wrong. He didn't have to say anything.

"I don't know." Zach felt like he could talk to him about what was going on. "I came home from school and my mom wasn't here. Not that she's always here when I get home, you know. But I just get the feeling that something's... wrong. Her car is here."

"Maybe she went shopping with someone and they picked her up." Johnny was trying to sound encouraging. It wasn't working.

"No. She would have left a note or something." He didn't know how to explain it, but he had this feeling deep down. And he was scared. Really scared. Not that he'd come right out and admit it.

"Would you like me to come over?"

"Could you?" Okay, so that sounded kind of desperate, but Zach didn't care. He really was worried. He'd never gone this long without hearing from his mom. And the fact that his grandparents weren't available only made it seem weirder.

"I'll be there as soon as I can." Johnny sounded like he was on his way already. Zach could almost picture him grabbing his keys and heading out to save the day. Kind of like when he headed out of the bullpen, after warming up to throw out the first pitch.

"Thanks." Zach felt better already. "I'm sure everything is fine, but I'm glad you're coming over."

He was glad Johnny was his dad.

Especially if something had happened to his mom. He'd been so mad at her last night. So much so, when she'd come into his room, he pretended to be asleep. He'd heard every word she'd said.

In the end he'd almost felt bad about not saying anything. But he needed time to think. This was major stuff here. He couldn't just forget about how she'd lied to him for basically his entire life. Even if he could kind of understand how she could think it was important to let Johnny—his dad—play baseball. To let him become the All-Star he was meant to be.

Zach tried to work on his homework while he waited for Johnny, but couldn't concentrate. So he gave up and paced around the living room, his worry growing with each passing minute.

Most of the time, he thought it was lame having his mom check in with him all the time. That she was always around. He could count on her being there when he woke up in the morning. When he got home from school. When he needed her.

So where was she now? It would be one thing if she'd been off with Johnny. Doing whatever it was that he didn't want to think about his mother doing with any guy, not even his dad.

It would be different, if she was more like Ty's mom. Always looking for a guy to make her life complete. He could totally see her running off and not bothering to tell her son where she was going. The way Ty told it, she was more interested in finding a guy to take care of her than taking care of her kid. Then again, Ty had pretty much been pissed off at his parents ever since they got divorced.

Zach wondered what it would have been like if his mom had married Johnny instead of Mel. Okay, so it was still weird to call him by his name, but calling him *Dad* seemed even weirder. Would she and Johnny have ended up hating each other like Ty's parents?

It seemed unlikely, considering how happy she'd been just the other day. Right after she'd spent the night with Johnny. She was happier than Zach had ever seen her. And for a brief moment, he'd thought maybe there would be one of those storybook endings. Where they would end up happy together. All of them. One. Big. Happy. Family.

Yeah. And he'd get drafted by the Goliaths right out of high school. In the first round.

The phone rang. He walked in slow motion to pick up the receiver. He didn't recognize the number, but it was local.

"Hello?" He tried to sound like the man of the house.

"Zach?" It was Mom. Like anyone else would pick up the phone. "Zach, is that you?"

"Yeah." He worked really hard at sounding like he wasn't scared to death.

"Oh, Zach. Thank God you're okay." She exhaled, sounding like she was the one who had no freaking idea where the other one had been all afternoon.

"Yeah. I'm fine. Just hanging out. I was just going to start my homework." Something he could do now he knew his mom was at least alive.

"Zach, I have some news." She sounded like she was afraid to tell him. "About your grandfather."

His heart stopped for an instant. His eyes got a little blurry and he felt moisture leaking out at the corners.

"Grandpa Mel had a heart attack. He's okay, but we had to take him to the hospital. I'm sorry I wasn't there when you got home from school."

Seriously? She was worried about not being home when he got out of school? Like that was a real problem.

"Are you sure he's going to be okay?" Zach's voice seemed like it was coming from someone else.

"Yes. I'm sorry I didn't call you sooner."

"No. It's okay. I didn't even notice you were gone." He lied, but thought it would make her feel better. She sounded so worried over the phone.

"Are you sure you're okay?"

The doorbell rang. He wasn't alone anymore.

"Yeah. I'm fine. I gotta go." Zach hung up the phone and had to restrain himself from running to get the door. The relief that washed over him was almost too much. First, knowing his mom was okay. And second, finding Johnny Scottsdale—his dad—at the front door.

Oh, and he was glad that his grandpa was going to be okay.

Even if he wasn't really his grandpa.

"I'm sorry I took so long to get here." Johnny must have flown, considering he lived clear on the other side of the city.

"It's okay." Zach couldn't help it; he threw his arms around Johnny. "I'm just glad you came."

Johnny wrapped his arms around the boy. His son. Still seemed unreal to him, but as he felt Zach's breathing slow and his body relax against him, he figured he must be doing something right. Even if it was just being there.

"So, what do you need me to do?" Johnny wanted to take charge. Find a solution. "Where should we look for your mom?"

"She's at the hospital." Zach released him and stepped back.

Johnny clenched his jaw; he knew he needed to be strong for his son.

"My grandpa had a heart attack." Zach relayed the news and Johnny immediately felt relieved. He couldn't imagine what he'd do if anything happened to Alice. Sure, he was pretty upset with her right now, but... He loved her.

"He's going to be alright. At least I think he is." Zach shoved his hands in his pockets, a move Johnny could relate to. "Sometimes my mom tries to protect me. She holds stuff back. She thinks I can't handle things. But I can. If it's really serious, I'd rather know, you know?"

"I can see your mom doing that." Johnny could see it all too clearly. She wanted to protect those she loved. Even if it meant withholding the truth. "Would you feel better if we went down there, and we could see for ourselves he's really okay?"

"You'd do that? You'd take me to the hospital?"

"Sure. Let's go." Johnny stood in the doorway while Zach grabbed a jacket.

"Has your grandpa had heart problems before?" Johnny had waited until they were on their way before asking.

"I don't think so." Zach shook his head. "He's pretty active for an old guy. I mean, for someone his age."

"That's good." Johnny tried to keep the conversation flowing, but it wasn't easy. "You're pretty close to your grandparents."

"Yeah. Is that weird?" He sounded as if he thought he should be embarrassed to like his family. "It's not just because they buy me stuff. I mean, they treat me like I'm a real person, you know?"

"Yeah. I know." Johnny flipped on his blinker to turn into the hospital parking lot. "I felt the same way when I first met them. I was real nervous. I didn't have a lot of money back then. I didn't have any money, and they had this big fancy house in the city. But they made me feel like I was important. Even before I was."

"If you were their son's friend, then you were important to them."

"You know, I think you're right." Johnny whipped his Jeep into a parking spot. "Are you ready for this?"

"Yes." Zach tried to sound brave. It must be hard on a kid his age to face the possibility of losing someone close to him. "Do you think he's really okay?"

"I hope so." Johnny never had a grandfather to be close to. He didn't have any family at all except for his mother.

And now Zach.

As he approached the front desk, Johnny wondered if coming here was the right thing to do. He'd just thought Zach must be worried, and sitting around the house all by himself only made the situation worse. So he'd jumped into action without thinking it through. Maybe visiting hours were over. Maybe they'd be in the way. But he couldn't stand by watching his kid imagine the worst.

They were directed to the family waiting room down the hall. Alice stood at the window, looking out.

"Mom." Zach ran to her and threw his arms around her waist.

"Zach, how did you . . ." She looked up at Johnny and for a moment he wondered if she'd be angry with him. Then her features softened. "Thank you, Johnny. Thank you."

"Is Grandpa going to be okay?" It broke Johnny's heart to hear the uncertainty in his voice.

"I think so." She sounded like she was trying to reassure herself as much as Zach. "They're running some tests to see how much damage it caused and what they need to do to treat him."

"Did you have to do CPR?" Zach's eyes were wide with fear.

"No. He never lost consciousness. He was having trouble catching his breath, and that's something you don't take chances with."

"Oh, okay." Zach seemed satisfied with her explanation. "Johnny brought me here because I was worried about Grandpa. And I didn't want you to be alone."

"Thank you." She smiled first at Zach, and then at Johnny. "Frannie is in there with him, and it is nerve wracking waiting out here all by myself."

She held his gaze for a moment. He couldn't be sure if it was guilt or simple weariness in her eyes. She held herself accountable for the health and well-being of everyone she cared about.

Frannie entered the waiting room and the three of them looked up at her expectantly.

"He's going to be fine." Her eyes still showed signs of worry. "It was a heart attack, but a mild one. Nothing we can't take care of with diet and lifestyle changes."

"That's a relief." Alice didn't look relieved. More like someone had just handed her an arrest warrant. "I mean, that it's not too serious. Is there medication? Or something we can do to fix this?"

"We'll follow up with his regular doctor." Frannie gave her a sympathetic glance. It should have been the other way around.

Alice nodded. She stood stiff, like she was awaiting sentence for a crime.

"Zach, I'm so glad you're here." Frannie beamed at her grandson. "Thank you Johnny, for bringing him."

Johnny nodded, feeling like an outsider.

"I'll bet Grandpa would love to see you." She put her arm around Zach's shoulder and led him out of the room.

"Thank you for coming." Alice was still shaken by the day's events. "I'm glad Zach called you."

"I'm glad I could be there for him." It didn't make up for all the times he wasn't, but it was something.

She leaned back against the wall. All the strength she'd been trying to display seemed to have left her.

Johnny was at her side in a heartbeat.

"Ali, I'm here for you, too." He put his arms around her and she fell into his embrace.

"It's my fault." Her words were barely a whisper.

"No, it's not." Johnny stroked her hair, wanting more than anything to take away her worry.

"It is. I was telling Frannie that Zach might be your son, and Mel overheard and . . . and he just collapsed." She pulled away from him. "It's all my fault."

"No. Alice. I'm sure it was only . . ." What? Bad timing? Coincidence? "I'm sure Mel's condition had nothing to do with you. With us."

"No, you're wrong. It has everything to do with it." Alice looked down at the floor, studying the vinyl tiles, as if she was searching for solace in the random pattern.

"Ali, you're not responsible for him."

"Oh, but I am. You weren't there." She shook her head. "After the accident. It was awful. I wasn't sure if he'd get through those early days. If it wasn't for Zach . . ."

She wrapped her arms around herself, holding her feelings inside.

Johnny stepped closer. He wanted to reach out to her, but she was shutting him out. Again.

"Zach is the light of his life." She shook her head. "I can't take that away from him."

"No one said you had to."

She turned toward Johnny, her face pale. Worry lined her eyes, and she shuddered with guilt. "I could have killed him."

She dissolved into tears, collapsing in the nearest chair.

He sat beside her and put his arms around her. She closed her eyes and leaned against him. He held her as she sobbed. She trembled, and it was all he could do not to lift her in his arms and carry her out of there. He wanted to tell her everything was going to be alright. Even if she wasn't ready to believe it.

"Johnny, please . . ." She wriggled out of his grasp. Again. "You're only making this harder than it already is."

"Making what harder?" It was just like before. When she'd told him they should start seeing other people and he'd be better off without her. He hadn't been. He'd been alone.

"Johnny, I'm glad you're still here." Frannie returned before he could say anything else. Before she could push him away even more. "They're going to keep Mel overnight for observation. I'm staying with him."

"Is there anything you need?" Johnny asked.

"Yes, would you please make sure Alice and Zach get home?"

"Sure. No problem. Anything else?" He almost wished for another errand. He wanted to do something. Anything, to keep Alice from pushing him away.

"No. Just knowing the two of them are taken care of is all I need."

"I'll do my best." He accepted the mission.

"Frannie, can I get you something to eat? Some tea?" Alice jumped in, probably trying to feel useful.

"No. I have everything I need right here." She glanced back at the hallway, showing them Mel was all she needed. "You get some rest, okay? This has been a scare, but maybe it's a blessing in disguise. You know how I've been pushing for him to retire."

"Yes. Yes, of course."

Frannie approached Johnny and stood on her tiptoes to whisper in his ear. "Take care of our girl, will you?"

"I will." Johnny gave her a quick hug before stepping back. "I most certainly will."

If she'd let him.

Chapter 14

Alice busied herself getting Zach ready for bed. Like he was eight years old again. She knew she was fussing, she knew he was annoyed, but she couldn't help herself. She needed to feel in control of something, and making sure he brushed his teeth was about the only thing she could control.

Zach, bless his heart, didn't protest like he normally did. He just went about his routine and even remembered to put his clothes in the hamper. He was either trying to impress Johnny or was as worried as she about his grandfather's condition.

"Goodnight, Mom." He gave her a hug. A real hug, not the half-hearted obligatory type he'd been giving her lately. "Goodnight, Johnny. Thanks for coming to get me and everything."

"No problem, sport. I'm glad I could help." Johnny seemed surprised when Zach gave him a quick hug before turning in.

They both watched Zach head upstairs.

"Well, I should get going." Johnny shrugged, as if he thought he was in the way. "I hope everything turns out okay for Mel."

"Johnny, wait." She'd been unfair to him. In so many ways.

He looked tired. He couldn't be half as worn out as she was, but a lot had happened today. Between them, around them, and because of them.

"Alice, I think . . . I think we should take a step back. Not try to force this." He was going to let her push him away again. Damn it, why didn't he fight for them? Why hadn't he ever fought for them?

"No. I was wrong. About so many things." She tugged on his arm, led him into the family room. They needed to finish this. Tonight. No matter how much they wanted to pretend the past was in the past and the future didn't matter.

"Alice, I don't want to fight with you."

"I don't want to fight either."

"Then maybe I should go. We can talk later. When things have calmed down."

"Things aren't going to calm down." She sat on the sofa, wishing he'd sit next to her, but knowing he'd choose the chair opposite her.

"I'm sure Mel will be fine and they can control it with medication or diet or a combination of the two."

"I'm not talking about him. I mean us." She was tired of pretending. Tired of loving Johnny from the sidelines. "Things aren't going to calm down between us. There's still something there. Something very powerful."

"I was horny. You were wearing that dress."

"Yeah. That's what happened. Johnny, I know you. I know you better than you know yourself sometimes."

"Then why do you think I could have hurt you?" He leaned forward, resting his hands on his knees. "Why do you think I could have been anything other than faithful to you?"

"I was young and insecure. I thought once you made the big leagues you'd forget about me." How could she explain how she never felt good enough for him? How she would have given anything for some sort of reassurance. Some kind of promise.

"How could I forget you?" He moved closer, perched on the edge his seat. "It would have been easier for me to forget how to throw a baseball."

"Maybe if you'd . . ." She looked up at him, at the bewilderment still in his eyes. "You never told me you loved me. You never even hinted at wanting a future with me."

"At the time I didn't know if I even had a future." Johnny's voice was tinged with the old insecurity they'd both felt. "I had one shot at having anything to offer you. I wasn't going to make any promises I couldn't keep."

"I would have liked the promise. The hope." But she hadn't been strong enough to ask for it.

"So all that stuff about groupies and women throwing themselves at me?"

"I wanted you to fight for me." She sighed. "To fight for us. To assure me that you could resist temptation because I was the only woman for you."

"You were the only woman for me." Johnny got up and sat on the sofa next to her. "You've always been the only woman for me."

"Johnny." She needed to know how many. "Don't tell me you've been celibate this whole time. I heard the rumors, but..."

"I tried." He looked down at the floor. "I mean, I tried to move on. To have a relationship with someone else. But I couldn't find anyone who could make me forget about you."

"Don't say things like that."

"I thought you wanted the truth." He looked up at her. His dark chocolate eyes made her melt. "You're the only woman I've ever really wanted."

"Even now?" The question almost died on her lips. "Even after I left you. After I hurt you..."

"Even now." He reached a trembling hand toward her and placed a finger over her lips. "You're right. I should've fought for you. I should've fought for us. I should've told you every day how much you meant to me."

He lifted her from the sofa and pulled her into his arms. He kissed her. Slowly. Thoroughly. Passionately. She had no choice but give in to him. Give in to the feelings he stirred in her. She wanted this man. Needed him. Wondered how she'd managed to live so long without him.

"Let's go upstairs," she whispered. She hoped Zach was already asleep, but she needed to be discreet.

"Sounds perfect."

Her heart pounded as she led him up the stairs to her bedroom. She didn't know how she deserved yet another chance with him, but was determined to make the most of it. Once they were inside, she quietly closed the door and turned the lock. She was almost surprised it still worked, since she'd never needed to lock her bedroom door before. Zach wouldn't enter her room without permission. Or without being summoned, and even then, he always made his presence known. Still, she'd hate for him to make tonight the one exception.

She stood still, staring back at Johnny. He was watching her, taking her in like he wanted to study every detail of her face, her figure, her trembling hands.

"I'm sure you've noticed I've gained a little weight since college." She toyed nervously with the buttons on her blouse.

"So have I." He stepped forward to assist her. He slid the silky fabric over her shoulders, letting it fall to the floor. He carefully tugged at the waistband of her skirt, inching it down her hips until it pooled at her ankles.

"But in your case, it's all muscle."

"You're beautiful." He reached for her, sliding his hands down her belly. He bent down and kissed her, there, right where Zach had grown inside her. "Even more beautiful than you were in college."

"So are you." She ran her hands over the old faded Wolf Pack baseball t-shirt he wore. "I remember this shirt. I can't believe you still have it."

"Some things are worth hanging on to." His voice was deep, smooth, sexy.

"And some things should have never been let go."

"Ali, let's just focus on the here. The now." His voice was so calm. So commanding. So in control.

She felt like she was going to fly out of her skin at any moment.

"Touch me, Ali." He guided her hands under his shirt. She felt the solid muscle of his abs. The silky, rough texture of the hair on his chest. The hard nipples that responded instantly to her touch.

She shoved the t-shirt over his shoulders. He tore it off and tossed it aside. She let her gaze travel over his torso. He really was beautiful. A near perfect male specimen. His shoulders and arms were sculpted from years of throwing. His abs were solid, with a fine trail of hair dipping below the waistband of his jeans

She grabbed his wrist and tugged him toward the bed.

"Do you think you have enough pillows?" Johnny cocked his head toward the dozens of satiny pillows in every shape lined up against the headboard. Round, square, rectangular and cylindrical. She liked to think they kept her bed from looking so lonely.

"I'll get rid of them." She laughed as she tossed pillow after pillow to the floor.

"As long as you don't get rid of me so easily." Johnny grabbed one of the satin squares from her and pushed her down on the bed, knocking the remaining pillows over the edge.

Alice tried to stifle a giggle, something she'd had trouble with in the past. Of course, the walls of Johnny's college apartment were much thinner and Mel knew what she and Johnny were up to each night. Zach slept two rooms down, but she especially didn't want him figuring out what she and Johnny were doing in her bedroom.

They quickly dispensed with the rest of their clothing. She reached into the bedside table where she'd put the condoms she purchased before their Saturday night date. Now she was glad she'd sprung for the big box.

Johnny moved over her, kissing her first on the mouth, then moving his way down her body. He lingered on her breasts for a while, before exploring elsewhere. He smiled as he kissed the rounded, somewhat stretched skin of her belly. He swirled his tongue into her navel, making her quiver in anticipation of where he'd kiss her next.

He didn't disappoint. He spread her legs and dipped his head. Kissing her. Tasting her. Driving her over the edge. She moaned, wanting to tell him to hurry, but there was no need. He knew. He read her mind. Or read her body at least.

After putting on the condom, he positioned himself over her. Propped up on his elbows, he stared into her eyes as he slowly entered her.

Their lovemaking was different than the other night. The frantic hunger was replaced by a resounding longing. Their connection ran deeper, more intense than ever before.

With her heart at the epicenter, she shook with the most powerful pleasure she'd ever known. She was surprised it didn't rattle the windows or set off seismic warning alarms throughout the city. All she knew was, she had Johnny back, and she wasn't going to let fear come between them ever again.

Alice dreamed there was a man in her bed. Not just any man—Johnny Scottsdale. If only she could stay in bed a little longer and enjoy this dream.

"Morning." Strong male arms wrapped around her and she opened her eyes. It wasn't a dream. Johnny was in her bed.

"Good morning." She snuggled against him. His erection pressed against her thigh. She shifted her weight and smiled wickedly before sliding down on top of him.

It wasn't very often she could catch him by surprise. The look on his face showed shock and awe. He grabbed her hips, trying to take control of the situation, but she shook her head. She gently, but forcefully, took his wrists and raised his arms over his head.

She was in charge now. He'd better get used to it.

She moved slowly, taking her time, making the most of every movement. Every sound of pleasure that escaped from his throat. He was losing control already. It took a lot for Johnny Scottsdale to let go.

Emboldened by that thought, she picked up her pace, grinding her hips against him, determined to drive him out of his mind. But she was going to get there first.

Johnny took over, thrusting once. Twice. And then she couldn't count any higher, the pleasure was too much.

"Oh, Johnny." She shuddered and collapsed on top of him as he gave one last thrust and groaned with his release.

She rolled off him and caught a glimpse of the clock by her bed. "Oh no. It's late. Very late. I've got to get in the shower."

She bolted out of bed. Turned on the shower and stepped under the warm spray. She squirted shampoo in her hand and had started to lather, when Johnny slipped into the shower behind her.

"Let me help you with that." He slid his fingers through her hair. He pressed up against her and it was tempting. Oh, so tempting to let him take control of the situation. To take control of her and her body.

"We can't. I have to take Zach to school. Besides, we don't have any protection." Like a blast of cold water, she realized they'd already made love once without it.

Johnny stepped back, knocking against the shower door.

"Rinse." He grabbed the shampoo and lathered his own hair. "I'll be done in a minute. Then I can start breakfast and we'll take Zach to school together. If that's okay with you?"

"Yeah. That would be great."

She finished rinsing and then stepped aside so Johnny could finish washing up. He was out of the shower before she had a chance to work the conditioner through her hair. And long before she could bring up the question of what would happen if she'd conceived that morning.

A new baby.

A chance to do it right this time.

With Johnny's full participation.

The thought excited and terrified her at the same time.

She quickly dressed, dried her hair and applied her makeup.

Downstairs, she found Johnny and Zach once again bonding over breakfast. Bagels with cream cheese and strawberry preserves. Zach poured himself a giant glass of milk and Johnny made coffee.

He'd also made Zach's lunch.

"So. You two are a couple, now?" Zach spoke through a mouthful of bagel and cream cheese. "That's cool."

Johnny handed Alice a cup of coffee, with cream and sugar just the way she liked it. It all felt so domestic. So natural. He slipped his arm around her shoulder, giving her strength to bring up the one subject they all needed to discuss.

"I'm glad you're okay with having Johnny in our lives." A reassuring squeeze and she felt brave enough to continue. "Because there is something we need to talk about."

"What? Are you guys getting married or something?" Zach popped the last of his bagel into his mouth and took a long swallow of milk.

"We haven't discussed that." She could hear amusement in Johnny's voice. "Yet."

"Oh. Okay." Zach chugged the rest of his milk and set the glass down on the table with a loud bang.

"You see . . ." Oh, this was going to be harder than she thought. "Well, you know Johnny and I used to date? Back in college."

"Yeah. I know." He lifted his shoulders in an exaggerated shrug.

"Well . . ." She swallowed the giant lump in her throat.

"What your mother is trying to say . . ." Johnny couldn't do it either.

Zach just sat there, all innocent and trusting. Not having a clue that his life was about to change within the next few minutes.

"So, are you guys, like, trying to tell me that Johnny's my real dad?" Zach slid out of his chair, carrying his dishes to the sink. "Because, I kind of figured it out already."

Johnny's arm slid off her shoulder. They stood there, shocked by how casual Zach made it sound.

"So, who's taking me to school?" Zach picked up his lunch sack and shoved it in his backpack. "Or should I walk?"

"No. We'll take you. We'll both take you." Alice set her coffee on the counter. "How did you . . . figure it out?"

"I don't know." Zach shrugged again, in his no-big-deal kind of way. "I just put things together. I mean, come on. Anyone could see that I'm, like, his mini-me."

"Yeah, well, it might come out on the news." Alice took charge of the conversation, now that the truth was out there. "So, we wanted to prepare you. And see if you had any questions."

"Why would it be on the news?" Zach asked, but then he seemed to remember that Johnny was a famous ballplayer. "Oh, right. So can we talk about this later? I've got Ms. Westfield first period and you know how she is about tardies."

"Sure." Alice figured she'd have her bagel later. She didn't think she'd be able to eat it now, anyway.

"I'll drive." Johnny reached in his pocket for his keys. "Just point me in the right direction."

"Cool." Zach slung his backpack over one shoulder and headed toward the door.

"You should eat." Johnny leaned over and whispered in her ear. "Bring it with you. I have a few stops to make after we drop the kid off."

"Okay." She slathered some cream cheese on half a bagel and grabbed a napkin. She choked down the last of her coffee and followed her two guys out the back door.

Zach thanked Johnny for driving him to school. Or should he call him Dad? He wasn't sure how he felt about it still, but he was glad they'd finally told him. Not that they'd really told him. He kind of let them off the hook by admitting he'd already guessed. In a way, he was relieved they'd done it together. By having Johnny—his dad—there, it kept his mom from getting all weird and asking him how he felt and when he'd tell her he didn't know, she would keep prodding until he got mad.

This was better. They knew that he knew and now he could just get on with his day.

Except for wondering if everyone else knew, too. He walked down the hall, expecting people to look at him differently. Or whispering behind his back, but he made it to his locker without any of that. Hopefully he'd have a little more time to get used to the idea before having to explain it to people.

He should tell someone, though. It used to be Tyler who he'd want to talk to first, but he had the feeling Ty wouldn't care. Or he'd act like he wouldn't care but be mad at him for not telling him sooner.

"Hey, Zach." Ashley Turner smiled shyly at him. "How's it going?"

"Good." He'd only known her since, like, second grade. Why was it all of a sudden hard to talk to her? Other than the fact that she was a girl? And okay, he'd admit it, he kind of liked her.

"Cool." She smiled more like a real smile. Like she was happy to see him. Or something.

"Yeah. How's it going with you?" Oh, real smooth. So original. "I mean, hey, can I tell you something?"

"Sure." She stepped closer and kind of flipped her hair over her shoulder.

"You can't tell anyone. I mean it." Zach lowered his voice so people wouldn't hear him.

She looked kind of worried. "Is everything okay?"

"Yeah. I mean, everything's okay. Good news, I think." He wasn't sure why he felt like he needed to tell her this right now, but he thought he would burst if he kept it to himself. And who knew? Maybe this would be some way to make them, like, bonded or something.

"Okay. I like good news." She smiled again and Zach had to remind himself to breathe. "Even if it is a secret."

"Okay. Yeah. Um. So you know how my dad died a long time ago?" Stupid. She probably didn't know that. She probably didn't know anything about him.

"Yeah. I'm sorry about that." She started to put her hand out, like she was going to pat him on the shoulder or something. But she let it fall to her side.

"Well, he wasn't really my dad."

"Seriously?" She looked at him with curiosity, and an openness that made him think he wasn't stupid for wanting to tell her.

"Yeah. I just found out that my real dad is . . ." Would she even know who Johnny Scottsdale was?

Someone bumped into him, shoving him against her and knocking them into the wall.

"Are you okay?" He asked after the numbskull walked on by, not even bothering to apologize.

"Yeah. I'm fine." She shifted her backpack just as the warning bell rang. "But I gotta go to class. Can we talk later? I mean, like, at lunch?"

"Yeah. I eat lunch." Duh. Of course he ate lunch. Everyone did.

"Okay, I'll look for you. And you can finish telling me about your dad." She tucked her hair behind her ear and smiled at him. A real encouraging smile. Like maybe they could be friends. Or maybe something more.

"Do you have a lot of work to do this morning?" Johnny wasn't ready to take Alice home after dropping Zach off at school. There was too much going on between them.

"Nothing that can't wait until this afternoon. I should have the final numbers back from the accountants by then and we can start planning for next year's event."

"What about school?" Johnny asked. "I thought you were going to quit the foundation and get your teaching credential."

"It's just an idea I was toying with, but..." She gazed out the window.

"But what?"

"This year's camp was really special." She turned toward him and started to say something else. "I don't know, just some ideas running through my head."

"Why don't we go for a walk?" Johnny had some ideas of his own running though his head. But he needed to get out and stretch his legs. "I need to do a little shopping, too. Maybe you can help me pick out a few things."

"Sure. I'd love to help." She smiled at him, probably thinking they would be looking at lamps or maybe some throw pillows for his apartment.

"Then, I thought we could have lunch on Union Square. Somewhere I never could afford to take you before."

"That sounds wonderful."

He found a place to park and helped her out of her seat. They walked around, doing a little window-shopping and people watching.

They cut across the park. Johnny found an unoccupied bench and motioned for her to sit down. They sat watching pigeons peck around the sidewalk, searching for a meal.

"So, this morning..." Johnny wasn't sure how to bring up the subject. First of all, it had been amazing. What a way to start the day. But they hadn't used a condom.

"Look, I'm sure it's fine. Let's not get too worried until we have to."

"I'm not worried." He'd been thinking about it. Especially after seeing all the kids at Zach's private school. From kindergarteners with backpacks bigger than they were, to eighth graders with attitude leaking from every pore. "I kind of like the idea of having a baby with you."

"Oh really?" She had a teasing note in her voice, but also a tiny hint of fear.

"Yeah. I missed out the first time. I think it would be fun." Sure, easy for him to say. He wouldn't be the one carrying the baby. Delivering the baby. Nursing the baby.

"Fun?" She didn't sound so convinced.

"Just so you know . . ." He hesitated, because once he said his plans out loud, there was no taking them back. "I'm retiring at the end of this season. Win or lose. No matter what. I'm hanging up my cleats after the last pitch."

"Oh, Johnny, you still have a lot of baseball left in you." She was always his number one fan.

"Maybe. But if I keep playing baseball, I'm afraid that's all I'll have." He'd traded his relationship with Ali for his career. It had been a damn fine career, but now that he knew everything he'd given up, it didn't seem like such a good trade after all.

"Have you told anyone your plans?" She rested her hand on his forearm. Like maybe she could change his mind.

"Only you." He leaned forward, resting his forearms on his knees. "I want more. I want to be there for you and Zach. And if there is a player to be named later . . . Well, I think we should get married."

"Married?" She sounded so shocked. As if he wasn't capable of even thinking about marrying her. Hell, he'd thought about it a lot. There were so many times he'd wanted to just haul her off to one of those all-night wedding chapels in Reno. He'd just never had the money.

"Yes. I think we should get married." He stood up, reaching for her hand. He hoped she'd think it romantic to walk across Union Square into Tiffany & Co. She could pick out any diamond she wanted and he'd drop down on one knee to make it official.

"Let's not rush into anything." She stayed rooted to the bench. "I mean, it was only one time, and—"

"Not rush into anything?" Johnny felt like he'd been drilled by a fastball right to the chest. "Sure. How much more time do you need? Another fourteen years?"

"That's not what I meant." She stood, but Tiffany's was the last place he wanted to go to now. "This is exactly why I didn't . . . Look, can we not do this right now?"

"Is this why you never told me about Zach? You didn't want to marry me? You never wanted to marry me? I wish I'd known that years ago. I might have been able to have a life." He started to walk back to his Jeep. He didn't want her to see how much she'd hurt him.

"Johnny, wait," she pleaded, with enough remorse in her voice that he stopped, turned around.

"I leave for Arizona the day after tomorrow," he informed her. All his emotions shut down. He was The Monk. Unable to feel anything other than perfect control. "I want a paternity test before I go."

"Of course." She shouldered her bag and walked off across the square.

Fine. He should let her go. Just let her walk out of his life for good.

But if they had a child together, he couldn't do that. And if they had another on the way?

He needed to find out for sure about Zach, first. He'd worry about whether or not Alice was pregnant later.

Chapter 15

"Hey man, I need a favor." Johnny had called Bryce as soon as he'd gotten home.

"Already taken care of." Bryce was too laid-back. Nothing bothered him. Life was one big party. "I had to sacrifice my body, but I convinced Ms. Parker to keep the story to herself."

"Thanks. I appreciate that." Johnny could at least put that worry to rest. "But that's not why I called."

"Shoot. Whatever you need, I'll see what I can do."

"I was just going to go for a run." Johnny never did like to talk over the phone. He'd rather be doing something. Especially when he had something important to say.

"You need a running partner." Johnny liked that Bryce got it. He didn't have to ask. "I'll lace up my shoes and meet you at the statue in front of the ballpark."

"Sounds good." His apartment was conveniently located near his work. Bryce must have made the same consideration when choosing his place. Or maybe it was just that the construction of the ballpark had revitalized that part of the city. They'd built a lot of luxury condos nearby.

They met in front of the stadium. The brick structure looked a little lonely this time of year. But come April, the place would be a hubbub of activity. Home stands ranging from three to nine games would bring in the crowds. Last year well over three million fans had packed into the ballpark. Twice the attendance of Johnny's last team.

The closer they got to the season, the more Johnny worried about living up to their expectations. Did he have enough left to justify what they were paying him? Could he stay focused on his game when he had so much going on in his personal life? For years, he didn't have a personal life. Now he had too much of one. Alice had hurt him, yet again. And if it wasn't for the kid, he'd say to hell with it. A guy could only take so much grief.

He wanted to do right by Zach. If he really was his kid. Hell, even if he wasn't. He liked the boy.

They ran at least a mile before Johnny felt comfortable bringing up his issues.

"I need a paternity test. One that will hold up in court." Not that he intended to sue for custody, but he wanted to have all his bases covered. "You said you don't need to draw blood, right?"

"That's right. They do a simple cheek swab. Totally painless." Bryce took the opportunity to grab a quick gulp of water. They were heading downhill, and neither of them had been running at full speed. Not much more than a jog, really.

"How soon can I get the results?" Johnny would like to have them before he left town and needed to focus entirely on work.

"I think two to three days." Bryce slowed his pace, seeming to understand they weren't really there for a workout. "It helps that you and the kid are in the same town. You could even go in together if you want."

"That's what I want." No. Not exactly. But since he couldn't go back in time, it was as close as he was going to get.

Bryce pulled his phone out of his jacket pocket.

"Let me pull up the website for the company I used. I'm pretty sure they're nationwide, so they should have a lab here in town." He made it sound so simple. Like he was referring a friend to a dentist or an auto repair shop. "Yes. They have a lab here. I'll email you the link. You can check out the website. There's even a YouTube video that walks you through the process."

"Thanks, man. I appreciate your help with this." Johnny was glad he had someone he could turn to right now.

"No problem. What are friends for?" Bryce asked and Johnny realized he hadn't had anyone call him a friend since Mel. Sure, they'd all said he was a good guy. A good teammate. But never a good friend.

"Hey, how is everything else going? I mean with Alice?"

"It's not." Johnny exhaled in frustration. He pretended to stretch out a cramp. "I thought it was good. Hell, it was great."

Bryce just nodded. Like he understood.

"But then when I found out that Zach might be my kid . . ." Johnny was still reeling from it, alternating between pride and absolute terror at the thought of being a father. "I guess I pulled back a little too much. But it was kind of a shock."

"Especially for you." Bryce chuckled. "Who would have thought 'The Monk' would have a love child?"

"Yeah, that whole monk thing has gotten old." Johnny had taken the nickname in stride at first. It was all part of the game. Spending that much time with a group of guys, it was bound to happen. It was meant in fun, but once the media got hold of it, and the public embraced it, he couldn't shake it.

In a way, he'd used the image to his advantage. No one expected clever sound bites. That whole vow of silence thing came in handy there. And no one expected him to party when they went on the road. He kept to himself mostly and since he wasn't critical of his wilder teammates, they left him alone.

But he was tired of being alone.

"It was enough of a shock that she's convinced it led to her father-in-law's heart attack."

"Is he alright?"

"Yeah. It had nothing to do with our news. But she was pretty torn up about it."

"So here's your chance to be there for her." Bryce was trying to be helpful. "She could probably use some comfort."

"Oh, I was there. And I offered my comfort." Johnny closed his eyes, recalling the night they'd spent together. And the morning. Had it only been a few hours ago? Hell, it felt like a lifetime.

"So, maybe she's still feeling guilty about her ex's family." Bryce tossed out the idea. "I was never close to my in-laws, but I do know guys who stayed in touch with their exes' families."

"She's very close to them. I think that may be one of the reasons she never said anything sooner." Johnny was getting the hang of this sharing business. It was actually somewhat helpful. "The kid looks just like me. He's got my eyes, my dopey smile. Hell, he's even got my arm."

"That's great. A chip off the old block?"

"Yeah. But the Harrisons lost their only son." Remorse stabbed Johnny in the gut. For not being there when it happened. And for taking their grandson away. "Zach is all they have left."

"Look, I get that you feel bad. But that doesn't mean you shouldn't fight for what's yours."

Johnny thought about that for a minute. He wanted to fight for her. Something he hadn't had the courage to do fourteen years ago. But he didn't want to be like the guy who held on when everyone around him knew it was a losing cause. Whether it was hanging up his cleats or walking away from the only woman he'd ever loved, he didn't want to go out a loser.

"I don't know if she wants me to fight for her." He leaned over, sucking in a few deep breaths. "I thought she did. I thought maybe that was the one way I'd failed her all those years ago. I just walked away, thinking I had nothing to offer her anyway. I figured I'd make the big leagues and come back, dazzling her with a big contract and an even bigger ring."

"Didn't work out that way, did it?"

"It most certainly did not."

"But you didn't give up on her." Bryce started jogging in place. Ready to head back the way they'd come. "You were more faithful to her than most married guys in this league. So why give up now?"

"She said I'm rushing her." Johnny still couldn't believe that. "Fourteen years, I've been waiting for this woman. Waiting for the life that should have been mine all along. And she gets cold feet."

"I don't know, maybe it's because of the kid. Maybe she's afraid of making a mistake." Bryce started jogging back toward the ballpark.

"The thing is, we might've made another mistake." Johnny joined him stride for stride. It was so much easier to talk when he was moving. "Not that Zach's a mistake. He's a great kid."

"She could be pregnant?" Bryce didn't even miss a step.

"Yeah." Johnny kept jogging, the words coming easier with each step. "I tried to assure her I'll be there for her and the baby, if there is one. Told her I'm quitting after this season. And we can get married."

"Whoa. You're quitting?" Bryce stopped in his tracks. He shouldn't be surprised. It wasn't like Johnny was still a young player. "Wait. Did you propose?"

"I didn't get the chance. I told her I thought we should get married. And then I was going to take her to pick out a ring—"

"Before or after the discussion of the possible pregnancy?"

"After. I think." Johnny couldn't remember. He just knew he'd blown it. Did the order matter at this point?

"There's your mistake, man." Bryce gave him a hearty clap on the back.

"What?" It might as well have been a sucker punch.

"I don't care how practical a woman is, you never propose by saying it's the right thing to do." Bryce chuckled, like Johnny had somehow missed the most basic rule. "Women want romance. They don't want to think the only reason you're asking is because you knocked them up. Trust me, it will only make things worse. Even if she says yes."

"Well, it worked for Mel." Shit. Would he ever be able to let that go? "There's no way she would have married him if she hadn't been pregnant. She admitted as much."

"Even though she's in love with you."

"Apparently not."

"Give her some time to cool off." Bryce suggested. "Then you have to go all out. Make the most romantic gesture of all time."

"I've never been good at romance," Johnny admitted. "Back when we were dating, I couldn't afford things like flowers and nice dinners. I wasn't good with poetry either. I barely passed my English classes."

"That stuff's for amateurs anyways." Bryce acted like he knew what he was talking about. But Johnny didn't want to get laid. He'd managed that part fine on his own. He wanted something more permanent. Something his buddy hadn't been able to manage, either. "You need to come up with something original. Something that can live up to the legend that is Johnny Scottsdale."

Alice sometimes wished she'd leased office space downtown. Running the Harrison Foundation from her home office was convenient, sure, but also made it difficult to separate her personal and professional lives.

When Zach was little, it was the only way she could manage it all. She worked while he was in school, making phone calls, sending emails, meeting with donors. Then she'd pick him up, do the whole homework, dinner, activities routine. And once he was in bed, she'd tackle the paperwork. Reports, thank you letters, and all the attention to details best handled when the house was quiet and she was more than happy to have the distraction of work to keep her from dwelling on her loneliness.

As the work had become more routine, the loneliness became harder to quell. Zach was growing up, not needing her as much. Soon he wouldn't need her at all. Or at least, he wouldn't admit to it. And the foundation no longer filled the hole in her life.

It would be easy enough to hire someone to take over. An eager college grad, or perhaps a mother seeking to return to the workforce after years of volunteer service and school fundraising. It could even be a good fit for the semi-retired. Someone who needed to keep busy, but not have the kind of stress running, say, an investment firm required.

She knew the perfect person for the job.

The transition wouldn't take more than a few months. Certainly less than nine. She patted her lower abdomen. She might finally have the perfect excuse to walk away from the Mel Harrison Jr. Foundation.

She and Frannie had a standing lunch date. But since Mel hadn't been released from the hospital yet, they moved the location to the cafeteria instead of their usual restaurant. Frannie looked pretty good for a woman who'd no doubt slept in a chair.

"Alice, thank you for agreeing to meet here. Their clam chowder is actually not bad. I had some last night." Frannie was trying to be cheerful. Put a positive spin on things. But she was worried. No doubt about it.

"When is Mel going to be released?" Alice grabbed a tray and followed her mother-in-law through the cafeteria line.

"Later this afternoon." Frannie headed straight for the salad bar, and started loading up on organic greens. "But he's already getting anxious. I guess that's a good sign. That he's ready to get out of here."

"Yes. I can't imagine him staying here willingly if he's feeling better."

"That's what worries me. What is he going to do to fill his days?"

"He's really going to retire?" It was hard to imagine the man actually slowing down.

"He'd better." Frannie filled a small cup with balsamic vinaigrette and placed it next to her salad plate. She moved over to the soup tureen. "But how am I going to keep him out of my hair? Especially now that Zach is ... getting older, and wanting to spend more time with his friends."

"Maybe something will come up." Alice wanted to wait until they were seated before bringing up her idea. "And Zach will still be around."

"Oh, Alice, I appreciate that, but what if Johnny ends up going to another team? Will you follow him?"

"I don't know. He says he's planning to retire after this year. And ..." She ladled soup into her bowl and tossed some crackers on her tray. "It's not as easy as it was back in college."

"Of course it isn't easy." Frannie chuckled to herself. "Whatever made you think it would be?"

"It used to be." Alice poured herself an iced tea and approached the cashier.

"If it was so easy, why did you let him go?"

Okay. Good point. Especially since the difficulties had been mostly in her imagination.

"Johnny wants to get married." Alice waited until they sat before sharing that piece of information.

"And you don't?"

"No. I mean, I do. But ..."

What did she want? Once upon a time it had all been so simple. She'd dreamed of being a teacher. A mother. A wife. Johnny's wife. But in her vision it had been so different.

"I guess I wanted it to be perfect."

"Oh honey, nothing is ever perfect."

"Johnny was. Once." Alice smiled, recalling the night he pitched his perfect game.

"Yes. But that was just a game." Frannie touched her hand. "The rest of the time he's just a man. A good man. But still, only a man."

"I know. It's ... Every time I try to do the right thing, I end up hurting him."

"So you're going to let him go?" Frannie asked. "Won't that hurt him even more?"

"But then he can get on with his life."

"Honey, if he hasn't done that by now, he never will."

They each took a few bites of their lunch. It actually wasn't bad. In fact it was pretty good clam chowder. And the bread was fresh. If they hadn't been eating off plastic trays, she'd think they were in a nice restaurant instead of a hospital cafeteria.

"Did he actually propose?" Frannie asked.

"Well, no. I didn't give him a chance." Alice had pushed him away. Again.

"Well, a man has his pride." Frannie smiled knowingly. Then she let out a long sigh. "Sometimes it's a good thing. But sometimes..."

"You're worried about Mel." How could she have been so selfish, coming here and whining about her problems? Problems she'd gone out of her way to create.

"Of course, I am. He can't keep working full time, but..." She let out a weary sigh. "I don't know what he's going to do next."

"I'm sure you'll think of something." Alice scooped up the last of her clam chowder. Maybe now was a good time to throw out her idea. See if it would be a hit or a miss. "I think it's time for me to step away from the foundation."

"Oh, Alice, whatever will we do without you?" Frannie dropped her spoon.

"Maybe Mel could take over." The enthusiasm she'd felt when the idea first came to her was increasing. "We have a good team in place. The program practically runs itself. And I would feel better knowing the foundation was in the hands of someone who truly cared about it."

Frannie didn't say anything for a minute. She simply nodded, thinking about Alice's suggestion.

"You know, I think that might be a terrific idea." Frannie's face lit up. "Of course, you'll have to stay on for a little while, to oversee the transition."

"Of course." It was the least she could do.

"So, the only tricky part will be in convincing Mel that you need him to do this. That he'd be doing you the favor. Not the other way around."

"He would be doing me a favor," Alice admitted. "I've enjoyed my work with the foundation. But it is time for me to move on. With Johnny, if he'll have me."

The two women put their heads together to come up with a plan for letting Mel take over the Mel Harrison Jr. Foundation. Then Alice could focus her attention on winning Johnny's trust.

And maybe, just maybe have a chance at something better than perfect. The family she and Johnny should have had all along.

"Hey Zach, I'm sorry I didn't catch you at lunch." Ashley stopped by his locker after school. He was shoving the last of his stuff into his backpack. "But my friends were... Well, I thought you said what you wanted to tell me was private."

"No big deal." Zach shouldered his backpack and shrugged, tightening the strap.

"So, do you walk home every day?" She tilted her head to the side. Just enough for her hair to swing out and brush her shoulder.

He wondered if it was as soft as it looked. But it wasn't like he could just reach out and touch it. "Yeah, usually."

"Cool." Ashley smiled and it was like she hit him in the stomach. Hard enough that he couldn't catch his breath. "Can I walk with you?"

"Sure." Zach tried to think of what Johnny said on the mound. *Focus. Breathe.* Oh, yeah, that's what he was forgetting to do. *Breathe.* "Let's go."

They took their time leaving the campus. Some of the kids all left in a big rush right at the bell, but Zach wanted to have Ashley to himself. Or as much to himself as possible in broad daylight on a busy city street.

"So..." Ashley started to ask him something, but then changed her mind or something. "How did you do on Miss Rosenberg's test?"

"A-minus."

"Me too. She's tough."

"Yeah."

They walked on, but they didn't have too much farther to go before she would turn up the street and he would turn down.

"So, about your dad?" She stopped, tucking a strand of hair behind her ear. Zach never understood why girls wore their hair long and then they were always fussing with it. But right now, he liked her long hair. And the way she was fussing with it. He was glad he could look at it and not think about what he was about to tell her. His biggest secret.

"Yeah." Zach almost couldn't remember what he was going to tell her.

"Who is he?" She tilted her head, making her hair fall forward. Making him lose concentration. No wonder Johnny needed to be like a monk. Girls were very distracting.

"Johnny Scottsdale." He couldn't say the rest. It stuck in his throat. It was all he could do to say that much.

"The baseball player?" Her eyes got all wide. And even more blue, if that was even possible.

Zach nodded, like a dumb mute.

"Cool." She tucked her hair behind both ears now. "I remember when you did your biography report on him in fifth grade. And you didn't even know he was, like, your real dad?"

Zach shook his head. What if this was permanent? What if he'd never be able to speak again?

"Wow. I can't imagine." She tilted her head, making her hair swing and Zach kind of woke up.

"Neither could I, but I guess it's true." Zach looked at her shoes. They were bright pink. With purple sparkly laces. Why did girls have to sparkle so much? "And I think they might get back together, but I don't know. It's weird to think of them dating."

"Your mom and Johnny Scottsdale?"

"Yeah."

"Wow." She sighed. "I mean, your mom is cool and everything, but *Johnny Scottsdale*."

She sighed again. Like she thought he was hot or something.

"Hey, that's my dad you're talking about." Zach felt the heat rise in his cheeks.

"Oh. Right." She gave him a friendly little shove. "I forgot."

Man, girls were so weird.

"You know, you do look a lot like him." She smiled when she said that. "I guess I never really noticed."

Did that mean she was noticing him now?

He wasn't quite sure he wanted to know.

"So text me later, okay?" Ashley pulled out her phone to exchange numbers.

"Um, I don't have a phone." Zach felt about five years old. Why didn't he have a phone? It wasn't like they couldn't afford it or anything. He'd just never asked for one. Never thought he needed one.

"Oh, okay." She slid her phone into her back pocket. It was pink and sparkly, too. The phone. Not her pocket. He wasn't looking at her pockets. "I'll see you tomorrow."

And then she was on her way home. So much for playing it cool.

Chapter 16

Johnny waited for Zach to get home from school. As soon as he saw him walking up the street, he got out of his Jeep. Man, the kid even had his walk. At least the walk he'd had at that age. Right down to the slumped shoulders, which only made his long arms look even longer. He hoped none of the kids teased Zach the way he'd been teased.

"Hey, what's up?" Zach's smile brightened when he saw Johnny.

"Did you have a good day at school?"

"It was okay." Zach shifted his backpack from one shoulder to the other.

"So, you know I'm leaving for spring training soon." This was the first year he wasn't itching to get down there. Normally, he was bursting at the seams to get the season underway.

"Yeah. Are you excited? Nervous?"

"A little bit of both."

"Okay. Are you staying for dinner?" Zach asked eagerly. Right, he didn't know that things weren't going so well between Alice and him.

"Probably not." Johnny shoved his hands in his pockets. "I . . . um . . . Well, I have an appointment. We have an appointment to see if you're my son."

"Oh. Like a blood test?"

"No blood. But yeah, it's a DNA test." Johnny had never thought he'd be having a conversation like this. "That way I can add you to my insurance and stuff."

Sure. That was why he needed to know.

"So does my mom need to come?"

"Do you want her to?" He supposed that would make Zach more comfortable.

"Not really." Zach looked up at him with slight uncertainty in his features.

"I can have her sign a release form. If you don't want her to come."

"Yeah. Okay." Zach squared his shoulders and Johnny followed him into the house.

Alice signed the release and they were on their way.

"So what's the deal with you and my mom?" Zach was a smart kid. He'd picked up on the tension between the two of them. "Are you guys together or what?"

"Or what." Johnny mumbled as he slid behind the wheel of his Jeep.

"I'm confused. You guys like each other, right?" Zach clicked his seatbelt. "Maybe even love each other."

"Yes." Johnny couldn't deny it. At least not on his part.

"And you're, like, sleeping with her?"

Johnny nodded. He couldn't admit it out loud. But he couldn't lie to him either.

"So, you guys should be together." Zach offered his humble opinion.

"I wish it were that simple."

"It should be. You love each other. You're sleeping together. And we're on our way to find out if you have a kid together." Zach had a pretty good argument. Too bad Alice didn't see it that way. "You should be together. Simple."

"Like baseball is a simple game. One guy throws the ball and another tries to hit it. Easy, right?" Johnny hoped Zach would understand.

"Yeah. Except it isn't all that easy to hit the ball." Zach got it. "And even when you do hit the ball, sometimes someone catches it."

"I think relationships are the same. It takes a lot of hard work and a little bit of luck."

"So you work on it. Maybe you'll get lucky." Zach let out a nervous laugh. "I mean, not like that, but like, lucky to have it work out."

If only Johnny knew how to work on it. He didn't have a game plan. Didn't have a clue.

"I used to wonder why my mom never dated anyone after my dad died—or maybe he was my stepdad—but, whatever." Zach didn't look at Johnny. He stared straight ahead as they drove through the city. "But now I think I understand."

Johnny didn't know what to say. Instead he concentrated on navigating through the traffic to get to the clinic. To get this over with. To know one way or the other.

"I always knew she had a crush on you."

Really? Hope fluttered inside him. But he cut it off, like the jerk in the SUV crossing into his lane, forcing him to slam on his brakes.

"You okay?" Johnny turned to Zach, worried about the sudden stop.

Zach looked at him like he was being overprotective. At least he hadn't flung his arm across the seat, whacking Zach in the face when the seatbelt was perfectly capable of keeping the passenger from flying through the windshield.

"I just thought it was one of those things. Like in movies and stuff. Where you were the big hot shot on campus and she was some nerdy girl who was too shy to talk to you."

"What makes you think your mom was ever a nerd?" Johnny couldn't picture it. She was anything but.

"She did get straight A's. She dresses kind of boring. And, well, look at who she married." Zach sounded like a typical teenager, who thought the older generation was hopelessly out of touch.

"Your mom was not a nerd. Not at all." She was hot. And she'd been anything but shy. At least not with him.

"Yeah, well, how was I supposed to know that?" Zach was probably rolling his eyes. "Besides, I never knew she actually knew you. I thought maybe she worshipped you from the stands. But never had the nerve to tell you that she was totally into you."

Oh, she had the nerve alright. But Johnny wasn't going to tell her son that.

"That was a long time ago."

"She's still totally into you." Zach shifted uncomfortably in the passenger seat. "I think she never stopped."

"I don't know about that." Johnny thought about how quickly she'd retreated this morning. Sure, the physical attraction was still there. But it wasn't enough.

"We're here." Johnny pulled into the parking lot of the clinic. "Are you ready for this?"

"Are you?"

"Yeah. Look. If you are my son, no matter what happens with your mom and me, I want to be a part of your life."

"And what if I'm not?"

"Well, then you'll have to decide if you want me around. As a friend. A coach or mentor or something like that." Johnny didn't like the thought of not being there for Zach. Of not being there for Alice either.

"Okay. Let's go find out if I'm your kid." Zach tried to play it off like it was as simple as consulting the Magic 8 Ball. Like they could ask it a question and if the answer wasn't what they wanted, they could shake it again until it read *Without A Doubt*.

Johnny held open the door to the clinic. He'd never been more nervous in his life. Not when he made his Major League debut. Not his first All-Star appearance or his first post-season game. Hell, not even the first time he was interviewed live on national TV.

He filled out the forms, and picked up a magazine to thumb through.

"Hey, look." Zach held up an old issue of *Sports Illustrated*. "It's you."

Sure enough, it was the cover of his perfect game. It showed his stoic face after he'd recorded the final out. The article made him look like a man who just quietly went about his business, throwing perfect strikes and buckling the knees of the most confident hitters. The sportswriter portrayed a man so in control, so sure of himself, he didn't need words to add to the statement he'd made on the field.

What the article didn't show was how alone Johnny had felt at that moment. How what should have been one of the best days of his life had been one of the worst. He'd celebrated by having a beer with the grounds crew after they dug up the pitching rubber to send to Cooperstown. He hadn't had anyone else to celebrate with. And he certainly hadn't wanted to go home. Alone.

"Mr. Scottsdale?" The nurse called him and Zach back to the exam room. She waited until they were seated before briefly explaining how the test would work. She swiped a cotton swab in Johnny's mouth and placed it in a sealed container, following with a second swab and then repeating the process with Zach.

Simple. Painless. And over very quickly.

The hard part was coming up. Waiting for the results.

On their way out, the nurse stopped Johnny. He motioned for Zach to meet him in the lobby.

"I just wanted to let you know I'm a huge fan of yours." She gave him a giddy smile. "Huge. Oh-my-God, I can't believe you're here, in my lab, on my shift. And you're just as good-looking in real life. No, you're perfect. I will remember this day. For the rest of my life."

She placed her hand over her heart and looked up at him, eyes glistening with tears of admiration.

"Thank you." Johnny felt more than uncomfortable. Especially considering the time and place. If she asked for his autograph, he was going to lose it.

She didn't. Instead she promised to take extra care with his sample. She continued to gush over him as he made his way back to the lobby.

"So, do I call you 'Dad'? If, you know, you are?" Zach had waited until they'd left the building before asking that question.

"If you want to." Johnny felt a little dizzy at the thought. But he'd rather think about that than think about what he'd do if the results were negative.

"What about my name?" Zach stopped in front of the Jeep. "Would you want me to change it? Would it be okay if I went by Zach Scottsdale?"

He had to admit, he liked the sound of it. A legacy. Something he never thought he'd have outside baseball.

He'd always wondered where his name had come from. He'd overheard his mother describing her dream of living someplace warm. She wasn't sure where she'd come from, but he thought it might be Idaho or Utah or maybe she was from Canada, here illegally. She'd left home at the age of sixteen, thinking Scottsdale, Arizona would be a nice place to live.

She never made it past Reno. Or the neighboring county, where prostitution was legal. So Johnny always wondered if the only thing left of her dream was the name. She called herself Destiny Rose Scottsdale. He had a strong feeling she'd made it up and just passed the last name along when she had to put something on his birth certificate.

"Do you want to change your name?" Johnny asked.

"I don't know. Maybe." Zach opened the Jeep's door. "Is it hard being famous?"

"I'm not that famous." Johnny slid behind the wheel. "Out of uniform, most people don't even recognize me."

"But they recognize your name, don't they?"

"Sometimes. If they're serious baseball fans." Johnny wondered what it would be like to be the kid of someone famous. He'd known too well what it was like being the son of someone infamous. The whispers behind his back, the children who were suddenly not allowed to play with him. Later, the teasing and dirty comments about his mother.

Zach fastened his seatbelt.

"Don't feel like you have to decide anything right away." Johnny started the engine. "This is all kind of sudden."

"Yeah, a few months ago you were just some guy we were hoping would sign with the Goliaths." Zach leaned forward, resting his hands on his knees. "Only a week ago, I found out you and my mom were friends. And now? Now, you might be my dad."

"Yeah, I guess it's a lot to take in all at once." If Johnny's head was spinning at the sudden change, Zach must be really reeling. And Alice, too.

She wanted time. He'd give it to her. He'd report to spring training, giving them both the space they needed to figure out what they wanted. He knew he wanted Alice. And Zach. The baby, too, if there was one.

He looked over at Zach. The lady at the clinic told him to expect an email within two to three days. He should know the results before he stepped onto the field on Saturday. But he didn't need an email to tell him what he already felt in his heart. Zach was his son.

And they had a whole lot of catching up to do.

"Do you want to stop and get an ice cream or something?" Johnny suggested. He needed a little more time with Zach before dropping him off.

"Sure. I could eat." Zach patted his stomach. "I could definitely eat ice cream."

"As long as it won't ruin your appetite for dinner?"

"No. I'll still eat my dinner," Zach said. "Remember, my mom's a good cook."

He ordered an ice cream sundae. With hot fudge, caramel sauce, whipped cream and a cherry on top. Johnny ordered a plain vanilla cone.

"So do you think I could get a cell phone?" Zach asked after they'd settled in to eat their ice cream treats.

"You don't have one already?" Surely most kids his age did.

"Nope. I'm like, the only kid over ten who doesn't." Zach rolled his eyes. "My mom thinks I don't need one yet."

"So what's her name?" Johnny had a feeling there was a reason he wanted one now.

"It's not because of a girl." Zach blushed, telling Johnny there was a girl. "I just thought it would be a good way for us to keep in touch. You know, when you're on the road and stuff."

"That sounds like a good idea." Johnny was touched. Even if he knew Zach would be busy texting this mystery girl more than he'd text him. He liked the idea of being able to keep in contact with his son. "I'll talk to your mother about it."

"Yeah. Okay." Zach scooped up the last few bites of ice cream. "But maybe we should pick it out before you leave. So I can be sure to get your number and everything."

"I'd like that. But we still need to discuss it with your mom."

"Yeah, maybe you guys could go shopping for it tomorrow." Zach suggested. "You, know, while I'm at school."

"That sounds like a good plan." The kid was trying to get him and Alice back together. Johnny wasn't going to fight it. He wasn't going to push too hard, though.

"I suppose you guys are going to do a lot of discussing things about me." Zach licked the back of his spoon. He'd gotten his money's worth of the ice cream sundae.

"Hopefully we'll do a lot of discussion with you, too." Johnny had no idea how to do this parenting thing. But he did remember what it was like to be a teenage boy. Desperately in need of guidance but afraid and too proud to ask.

He hoped he could answer Zach's questions before they came up. If they had anything to do with baseball or working toward a goal or even how to juggle school and practice schedules, he felt pretty confident.

If the boy had questions about girls... Well, that was one area where Johnny hadn't been quite as successful. But he was starting to see where he'd gone wrong.

He'd have to work on fixing it. And Zach was an extra incentive to make sure he did not fail.

Alice picked up a huge bunch of daffodils at the market. They were so cheerful and sunny, she couldn't resist buying three dozen.

She stood on a chair, looking for a vase big enough to hold all of them when Zach and Johnny arrived home from the clinic.

"Ali, let me get that." Johnny was at her side, steadying her hips just seconds after walking in the door. Sending tremors throughout her body.

"It's okay. I've got it." She'd wondered what had him so protective and possessive all of a sudden, when she glanced down to see him gazing at her abdomen.

The baby. If there was one.

The timing was about right, but she was getting older. Surely if they were actively trying it would take months. But they weren't trying to get pregnant. And this morning they'd done nothing to prevent it, either.

"Here, take this." She handed the vase to Johnny.

He set it on the counter and held his hand for her to take as she climbed down.

"Be careful." Johnny's concern was touching, but a little bit too much. Especially if it was only because of her possible condition.

"So how did it go today?" She'd waited until she was on solid ground before asking.

"Good." Zach tossed his backpack on the kitchen table. "When's dinner?"

"I haven't thought about it, but I'll whip something up." She wondered if she should ask Johnny to stay. As a peace offering.

"And I was worried stopping for ice cream would spoil his appetite." Johnny looked at Zach with pride in his eyes. The test was simply a formality, for sure.

"How much homework do you have?" she asked Zach.

"Not much. I'll take it to my room." He gave Johnny a knowing smile. "So you two can talk."

He was up to something.

"So, what does he want?" Alice filled the vase and arranged the flowers in it. She placed it in the center of her kitchen table. Just the cheery effect she was looking for. The fog would roll in over the next few weeks and the flowers might be the only hint of spring for some time.

"A cell phone." Johnny shoved his hands in his pockets and leaned against the counter. "I told him I thought it was a good idea, but we had to discuss it first."

"I suppose I've put it off long enough." She brushed her hair off her forehead. "It's not that I have anything against cell phones. I find mine quite handy, but it's . . ."

"A sign he's growing up." Johnny gave her a sympathetic smile.

"Yeah. Too fast for me. Not fast enough for him."

Johnny nodded. Of course, it had been lightning speed for him.

"I'd like to take care of the phone. If you'll come with me to pick it out. I have no idea what is appropriate for a kid his age."

"Sure. Tomorrow?"

"Early works better for me." Johnny shifted from one foot to the other. "Maybe after you drop him off at school."

"Do you want to stay for dinner?"

Johnny shook his head, slowly. "I have a lot of packing to do." He shoved off the counter. "I'm driving down to spring training."

"It would be easier to fly."

"Yeah. But you know me. I like the open road. There's a lot of space between here and Arizona. And I've got a lot on my mind."

"Yeah. I guess you do." She wished she could take it back. All of it. Every single hurt she'd thrown at this man. Every time she'd let her fear get in the way of what could have been something pretty damn special.

"Should I meet you here or the phone store?" Johnny asked.

"Here."

"Nine thirty?"

"Sure. That would be great." She wondered if this was how it was going to be from now on. Making appointments for Zach's sake. Formal. Distant. Excruciating. "Are you sure you won't stay for dinner?"

His eyes lit up for a moment, but he shook his head. "I think that would be a mistake." Johnny had his mask on. The one he wore so often on the field. "You know what would happen if I stayed. And I think we both need a little time to cool off."

She tried to agree, but the words got stuck in her throat.

"We're not a couple of kids anymore," he reminded her.

"No. We're not."

"I want to do this right." He hooked his thumbs in his front pockets. "You asked for time. I'm going to give it to you. I think it's a good thing that I'm going to be in Arizona for a few weeks."

"A good thing." She repeated his words. Even though she knew she'd miss him. Terribly.

"Goodnight, Alice." He leaned toward her, as if he might kiss her, but then backed away.

"Goodnight, Johnny." She managed to refrain from throwing herself at him. To keep from begging him not to go. But she had to keep some semblance of pride.

He gave her a nod and slipped out her back door.

He would be back. But she wasn't sure if he'd be back for her, or just their son.

Chapter 17

Since Johnny's Jeep was already packed with his baseball equipment and everything he'd need for the month and a half he'd spend down in Arizona, they drove to the cell phone store in Alice's car. A cute little hybrid SUV that made sense in the city.

Johnny wanted to add Zach's phone to his plan. It seemed like the least he could do. He'd be sure to ask the salesperson what he'd need to do in terms of monitoring and parental controls. Alice probably already knew all about that kind of thing. Plus, she'd be around for good old-fashioned supervision of the looking-over-the-shoulder variety.

They weren't in the store five minutes when a twenty-something sales clerk approached them.

"Hi, my name is Jason. What can I do for you today?"

"We're looking for a phone for our son." Johnny felt perfectly natural using the term. "He's thirteen."

"So he'll be doing a lot of texting." The clerk smiled knowingly. "Do you already have a family plan? Or will this be a new service?"

"I want to add it to my plan." Johnny took charge of the conversation.

"Okay, did you want to pick out the phone first, or check to see what kind of options your plan covers?"

"We'll get the phone first." Johnny didn't have to worry about how he was going to pay for it. At least not until he retired. Even then, there weren't enough minutes in the day to blow through his savings before he figured out what he'd do next.

Jason led them to the display, showing everything from the basic model, to the flashiest smart phones with all the bells and whistles.

"If you have the one that will clean his room for him, we'll take that one," Alice said after listening to the wide variety of features.

"I'm afraid there isn't an app for that." Jason chuckled as if he'd heard that one a thousand times.

"We really just want something he can call or text us on." Alice seemed a little overwhelmed by the choices. Johnny put his hand on her shoulder and was grateful she didn't pull away.

"Kids don't call. At least, most of them don't." Jason pointed out. "Especially boys. Texting is so much easier."

"Yeah, if he's anything like me, he'd rather not talk on the phone." Johnny hooked his thumbs in his jeans pockets.

"Oh, he's exactly like you." Ali smiled up at him. And he felt the bonds of family tighten between them. "Especially when it comes to communication."

As much as Johnny didn't want to air their personal grievances in front of a stranger, he didn't mind the teasing note in her voice.

"Do you have a phone that can translate caveman grunts into poetry?" Johnny decided to play along.

"I don't think he needs to be reciting poetry any time soon." Alice had a hint of fear in her voice.

"Do you really think he wants a phone just so he can keep in touch with me when I'm on the road?" Johnny hadn't had the chance to find out more about this girl. But he knew there was one.

"Girls?" Alice clutched her chest, in a mock swoon.

"Afraid so." Johnny put his arm around her shoulder in case she really did faint. Yeah. Right. That's why. "Probably just a girl. If he's anything like me."

She sighed and leaned a little closer to him.

"I had no idea." She shook her head.

"You're his mom. You'll be the last to know."

"Oh, I'm being replaced already." She tilted her head and rested against Johnny's shoulder.

"I think you'll always be important to him." Johnny didn't need to add *if he's anything like me.*

After a little more kidding around with each other, and a few inside jokes that poor Jason could only stand there and pretend not to notice, they settled on a phone for Zach. Then it was time to pick the perfect plan. Again, far too many options were available.

"There is a two year commitment, to get the phone at this price," Jason reminded them.

"I think I can handle that." If Johnny had his way, he'd have more than that.

"Are you sure you don't want to put it on my plan?" Alice asked, but it felt like she was only trying to let him off the hook. Not that she wasn't willing to let him make the commitment.

"I'll take care of this." Johnny moved his hand to rest on the small of her back, and was relieved when she didn't pull away.

"I can add a third line for only nine ninety-nine." Jason flipped to the page in the brochure outlining the family plan. Three phones, unlimited texting, a large number of minutes and a combined data plan all for one price.

"Not at this time." Alice jumped in. "I still have time left on my current contract."

"I'd be happy to look it up for you."

"That's okay. We'll go ahead and add this phone to Johnny's plan now." She squirmed a little, probably hoping that they wouldn't have to explain their current relationship. "But it would be easy enough to add my line to theirs later, right?"

"Sure." Jason went back to the computer and started ringing up the phone, the case, the accidental damage insurance. No need for a car charger, since Zach didn't have a car.

Johnny paid for the phone, signed the next two years of his life away and got Jason to show him and Alice how to add their numbers into the phone's contacts.

"Don't worry, most thirteen-year-olds are plenty tech savvy. He'll have no trouble figuring out the features of the phone," Jason assured them. "But he can't turn on the blocked features without your password."

"Sounds like we're all set, then," Alice said.

Jason shook their hands and presented the new phone to Johnny.

"He's been wanting a phone for some time," Alice said as she slid behind the wheel. "I don't know why I haven't given in before now."

"I'm glad I could help." Johnny folded his legs into the passenger's side. He'd scooted the seat all the way back and there still wasn't a lot of room for him. "I'd like to do more."

"We can talk about all that later." She started the engine and pulled into the street. "You know, when it's official."

"I have no doubt that he's my son." Johnny put his hand on her arm. "Do you?"

She shook her head. "Not anymore."

"Good." Johnny left it at that. He didn't want to know if she still had doubts about him.

They drove through the city on their way to her home. That was something else he'd want to discuss. Later. There was no way he'd live in Mel's house. And his apartment didn't have room for all of them. Especially if they were going to add to their family.

"How are you feeling?" he asked, thinking about the baby they might have created together.

"It's only a phone." Alice gave a nervous little laugh. "It's not nearly as traumatic as him getting, say, his learner's permit."

"I meant, how are *you* feeling? No morning sickness, yet?"

"Oh. No. Too soon." Alice kept her eyes on the road. "Besides, I hardly had any with Zach. Just enough to make me feel like I was doing it right, but it wasn't bad."

"I wish I could have been there."

"But then you wouldn't be where you are now."

He hated to admit that might be true.

"Are you sure you can't wait and give Zach the phone when he gets home from school?"

"I'd like to at least get to Tonopah before they close up the streets." Johnny leaned his head against the headrest.

"You really want to drive all that way?"

"Yes." He had about a thousand things on his mind, and needed that many miles to sort through them all.

"Okay, I never do this but..." She turned her head to merge quickly into the other lane, made an abrupt turn and headed in the opposite direction.

"You're kidnapping me?" Johnny held on as the sound of blaring horns rang out behind them.

"No. I'm taking Zach out of school early." She eased onto the street she needed and proceeded to the school. "We can't let you go down to spring training without some kind of party."

"A party?"

"If this is your last season, we should send you off in style."

She pulled into the visitor's parking spot in front of the school. Dashed into the office and came out with Zach less than fifteen minutes later.

"You'll have to sit in the back," Alice told Zach once they approached the car.

"Are you sure Grandpa's alright?" He looked worried.

"Oh, yeah. The family emergency has nothing to do with him." She smiled at his thoughtfulness. "I'm sorry if I worried you."

"So why did you pull me out of school?"

"We're celebrating." She opened her door and watched Zach climb in behind her. A big smile appeared on his face once he saw Johnny.

"What are we celebrating?" Zach asked while he made himself comfortable, tossing his backpack aside and buckling his seat belt.

"Pitchers and catchers report to spring training in two days, twenty-one hours and seventeen minutes." She may have been off on the minutes.

"You're leaving." Zach slumped back into the seat.

"This afternoon." Johnny tried to smile, but couldn't quite pull it off. "I'm driving down. It will take two days to get there."

"Oh. Why don't you fly?"

"I like to drive. Besides, I'm hoping to stop by and see my mother."

"Oh." Zach leaned forward. "Where does she live?"

"Vegas."

"Cool." Zach seemed to sense that Johnny didn't want to talk about her. Just the fact he'd mentioned his mother was something.

"So, we have a surprise for you." Johnny changed the subject.

"More of a surprise than getting out of school early?"

"I think it's more of a present than a surprise." Alice maneuvered to their favorite hot dog place. Outside of the ballpark, that is.

"Cool." Zach probably figured they were getting him a phone. He'd asked for it, and they had no reason not to give it to him. "Oh, we're getting hot dogs. And it's not even Valentine's Day."

"What does Valentine's Day have to do with hot dogs?" Johnny turned around to look at Zach.

"Well, you know how pitchers and catchers always report to spring training around February fourteenth?"

"I never really pay attention to the date." Johnny still didn't see the connection.

"Instead of celebrating Valentine's Day, we celebrate that. We get hot dogs and other ballpark food, then we have Cracker Jack for dessert." Zach was excited to explain their special day. "It's, like, a tradition."

"Sounds like a nice tradition."

"It sure beats hearts and flowers and stuff." Zach said. "But sometimes I still get my mom chocolate."

"Well, you can never go wrong with chocolate," Alice added.

"I'll try to remember that." Johnny glanced over at her with a molten look in his eyes. Damn. Why did he have to leave so soon?

"So how do you usually celebrate—oh, stupid question." Zach palmed his forehead. "You're the one reporting to spring training. You're going to work."

"Yes. It is work, but it's kind of a celebration, too. There's nothing like getting back on the field. The grass is greener than you remember. The sky is bluer than any other time of year." Johnny made it sound almost mystical. "There's nothing better than getting back into the rhythm of the game. Seeing the guys you played with or against the previous year."

"Cool." Zach dreamed of being one of those guys someday. And maybe with Johnny's help he would have a chance.

She parked in front of the hot dog place and they headed inside for an early lunch and an impromptu goodbye party.

They placed their orders and found a seat by the window. Johnny presented the cell phone to Zach while they waited on hot dogs, fries and a chocolate shake for Zach.

"Oh, cool. Thank you." Zach's face lit up with the surprise. "So can I text you anytime?"

"Anytime." A warm smile spread across Johnny's face. "I'm not allowed to have my phone in the dugout, but I'll be sure to get back to you."

"Yeah, we can't use our phones in class, either." Zach did that half eye-roll he did when he thought he was being treated like a little kid. "They tried to make it so we couldn't have phones at school, but too many parents complained about not being able to get a hold of their kids."

"Just know that having a phone is a privilege," Alice reminded him. "And a responsibility."

"I know."

"There are some rules." She should have discussed them with Johnny. But she wasn't used to having a co-parent. A partner. "Such as no texting or calling after eight PM on school nights."

"Okay."

"And check to see if your friends have unlimited texting," Johnny suggested. "You wouldn't want to ring up their bill with non-stop texts if they can't afford it."

"Good point." Zach was familiarizing himself with the phone, but he was listening. "I've heard stories of kids getting huge bills and not even realizing it."

"What else have you heard about kids getting into trouble with phones?" She had to ask.

"Oh my gosh, Mom. Really?" Zach rolled his eyes and shook his head. "I'm not going to take pictures of myself naked or anything. Or anyone else, either. That's so lame."

Johnny looked a little surprised by the frankness of their conversation.

"And I won't text dirty messages, either." Zach gave Johnny a look. A can-you-believe-I-have-to-put-up-with-this kind of look. "I won't do anything Johnny wouldn't do."

Should she explain that there were times when she'd used Johnny's example on and off the field as a discipline tool? It had been pretty effective at curtailing tantrums and whining when Zach was younger. As he grew older, holding Johnny up as a role model had provided a good starting point for discussing some of the trickier subjects having to do with growing up.

He'd been there for Zach in many ways, even if he didn't know it.

Their order came up and they ate quickly. Zach polished off his jumbo hot dog, fries and he gulped down his shake.

"It's too bad you can't be here when I have my tryouts." Zach grabbed one of Alice's fries.

"You're ready," Johnny assured him. "Just remember what we worked on."

"Yeah. Okay."

"You're a good ballplayer." Johnny reached out and patted Zach's shoulder. "You have talent. It's up to you to make the most of it."

Zach's cheeks flushed as he sucked down the last of his milkshake.

"I still wish you could be there." He stared down at the table. "Not because you're famous and all, but just . . . because."

Because a boy needed his father.

Johnny reluctantly finished his lunch. He needed to hit the road, but wasn't ready to leave. Not when he finally had a family to miss.

He had no ritual when it came to saying goodbye. He usually hit the road early, giving himself plenty of time to get to spring training. To settle into his hotel room and start his workouts early.

Now he almost wished he'd chosen to fly. To spend the extra day with Alice and Zach.

But one more day wouldn't be enough. So he might as well get his goodbye over with.

They pulled into Alice's driveway.

"Hey, thanks for the phone." Zach was antsy to start fiddling with the thing. Not at all intimidated by the numerous features. "I hope I don't bug you too much."

"I don't think that's possible." Johnny's chest started to constrict. "I look forward to hearing from you."

"And good luck in spring training." Zach stood stiffly, like he was wondering if he should say more. Or maybe even hug Johnny.

"Thanks. But luck is the least of it. Preparation. Hard work. Dedication. These things are much more important than luck." Johnny put his hand on the boy's shoulder. "Remember that, when you have your tryouts."

"Right. That and our little secret saying." Zach flung his arms around Johnny's waist. So he'd decided to go for the hug after all.

Johnny returned the embrace with a pat on the back, for good measure.

"Well, I'm going to go play with my new phone."

"It's not a toy," Alice corrected. "It's a tool for communication."

"Then I'm going to go make sure I know how to use my new tool correctly." Zach gave Johnny a smile, and a look that said *she's all yours*.

"Come on in," Alice offered.

Johnny shook his head. "I need to get on the road."

"Are you really going to stop by and see your mom?"

"If I make good enough time. It's about ten hours to Vegas from here."

"That's a long way to drive all by yourself."

"I've got plenty to think about while I'm on the road." He shoved his hands in his pockets to keep from reaching for her. "I suppose you do, too."

"Yeah." She twisted a strand of hair, releasing the sweet scent of her shampoo. Damn, he didn't want to leave her. It was almost harder than the last time. When they'd been officially broken up. But he hadn't let her go without one last attempt at getting her back. He'd gotten her into bed, but hadn't had the courage to ask her to wait for him. In case he didn't make it, he hadn't wanted to hold her back from having some kind of life.

That must have been the night Zach was conceived.

"I should get the results by the end of the week." Johnny was looking forward to making it official.

"And then you'll be with your team."

"No. My team will be right here. You and Zach." He glanced down at her lower abdomen to where she might or might not be working on expanding their roster.

"Johnny, I—"

He placed a finger across her lips.

"Don't worry. We've got plenty of time." Johnny felt her tremble beneath his touch. She wanted him to kiss her. And he would have, but he didn't want to delay his departure any longer. "I won't pressure you. But I'm not going to let you get away. Not this time."

He placed a gentle kiss on her forehead.

"Drive safe." She had a catch in her voice, which told him so much more than her words.

"Take care of yourself. And our son."

"Johnny." She threw her arms around him. And he held her. Both of them wanting more, both of them hoping they'd have another chance.

It didn't feel like a goodbye after all.

He'd be back and they would finally be able to start the life together they'd put on hold for fourteen years.

Chapter 18

Nearly ten hours on the open road, and Johnny was no closer to the perfect proposal than he had been in Union Square. Offering Alice her choice of rings at Tiffany's was so far off the mark. The only thing that would have been worse was if he'd popped the question while they were in the shower.

Alice was a once in a lifetime woman. She deserved a once in a lifetime proposal.

Johnny was relieved to find the McDonald's still open when he pulled through the halfway point in Tonopah. He grabbed a quick bite to eat and drove four more hours to his mother's place. She'd been surprised, yet pleased, to hear from him and was more than willing to wait up for him.

"Johnny, you made it." She opened the door before he even had a chance to knock. "Look at you, so handsome."

He shook his head, feeling a little bit like Zach, embarrassed by his mother's praise.

She pulled him into an awkward hug. That was new. He couldn't remember the last time Destiny Rose Scottsdale showed him any physical affection.

"Did you have a nice trip?" She stepped aside so he could enter her home. "I still don't know why you'd drive rather than fly."

"I like to drive." He shrugged. He didn't want to worry her with the fact that he needed time to think. "There's something about being on the road with wide open spaces and oceans of sagebrush."

He was already feeling closed in by the city. Too many people. He'd missed the desert while he lived in Florida and Kansas City and all the places in between. Where some folks looked out and saw miles and miles of nothing, Johnny saw miles and miles of peace. No people meant no one to let down.

"There's someone I'd like you to meet." His mom smiled. No, she glowed. Then Johnny noticed a man, in his mid to late fifties, step forward. "Howard, this is my son Johnny."

"So nice to finally meet you." The other man extended his hand for a firm handshake.

"Nice to meet you." Johnny had never heard of the man, so there'd been no anticipation on his end.

"Rose talks about you all the time." Howard motioned for Johnny to sit down, as if he'd been the one to pay the mortgage. "She's awfully proud of you."

"Thank you." Johnny sat, but never took his eyes off the other man. He'd worried about men using her to get to him. It sickened him, the kind of guys who would crawl into bed with her just so they could say they rubbed elbows with the woman who'd given birth to the great Johnny Scottsdale. He thought she would have learned her lesson early on. But she had that look. The one that said she was thinking with something other than her brain.

"I hope this move to the west coast means we'll get to see more of you." She looked at Howard when she said it, not Johnny. They were a "we" now. Interesting.

"Actually . . ." Johnny wanted to break the news that she was a grandmother, but he didn't want an audience.

"Maybe I should let you two catch up." Howard, at least, sensed Johnny's discomfort. That, or he was hiding something.

"I'll keep the bed warm for you, Rose," he whispered, a little too loudly.

Johnny held on to all his control not to shudder. Or get up and punch the man in the face. "So he's living here?" Johnny didn't want to put restrictions on her, but still . . .

"Yes. And he pays his share, if that's what you're worried about." His mom folded her arms across her chest. Without the glow of whatever Howard inspired in her, she looked older. Weary.

"I don't want to pry where it isn't any of my business," Johnny said. "I just don't want you getting hurt. I don't want anyone using you."

She laughed. A rich, hearty, I've-been-around-the-block-more-than-once kind of laugh.

"Oh Johnny. How did you get so sweet?" She smiled at him with genuine surprise. And affection. "I never did deserve you. But I'm so grateful to have had you."

"Is that so?"

"Look, I know I'm not exactly anyone's ideal of motherhood." She fiddled with a rather large emerald ring on her left hand. An engagement ring? Or was it a wedding ring? "But I am proud of you. And not because of the baseball thing."

The baseball thing. Fourteen years as a professional, and she called it a thing, as if it was some passing fancy.

"Proud of me? Is that why you let me go and live with Coach Ryan?" Even though it was his idea, he'd still wanted her to at least put up a fight. "I thought you just wanted me out of your hair."

"Oh, Johnny." She rose and sat next to him on the sofa. "Is that what you thought? That I wanted to get rid of you?"

He shrugged, reminding himself of his thirteen-year-old son.

"I let you go because I loved you." She put her arm around him. It was the first time he'd ever heard her say anything about love. "I loved you so much, I wanted you to have a chance to make something of yourself. I couldn't help you with college, or scholarships. Hell, I never even went to school."

"You dropped out?" He'd figured as much, since she was barely sixteen when she'd had him.

"No. I never went. Ever."

"Were you homeschooled?" He didn't know much about her past. She'd never shared this much before.

"Something like that." She heaved a big sigh. "Oh, I know it's hard for you to imagine that the life I led after you were born was so much better than what I left behind."

"It must have been pretty bad." He didn't want to know. Yet he'd always been curious. "So you didn't start . . ."

"At the ranch?" She made it sound so easy. So normal.

"You didn't work at the ranch until after I was born?"

"No." She patted his shoulder. "Did you think your father was one of my customers?"

"I thought maybe I was named after him." Johnny tried to smile at the joke, but his lips were frozen.

"You were named after a boy I knew." She looked off into the distance. Into her past. Some small part that made her smile. "If we lived in a different world, he might have been a boyfriend."

He waited. Maybe she would reveal who his father really was.

"So tell me about you." She dropped the subject. "Have you seen your friend from school? He lives in San Francisco."

Johnny leaned back against the sofa.

"Oh, I forgot." She patted his knee. "He went and married your girl."

"Mel died. Several years ago." Johnny didn't know how to explain it all. But he needed to explain the most important part. "She married him because she was pregnant. With my son."

Not exactly the way he'd meant to tell her. But it was done.

"Your son?" He heard tears in her voice. "I'm a grandma?"

"Yes." He took a deep breath. "His name is Zach. He's thirteen. A baseball player, like me."

"Is he as handsome as you?" She squeezed his knee. "Of course he is."

"He's a great kid."

"No surprise there. He's your kid." She sounded excited for him. Happy almost. "But she never told you."

"No. She was already married when he was born."

"I saw the paper, her wedding announcement. You have no idea how much I wanted to march right over there and give her a piece of my mind."

"Mother. Please." He could picture it. Big fancy society wedding broken up by a fight between the bride and a burned-out prostitute.

"You still love her, don't you?"

"Yes. Yes, I do." Johnny had never felt comfortable talking to his mother about his love life. Maybe because she'd never known love. At least, not as far as he'd seen. But hopefully that had changed.

"So what are you going to do about it?" She reached up and brushed his hair off his forehead. Such a motherly thing to do. And so unlike his experience of their relationship.

"I don't know." He hated to admit uncertainty. Or weakness. And he always tried to be strong, especially around his mother. "It's not that simple."

"No. It is simple. It just ain't easy." She patted his knee. "Like baseball, right?"

"Yeah? Well, a lot of things that work for baseball, don't exactly translate to real life."

"I suppose. But you can take what you learned on the field and apply it anywhere."

"There is one thing I've learned." Johnny stared down at the floor. "If a guy steps in the batter's box thinking there's no way he can hit the ball, there's a good chance he won't hit it. I don't know if I can do this."

"So why try?" She patted his knee one more time. "I guess I should have let you quit when you were nine. The first time you faced live pitching. You struck out three, four times in a row. You wanted to quit."

"I don't remember that."

"No? That's funny, because I was so torn up over that. I thought I was too harsh, making you finish the season. Thought I was selfish for wanting you to get outside more. Burn off all that energy that had you bouncing off the walls."

"I don't remember ever wanting to quit." Johnny said. "I still don't. Not really."

"Baseball's been good to you."

"Yeah. You could say that."

"But it's not enough."

"No. It's not." He sighed, and leaned forward, raking his hands through his hair. "I'm planning on retiring after this season."

"What are you going to do after?"

"I have no idea." Johnny shook his head. "I honestly have no idea."

"Well, you think about it. I'm going to bed." She stood. It would have been nice if she could just tell him what to do. She never had. Not really. Always let him make his own decisions on things. "Help yourself to anything in the kitchen."

He grabbed a beer. He didn't know what he'd expected coming here. Maybe he thought he'd find out who his father was. But no. She hadn't given up any information, other than the fact that he wasn't a customer. In some ways that was a relief. In others, it only made it worse. How bad could it have been that she wouldn't even give him a name? Especially now she knew he was a father himself.

He heard voices overhead. His mother and Howard talking. Or something else. He finished his beer, to drown out the image trying to form in his mind. It wasn't enough. He got up to grab another.

"You want to grab me one, too?" Howard startled him as he stared into the well-stocked refrigerator. Johnny pulled out two bottles and handed one to Howard.

"Rose tells me she's a grandmother." He held his bottle up in a silent toast.

"It was news to me, too." Johnny lifted his beer in acknowledgement before knocking back a long swallow.

"My oldest is expecting her first child in July." Howard prattled on like they were the best of friends. "A girl. I can't wait. Rose is throwing her a shower."

"Rose?" Johnny felt protective of her for some reason. Here this man seemed to genuinely care about her, when all the others hadn't. So why was Johnny's instinct to make sure he wasn't going to hurt her?

"I started calling her that when we first started seeing each other." Howard gave him a lovesick grin. "It seems to suit her."

"How did you meet?" Johnny knew she'd long since retired, but he wondered how she'd made the transition from meeting men for money to meeting someone for real companionship.

"Costco." The man's smile widened. It must have been a good memory. "She helped me pick out a bottle of wine for a first date. Only the date never happened. She talked me into sending flowers as an apology. My date got flowers, and I got Rose."

"Is that so?" It sounded kind of... sweet.

"I care about her. Very much." Howard seemed to understand. "And believe me, my intentions are honorable."

"Really?"

"Yes, sir." Howard sounded like a schoolboy, wanting to take a girl to the prom. "I love her, Johnny. And she loves me."

"Do you know..." Was it his place to tell him? Or should he stay out of their business?

"Everything." Howard pressed his lips into a tight smile. "It's been a long road, and I think she's finally in a place where she can allow herself to be happy."

"Well, that's good." He wondered what that must feel like. "I'm happy for her. For both of you."

"She wants you to be happy, too." Howard rose, patted Johnny on the shoulder and headed back upstairs.

"You're up." Mom, or Rose, as she was now going by, was waiting for him in the kitchen. "I'll put on a fresh pot of coffee."

"Thanks." Johnny had planned on leaving early in the morning, but he couldn't manage to fall asleep until about three in the morning. He'd been thinking about his mother. About Alice. Both women claimed to love him. Yet they'd let him go. Both women kept their child from his father. But while Alice had sold herself in marriage, his mother simply sold her body.

"I wish we had more time together." She set a plate of bacon and eggs in front of him. "I'd like to know more about my grandson."

"He's a terrific kid." Johnny swallowed a lump of eggs. Then he pulled his cell out of his pocket. "Here's a picture of him."

"He's beautiful." Rose didn't hide the tears glistening in her eyes. "He looks so much like you when you were young."

"You think so?" Johnny wondered if Alice had known all along, or if she truly didn't know until she'd seen the two of them together.

"It's the eyes." She indicated one of the pictures he'd taken when they were at the ballpark together. "Not just the color, but the shape and the warmth. And he's got your smile, too."

"It makes me wonder how she could have thought he could be Mel's child." Johnny drained his coffee, the bitter taste lingering, like his feelings toward Mel.

"A woman can convince herself of almost anything," She handed him the phone, as if the memories they'd missed out on were too much. "She can convince herself of anything if she thinks she's protecting those she loves."

"Why would she need to protect Zach from me?"

"Maybe she was protecting him from me." She stood, cleared Johnny's plate even though he wasn't quite finished. "Or maybe she was protecting you."

"That's bullshit." He'd never sworn in front of her before. "She said the same thing when she left me. That she wanted me to start my career without any distractions. She wanted me to be able to focus on getting to the majors without having to worry about keeping her happy."

"Were you ready to be a father then?"

"No. But that's not the point." Johnny cleared the rest of the table, setting his coffee cup in the top rack of the dishwasher. "Were you ready to be a mother when you had me?"

"No, of course not. But it's different for women." She turned to face him. To meet him eye to eye. "We don't have a choice."

"Yeah, well I wasn't given a choice either." He hated the fact that he was taking this out on her. But Alice wasn't here. If she had been, he would have ended up in bed with her rather than face the emotions she stirred in him. "I wish she would have told me sooner. At least she could have told me when Mel died."

"Would that have made a difference?"

"No. Not really." Johnny would have still felt betrayed. "But at least I would have had those years. Even if I was on the other side of the country."

That would have been tough. Johnny had just signed his first big contract. She would have worried he'd assume she was only contacting him because he was suddenly rich. He'd also started a tentative relationship with a woman in his building. One of two failed attempts at getting over Alice. And Zach would have been too young to understand why his first "Daddy" was gone and a new "Daddy" could only see him during the winter.

"Shit." Johnny shook his head, realizing she might have had good reason to keep it from him a little longer. "Sorry."

"It's okay. I don't think I've ever heard you swear." She put her arm around his waist and leaned against him. "Even when you were fifteen. You were the only person I knew who respected me like that."

"I'm sorry. Not that I respected you, but that no one else did."

"Howard does." Rose patted his shoulder and finished cleaning up. "He's a good man."

"I'm glad."

"You're a good man, Johnny. A very good man." She sniffled and wiped her eyes with the back of her hand. "I've always been so proud of you."

"Really?"

"I guess I never told you enough. I was proud of you. I guess I just figured that didn't mean a lot . . ." She swallowed the emotion in her voice. "Coming from someone like me."

"You're still my mother."

"Yes. Even though you deserved better."

"You did your best." Johnny understood that now. And he was beginning to understand why Alice had made the choices she'd made.

Zach didn't get too far behind after missing half a day of school. Just extra math, but that was no big deal. Especially since Ashley said she'd help him with it if he got stuck. She gave him her number and took his. Said she'd text him later.

He'd already texted back and forth with Johnny a couple of times. He'd made it to his mother's house in Vegas and was on his way to Arizona. He'd check into his hotel tonight and then he'd have all day tomorrow to settle in.

He should hear about the test by then, too.

But Zach wasn't worried. The more he thought about it, the more he was sure Johnny was his real dad and the only thing left to do was get him and his mom back together. For good.

"Do you have a lot of homework?" Mom came home while he was getting a snack.

"Not too bad." He shrugged. "A little more than normal, but it was worth it. I'm glad I got to say goodbye to Johnny."

"Me too." She gave him a dopey smile. "I think it meant a lot to him, too."

"I'm just not sure what I should call him." Zach looked down at the sandwich he'd made. Peanut butter and jelly on whole wheat. "It seems weird to call him Johnny, but I'm not sure if he wants me to call him Dad yet."

"The good news is, you've got plenty of time to figure it out." She patted him on the shoulder and grabbed the milk for him.

"I guess." He took a glass from the cupboard and filled it to the top. "Maybe it would feel more natural if you two were, like, married."

"Oh, really?" She had that tone, like she thought he was getting a little too big for his britches. "You think Johnny and I should get married."

"Yes. Definitely." Zach took a bite of his sandwich and washed it down with a gulp of cold milk. "But not just because of me. I mean, it's obvious you two like each other. A lot."

"Yes. We do. But . . ." She put the container back in the fridge, because he'd forgot.

"And if you're going to sleep together, you should be married." Isn't that what she'd always said? That people shouldn't have sex unless they were married. Or was that what she thought she should say when they watched movies or TV shows that showed people having casual sex?

"Is that so?" Her voice sounded a little like she'd sucked on a helium balloon. "Is that the only reason to get married?"

"No. I mean, you guys love each other. And we should be a family."

"Sounds like you have it all figured out." She sat down at the kitchen table. "Or have the two of you been conspiring?"

She pointed to his phone, which lay on the table next to his binder.

"No. I mean, not really. Just you know, we talked a little." He felt his cheeks get warm. "I told him that I'm good with the two of you being together."

"Well, that's . . ." She leaned back in her chair, closing her eyes like she was thinking about how to finish what she wanted to say. "That's one less thing to worry about, I guess."

"What are you worried about?"

"I don't want to hurt him any more than I already have."

"So don't."

"I wish it were that simple." She sounded like there was something else going on. Something that meant they might not make it.

"So why do you think you're going to hurt him? You wouldn't cheat on him, right?"

"No. But I guess I feel like I already have. Even though we weren't together when I married your . . . when I married Mel."

"If it bothered him so much, he wouldn't have gotten back together with you." Why did grownups have to make everything so complicated?

"Maybe." She was still worried though.

"You should tell him you love him. Tell him you want to be with him."

"He's in Arizona." She shook her head. "I'm here."

"So. Go down there. We've always talked about going to spring training someday. You should totally go this year."

"You have school." She was stalling. Looking for excuses.

"Go without me."

"Really?" She smiled at him. "It's that important to you, you'd have me go to spring training without you?"

"Well, yeah." Why was she making such a big deal about this? "I mean, if you guys get married we'll be able to go down there anytime."

"What if this is Johnny's last season?"

He hadn't thought about that.

"No big deal." He shrugged. If it was, then it would just mean Johnny would need a reason to stay in San Francisco. She needed to give him a reason to stay.

Chapter 19

Johnny checked into his hotel room and collapsed on the bed after a long, hot shower. He slept a full eight hours and woke feeling refreshed and eager to start the season.

Zach had texted him a few times. He was up to something. Trying to make sure Johnny didn't forget about them. But Johnny was proud of the boy. His son. The concept was becoming more and more real, and more and more satisfying as the days went by. He couldn't wait to get the official confirmation.

Bryce Baxter had also been in touch. He'd come down early, to report along with the pitchers and catchers and injured players. He was staying in the same hotel and had even arranged to get a room on the same floor. Johnny was actually glad to have a friend around to keep him loose. And after the way he'd convinced that reporter to back off on his relationship with Zach, Johnny figured he owed him one. They'd planned on meeting for dinner and a couple of beers on their last night of the offseason.

Having an extra day meant Johnny could take a leisurely swim before lunch and a light workout. He'd checked his phone several times, but still hadn't received the email confirming the test results. If he didn't get it today, he'd have to go the whole weekend not knowing.

Really, it didn't matter. Just a formality. He knew without a doubt that Zach was his son.

Maybe with the official results, he'd finally be able to forgive Mel for taking Alice away from him. He could forgive him now, but he would've liked to thank him for taking care of his son. The fact that Zach was happy, healthy and so well-adjusted was a testament to the kind of early childhood he'd been able to have, thanks to Mel.

It also helped him let go of his jealousy of Mel's relationship with Alice now that he realized she hadn't been able to get over Johnny any more than he'd been able to forget her.

He repeated his mantra in an effort to clear his head. To focus on the job ahead of him.

This was going to be a good season. His best ever. He could feel it. Deep in his core. This was the year he'd finally prove to himself that he was for real. That the awards he'd won weren't a fluke. That he hadn't just been lucky—or worse, everyone felt sorry for him so they let him win. Yeah, they let him win one hundred and forty-five times, versus a hundred and twenty-two losses.

He was feeling so optimistic about the upcoming season, he almost wanted to ask Bryce to invite his reporter friend along to dinner with them. Almost.

Johnny grabbed his phone, but didn't check for messages as he headed down to the hotel's restaurant where he would meet Bryce. An early meal, and hopefully another good night's sleep would be all he needed to be ready to report for duty first thing tomorrow.

"Yo, Johnny." Bryce was seated at the bar, already working on a beer when Johnny arrived. "Glad you could make it."

"Me, too." Johnny slid onto the barstool next to Bryce and indicated to the bartender that he'd take whatever Bryce was having.

"Man, can you feel it? This year is going to be something special." Bryce tried to pay for Johnny's drink, but Johnny shook him off. He reached for his wallet and tossed his phone on the bar next to it.

There was an email. Just waiting for him to open it.

He took a long pull on his beer before clicking on the icon.

He read the report. Blinked. Twice. And read it again.

It couldn't be. But there it was in PDF form. The results of the DNA test were negative.

Negative.

Zach wasn't his son after all.

The air sucked out of his lungs like he'd been sucker punched. His vision clouded and he worried he might be sick right there on the bar.

He gulped down the rest of his beer and then knocked over the bottle in his attempt to set in on the bar. He stood, a little wobbly, as if he'd had several drinks instead of just the one. He staggered toward the men's room.

Once there, he had no idea why he didn't just bolt for his room. The wave of nausea passed and he splashed cold water on his face.

"Hey, bro. What's the matter?" Bryce had followed him.

Johnny couldn't decide if he was grateful or pissed that he wasn't alone right now.

"I'm fine." Johnny got himself under control. *Focus. Breathe. Let it go.*

"Okay. Let's eat, then." Bryce patted him on the shoulder and kept his hand there as they walked back to the restaurant.

"Right." Whether Zach was his kid or not, Johnny needed to keep his strength up. He had a job to do. And once again, that was all he had.

"So is everything alright at home?" Bryce unfolded his menu and scanned the options.

"For the next six weeks, this is my home." Johnny barely glanced at the menu. He'd order the usual. Steak. Salad. Baked potato.

"You got some news. Something to do with Alice. Or the kid?"

"He's not my kid." Johnny closed the menu and placed it on the edge of the table. "That's the news."

"No way." Bryce turned the menu to the next page. "I'm sorry, man."

"Yeah. Well, it's probably for the best, right?" Johnny sipped his water and wished the waitress would return with their drinks. "I don't know a damn thing about being a father."

"You can still be there for the kid." Bryce was trying to be helpful. "You just won't be related."

"No. It's better if I step away. From both of them." All the old emotions came flooding back. The resentment. The jealousy. Mel was Zach's father. And in a way, it was worse after believing the kid could have been his. That Alice and Zach could've been the family he'd secretly longed for his whole life.

Only to have that hope once again crushed. Like a two-out, two-strike homer in the bottom of the ninth that would have broken up his perfect game.

Right now Johnny was too hurt to trust himself to be around them. To be able to look at Zach and not see his father's betrayal. It was like getting the wedding announcement in the mail all over again, serving as a reminder of what he'd lost.

"If you say so." Bryce finally closed his menu when the waitress returned with their beers. She took their orders, and they finished the meal talking about baseball and movies and music. Anything but the subject that was so painful for Johnny.

"Any dessert?" The waitress smiled first at Johnny, then turned her attention to Bryce when it was clear he wasn't interested.

"No. Just the bill. Thanks." Bryce gave her a polite smile. Very different from his usual charming grin.

"Look, if you're interested, don't let me stop you." Johnny could care less if his friend wanted to get laid.

"Nah. I'm a little worn out." Bryce leaned back in his chair, a satisfied smile on his face.

"Rachel Parker?" Johnny had a feeling there was more going on between those two than just a one-time thing.

Bryce beamed like a love-struck teenager.

"I wish I'd never met her." Johnny couldn't help but place some of the blame on her. "Wish she'd never conjured up the story that Zach might be my kid. Now every time I see her, I'll be reminded of dragging him down to that clinic. Having a discussion on whether or not he should call me 'Dad.' Then going out for ice cream afterward."

"Oh man, I'm sorry you had to go through all that." Bryce grabbed the bill.

Johnny was too defeated to fight him for it.

"Look, if you want me to stop seeing her, I will." Bryce scrawled his signature across the credit card slip. "She's becoming a distraction anyway, and it's time to get my head in the game."

"I know what you mean. Nothing but baseball from now until October."

"Yeah. I need your help to stay focused." Bryce walked with him to the elevators. "I need to be more monk-like."

"Maybe I should try to be more like you." Johnny couldn't see it. "Try and score with some of the hot babes down here."

Bryce chuckled and clapped him on the back.

"I like you, Johnny. You're a good guy. I've got a six-pack in my room. You want to come up and help me drink it?"

"I'm just going to go to bed." Johnny shook his head.

"Will you sleep?" Bryce wasn't going to let him off the hook so easily.

"Probably not."

"Then have a beer with me. We could hang out. Watch a movie. Keep me from slipping into my old ways. That waitress was pretty fine..." He craned his neck as if he was searching for her.

"Sure. Why not?" He wasn't going to sleep, so he might as well keep Bryce out of trouble.

Johnny followed Bryce to his room, which happened to be across the hall from his. He might as well get used to having Baxter around.

"Hey Mom, have you heard from Johnny?" Zach kept checking his phone, but shoving it back into his pocket with a disappointed look on his face.

"I know he made it to Arizona. But he's busy, you know." She hated to see her son so dependent on just a word from Johnny. "He's started his workouts and I'm sure there's a lot going on. He'll be in touch when he gets a chance."

"Yeah, I guess." Zach started to pull his phone out of his pocket but then thought better of it. "I suppose I'm being a pest."

She wasn't going to say anything, but she was a little frustrated with Johnny for not getting back to either of them. She also had unreturned texts. And she'd expected to get the results from the paternity test by now.

He was probably busy with his workouts and getting to know his teammates. He was the new guy, and she had a feeling he was concerned about his age and whether or not he still had what it takes. She imagined he'd work harder and longer than the rest of the team, leaving little time for anything else.

Still, it would be nice if he sent a text or two acknowledging his family.

It had been over a week. And Alice was getting tired of having to distract Zach. She was tempted to take his phone, but he'd gotten a few texts from a girl at school. Just a friend, according to Zach, but the way he grinned when he heard from her meant it might not stay that way for long.

Oh, she wasn't ready for girls. But Zach was getting there.

And she wished Johnny was here to help them through this stage.

She waited until Zach was in bed before making one more phone call. This time Johnny answered.

"Finally." She didn't even try to hide her exasperation. "I was starting to wonder if you'd been kidnapped by aliens."

"No. Just busy." Johnny's voice was tight. He was avoiding them.

"Too busy to acknowledge your son." She wanted him to know how Zach felt about being ignored.

"He's not my son."

She must have heard him wrong. His voice was barely audible.

"I got the results last Friday. They were negative."

"That can't be." She was so sure after seeing the two of them together these last two weeks. "There must be some kind of mistake."

"There's no mistake." Johnny's voice was completely devoid of emotion. "They took two samples from each of us. Placed them in a sealed container. Zach is not my son."

"Oh, Johnny. I'm so sorry." She felt a wave of nausea and she lowered herself to a chair.

"Yeah. Me too. He's a great kid." Johnny had all his defenses up. He sounded so calm. So controlled. "But I don't think I can deal with playing dad right now. I have to go."

He hung up before she could say anything else. Before she could break through his monk-like trance. He was hurting. He'd wanted to be Zach's father. Wanted it more than he'd admitted even to himself, and was devastated to find out he wasn't.

She waited for the nausea to pass. Now wasn't the time to think about the fact she was two days late. Nor would the news she could be pregnant soften the blow for Johnny.

But she did have to tell Zach. He needed to hear the truth. And maybe he would be comforted that Johnny was too upset about the knowledge to tell him.

Yeah. Right. That would make it easier.

She knocked on Zach's door. He quickly shoved his phone under the covers. He'd been texting, even though it was after nine.

"Don't get your friend in trouble by texting her too late." She smiled, letting him know she wasn't mad. "I'd hate for her to have her phone taken away."

"Sorry. I forgot."

She raised an eyebrow. She wanted him to know that he couldn't get away with excuses. "Don't forget again, or you'll be the one with no phone privileges."

"Yeah, okay." He sat up. "What's going on?"

He sensed when she had something unpleasant to say. Probably because she squirmed and made it that much harder by trying to be gentle.

"I just spoke with Johnny." And her heart was a little bit broken for him. For all of them. "He got the results back from the paternity test."

She couldn't say it. Couldn't shatter her little boy's heart. Not when he'd been so happy to have Johnny in his life.

"And?" He crossed his arms over his chest. Bracing for the bad news.

"He's not your dad." She had to squeeze her eyes shut to keep the moisture at bay.

"You're lying." Zach grabbed the blanket and balled it in both fists. "Of course he's my dad. You're just freaked out because you're so used to having me to yourself. You don't want to have to share my attention."

"Oh, Zach, I wish that were true. I really do." She reached out to brush his hair off his forehead, but he recoiled from her touch.

"Leave me alone." Zach flopped onto the mattress and pulled the covers over his head.

"I'm sorry. I know how much you like Johnny. How much he likes you. But . . ." Really, there wasn't anything more she could say. She couldn't just kiss it all better or slap a bandage on this kind of hurt.

She slipped quietly out of his room, hoping the new baby wouldn't make things worse.

Maybe she was wrong. Maybe she wasn't pregnant. Even though she was sure she was. She'd pick up a home pregnancy test in a couple of days. But she already knew what the results would be.

Then again, she'd been absolutely certain what the results of the paternity test would be, but she'd been wrong.

So wrong.

No. Freaking. Way.

Zach punched his pillow after he was sure his mom was downstairs. He couldn't believe Johnny wasn't his father. They had so much in common. They were so much alike. And he really, really, really wanted Johnny Scottsdale to be his dad.

There had to be a mistake. A mix-up at the lab.

But he'd been there. They were careful. Put everything in pre-labeled containers that were sealed before they left the room.

So yeah. It had to be true.

Man, this sucked. And he couldn't even tell Ashley right now. It was late. He didn't want to get her into trouble. But he needed someone to talk to.

He pulled out his phone, opened the text screen and typed.

Hey. Even if you aren't my dad. I still think you're cool.

He wondered if Johnny would text him back. Or if he'd even let him keep the phone. He'd signed a two-year contract, so he couldn't just give it back. And it wasn't like he had another kid he could give it to.

His phone buzzed.

Sorry kid. I gotta get to work. Look after your mom.

So that was it? Johnny was sorry. And he asked Zach to look after his mom. Meaning he wouldn't be coming around anymore.

Yeah. This sucked big time.

At least his grandparents would be happy. They were still his grandparents.

So life would go back to normal. He'd be busy with school. And then in a couple of weeks, he'd have baseball tryouts and even if he wasn't Johnny Scottsdale's son, he could remember what he'd learned. He'd do okay. He might not ever make it to the majors, but he'd at least be ready for this season.

Zach got out of bed. He walked over to his desk and grabbed his glove. He put it on. Punched the pocket and held it up to his face. He inhaled the familiar smell of leather. Only instead of comforting him, like it usually did, it made him feel a little sick.

Finding out Johnny wasn't really his dad should mean that everything would be the same as it was before. But everything felt different. Wrong, even.

For a few days anyway, he'd been somebody special. He was the son of the great Johnny Scottsdale. He'd had dreams of following in his father's footsteps all the way to the majors. With Johnny guiding him the next few years as he played high school ball, Zach knew he'd have a better than average chance of at least getting a look from college and Major League scouts. And having his name wouldn't have hurt. No, it would probably have given them enough reason to look a little closer and maybe give him an edge over the competition.

Sure, he still would have had to work hard to prove himself, but at least they wouldn't have just looked at his skinny legs or the fact that he played for a small private school instead of one of the big high schools that made the playoffs every season.

But no. Now he had to find out he wasn't even Johnny's son. Not only that, but Johnny didn't seem to want anything to do with him anymore. Or his mom.

It made Zach wonder if everything Johnny had told him was total BS. He'd told Zach that he would be around, even if he wasn't his dad. He'd also said he cared about Mom.

But Johnny found out that Zach wasn't his son and now he'd stopped texting him. Stopped talking to Mom. Like he'd been lying to them both.

And if he was lying about caring about them, then maybe he lied about everything else, too.

Like Zach being a good pitcher. That he had potential. That he could be really good if he worked on the things he'd taught him.

Well, maybe he'd taught him what his friend Ty had figured out on his own. That men would say or do anything to get into a woman's bed. And once they got there, they'd take off.

If Johnny lied to Zach just so he could back together with his mom—or worse, so he could get back at her for marrying someone else—then maybe Zach would end up looking like a complete idiot when he showed up for baseball tryouts.

Screw that. He wasn't going to try out. He didn't want to play baseball anymore. It would only remind him of Johnny Scottsdale. The guy who used to be his hero. The guy who'd almost been his dad.

Chapter 20

Johnny sat on the bench for the first game of spring training. He wasn't scheduled to pitch, so he kicked back in the dugout, eating sunflower seeds and watching his teammates get action on the field. The Goliaths' ace, Mark Carson, had a solid three-inning performance. Then the number two starter came in for two innings before the relievers got their shot.

Johnny hoped to get into a game tomorrow or the next day at the latest. He was in no hurry. In fact, he didn't really care if he played. He'd talked to Alice last night. After avoiding her for days, he'd finally broken down and told her the news. He'd tried to explain why he couldn't be with her—and Zach—at least not right now.

Zach had texted him. Told Johnny he didn't care that he wasn't his son. But he couldn't keep stringing the kid along. It would be better in the long run if he cut his ties sooner, before either of them got too attached.

Only problem was, Johnny was already attached.

He missed the kid. But he didn't want to ever make him feel like there was something wrong with him. Johnny knew that someday his feelings for Mel would show through. Like an old grass stain that couldn't be bleached away.

The game ended with a 7-6 Goliaths' victory. Bryce had a pretty good game. And he worked the crowd. Waving to fans and tipping his hat. He'd been more than happy to sign baseballs, posters and anything the fans put in front of him before the game. Especially t-shirts. While the women were still wearing them.

Johnny had a feeling he would be having dinner alone tonight. There were at least a half-dozen single women lined up for Bryce's attention. He'd made it ten days or so without hooking up with anyone. Johnny doubted he'd hold out much longer.

"What do you think? Italian or Tex-Mex for dinner tonight?" Bryce had stopped by Johnny's locker after his shower. "I'm starving, so either sounds good to me."

"Are you sure? You didn't get a better offer?"

"Several. But I'm not interested. I had a good game. Need to keep my focus on that."

"Yeah. Sure." Johnny laced up his shoes and told Bryce he'd meet him back at the hotel. He wasn't quite ready to leave the sanctuary of the ballpark. He hadn't kept his mind entirely on the game, but it was worse when he was alone in his hotel room. He missed Alice. Ached for her in a way that was a whole lot worse than the first time around.

"Oh. My. God." A female voice pierced the quiet of the clubhouse. "I can't believe I'm really here. In the locker room. It's just like I imagined. Only better. Because you're here. *The* Johnny Scottsdale."

"I'm sorry, but you're not supposed to be here." There was something vaguely familiar about the woman who'd snuck past security. "You could get into trouble."

"It's worth it." She was giddy. And a little scary. "You're worth it. I just had to see you. To be alone with you and tell you how *amazing* you are. How . . . how *perfect* . . ."

"Excuse me, I'm on my way out." He had no idea what she wanted from him. Oh, he had a little bit of an idea, but in case she was after something more than his body, he headed toward the exit.

"Aren't you going to thank me?" She stepped between him and the door and looked up at him expectantly, like a dog who'd performed a trick and was waiting for a pat on the head.

"For what?" The hair on the back of his neck prickled.

"For making sure that gold-digging bitch doesn't ruin your reputation and take you for every penny you're worth." Her expression went cold, calculating. She rested her hands on her hips and leaned forward. Probably hoping to entice him with her low-cut tank top. She reminded him of one of those women on those talk shows that seemed to be on late at night when he couldn't sleep. The ones where everyone screamed at each other and every other word had to be bleeped out.

"I'm sorry. I have no idea what you're talking about." Johnny tried to keep his voice calm in case this woman overran fanatic and rounded the bases toward crazy.

"The paternity test." She stepped toward him, a calculating smile plastered on her face. The pieces started to fall into place. "Of course that boy's mother is only after your money. But I saved you from her."

"You work at that clinic. You administered the paternity test." Johnny had to breathe real slow to keep from dragging this woman straight to the police.

"Yes. I knew—the minute you stepped in my exam room—I knew it was . . . fate. I knew it was meant to be. We are meant to be." She stepped closer, and Johnny backed up against his locker. "I couldn't stand to see your reputation tarnished. So, you had a little indiscretion. A long time ago. But the good news is that no one has to know. I'll keep our little secret."

"No. You won't." Johnny sidestepped as she reached for him. His flesh crawled as her fingers brushed his arm.

"Oh, come on. I did you a huge favor." She licked her lips, in what she must have thought was a sexy invitation. "I . . . I saved you."

"No, you messed with my life." He backed away toward the exit. "You hurt my family. You hurt my son."

"I was trying to protect you." She looked confused. Like she couldn't understand why he hadn't dropped to his knees and thanked her.

"Protect me? Lady, you don't even know me. You don't know what I want. What I need." He was fed up with this perception that because he was a public figure, people thought they had a right to his business.

"I know what you need." She lunged for him and he jumped out of the way. She fell to the floor with a cry of surprise.

"Hey, Johnny, I forgot my phone." Bryce came back in time to watch the woman pick herself off the floor. "Is everything alright in here?"

"No." Johnny didn't even reach out to help her up. "Everything is not alright."

Bryce grabbed his phone out of his locker. "I'll call security."

The woman looked down at her scraped palms. A small, pitiful cry escaped her throat.

"What's going on?" Bryce stepped between Johnny and his so-called fan.

"Do you want to tell him?" Johnny asked. "Or should we wait for the police?"

"Police?" Her eyes filled with tears. "I was only trying to help. I switched the samples, so there was no way the kid would come up as yours."

"She what?" Bryce clenched his fist, but held back. No doubt, he realized he couldn't touch her. No matter how badly she'd screwed with his friend.

"She tampered with the paternity test. Zach could be my son after all." Johnny's voice was thick. His throat felt clogged with emotion. "She almost ruined my life."

Security arrived and they were treated to a full blown crying fit. She blubbered and tried to wipe her face with her sleeve, but with the restraints, she only managed to make an even bigger mess of herself.

Bryce retrieved a wad of toilet paper and handed it to her. She blew her nose, then dropped the tissue to the ground.

"I love you, Johnny Scottsdale," she said over her shoulder as she was led away. "Just know I only did it because I love you. I am, and always will be, your number one fan."

"Oh man. I am so sorry." Bryce shoved a chair under Johnny once the locker room was empty. "Was that your first stalker?"

"Yeah. I guess." Johnny was glad he sat when he did. His legs were starting to shake. "Can you believe someone would do such a thing?"

"Wonder where she put your DNA. She probably hid it in her underwear drawer." Bryce pulled up another chair, and plopped down next to him.

"That's just sick." Johnny couldn't help but smile at his friend's attempt at cheering him up. It worked. A little. "So what's the weirdest thing a fan has done to you?"

"We'd better order a pitcher. I have quite a list." Bryce helped him up. "Of course, some of it was not so much stalking as revenge."

"Alright. I want to hear your stories." Johnny stood. "I could use some laughs."

"You got it." Bryce grinned. "Dinner and drinks are on me."

"I think it's my turn." Johnny had lost track of who had picked up the tab last.

"No, man. You've got a family to take care of. Let me treat."

"Mr. Scottsdale. Can we get a statement before you go?" One of the security officers returned before they were able to clear out.

"Sure." Johnny relayed the details as best as he could. The security guard didn't even bat an eye when he told him about the paternity test. At this point, Johnny didn't give a damn about his reputation. He just wanted to make sure this didn't happen to another family.

He and Bryce took a cab to a popular Tex-Mex restaurant. Over margaritas, Bryce entertained Johnny with tales of wild and crazy things women had done to get his attention. Everything from mailing their panties to showing up at his hotel rooms wearing nothing but the team's flag. The idea was to cheer Johnny up, make him laugh and get his mind off the crazed fan who'd turned Johnny's life inside out.

"You gonna be alright, man?" Bryce insisted on paying the bill and Johnny let him. He'd have more than enough time to repay the favor.

"Yeah. I just wish I'd been a bigger man when I got those false results."

"You were pretty upset."

"I didn't have to push them away." Even though he'd been devastated by the news. And even now, he didn't know for sure if Zach was his kid. "I shouldn't have let my feelings depend on a stupid piece of paper."

"So now you know how much they mean to you, what are you going to do about it?"

"Grovel." Johnny hoped it would be enough.

"Somehow I get the feeling you haven't had much practice."

"Nope. Any advice?"

"What makes you think I know anything about groveling?" Bryce flashed his trademark devil-may-care grin.

"Just a hunch."

"I guess I've had to get down on my knees once or twice." Bryce laughed.

"Damn. I wish she wasn't still in San Francisco."

"So, figure out a way to get her down here."

* * *

Dinner with the Harrisons had never been more awkward. No one wanted to talk about Mel's sudden retirement. He hadn't gone willingly, but he hadn't put up a fight, either. After spending his entire adult life working in the high pressure environment of the finance industry, he didn't seem to know what to do with himself.

He'd also had to change his diet, so the meal itself was different than what they were used to. Lean fish instead of roast beef. A single glass of wine instead of his usual before and during and after dinner cocktails. A hearty salad replaced his crusty loaf of sourdough bread.

At least they ate on familiar china, in the usual dining room.

And one other thing was the same as always.

Zach was still their grandson.

"So how's school?" Frannie asked, trying to draw Zach out of his funk.

"Fine." He'd been sullen and withdrawn since they found out the test results.

"Any big tests or projects coming up?" Frannie kept trying.

"No."

"So, I bet you're looking forward to baseball tryouts." Mel tried to steer the conversation to Zach's favorite subject. "Especially since you've been working with the best."

"I might not try out."

Shocked silence filled the room.

"What do you mean you might not try out?" Mel picked up his fork. "Baseball is life. At least that what all your t-shirts say."

"I don't want to play anymore," Zach mumbled before shoving food into his mouth.

"Why not?" Alice had a feeling it had everything to do with Johnny.

"Because." He gulped down a big swallow of milk. "Because I just don't, okay? Why does everyone have to get on my case about it?"

"No one's on your case." Frannie kept her voice calm, sounding like this was any other conversation at any other dinner.

He shoved back from the table. "May I be excused?"

Zach didn't wait for an answer before leaving the dining room. He headed for the door. One thing about living two doors away, he could walk home if he wanted to. It seemed like he wanted to right now.

"Let him go," Frannie cautioned. "He's just lost his hero."

True, but that didn't give him the right to be rude.

"I need to go after him." She stood, getting a little lightheaded. She felt feverish, her palms clammy, and then the room started to spin. She made a mad dash for the powder room, barely making it in time.

Hello, morning sickness. Even if it was evening.

Oh joy. Because her life wasn't complicated enough. No. Maybe it was about to become really simple. She loved Johnny. And she was going to have his baby. This time, she was strong enough to go after him.

As soon as she stopped puking.

Alice rinsed her mouth and reappeared in the dining room. She had a plan. Now she just needed a few pieces to fall into place.

"Are you alright, dear?" Frannie's concern showed on her face.

"Yes. I'm fine. I think maybe I've been overdoing it a bit." She wanted to make sure Mel overheard the conversation, but didn't want to make it too obvious. "I've been so busy with Zach's school and sports schedules. Getting ready for his graduation coming up. Now with Johnny coming back into our lives and then leaving again. Not to mention, all the work I have for the foundation."

"You do have a lot on your plate." Frannie kept her poker face. She must have sensed where the conversation was heading. "And it really is a shame that Johnny is all the way in Arizona. I think you two could work things out a lot easier if you could only spend more time together without all these distractions."

"Yes, but Zach needs me and I have to start working on next year's camp. We have a good start on the fundraising, but maybe there's a way to do more. Serve more kids." She did her best damsel in distress imitation. Hopefully she didn't sound too melodramatic.

"Do you have to do it all right now?" Frannie asked, completely and purposefully ignoring Mel.

"I have to meet with the major donors. It's the personal touch that keeps them coming back."

"It's too bad there wasn't someone who could help with that part." Frannie cast a glance in Mel's direction. "Someone with ties to the foundation. Someone who believes in it."

"I could do it," Mel volunteered. "I've got nothing better to do."

"Oh, I couldn't ask that of you. It's more than just meetings face to face. It's writing thank you letters and making phone calls." Alice held back a smile. "You should relax and enjoy your retirement."

"I'd enjoy it a lot more if I had something to keep me busy," Mel said. "Besides, I'm sure you kept such good notes, I could step right in and not even skip a beat."

"You know she has. In fact, she could probably even step away completely and we could keep it going. Couldn't we?" Frannie smiled sweetly at her husband.

"We could." If Mel had caught on to their scheme, he was willing to play along. "If our girl needed to pursue other interests."

"Why don't you take a few days, dear. We'll look after Zach and the foundation. You look after Johnny Scottsdale."

"Thank you." Alice didn't even help with the cleanup. She practically ran home. She'd pulled up the airline's website on her phone and by the time she unlocked the door, she was ready to type in her credit card for the next available flight to Phoenix.

"I'm sorry I ran out like that." Zach came out of his room when he heard her arrive. "I just couldn't pretend like nothing happened. Like I didn't get my hopes up only to find out that Johnny isn't my dad. And I don't want to feel bad for feeling bad about it."

"It's okay to feel bad. But it's not okay to take it out on the rest of us."

"I know." He looked down at his feet, kicking at the carpet.

"And we all understand that you're feeling disappointed." She put her hand on his shoulder. She had to reach up to do it. "What we don't understand is why you would want to quit baseball."

"It's just too hard. Thinking about Johnny and everything."

"It's even harder to give up something you love because you don't want to get hurt." She should know.

"I guess." He let out a long sigh.

"I'd like to stay and talk to you about this, but we have to pack."

"Pack?"

"Yes. You're going to stay with your grandparents, and I have a nine o'clock flight to Phoenix."

"You're going to go get Johnny back?" His face lit up.

"I'm going to try."

"Good. Because it's lame for you to give up someone you love, just because you don't want to get hurt." He repeated her words of wisdom.

"Is that so?"

"Yes. Besides, even if Johnny's not my dad, he'd still make an awesome stepfather." He sounded a tad uncertain, like maybe he didn't want to get his hopes up too much.

"You know, I think you're right." Her own hopes were soaring.

"Do you want to take my lucky glove?" Zach offered. He put his arm around her shoulder and started walking her toward her room.

"No. I think I'll rely on something better than luck."

"Hard work, preparation and dedication?" He dropped his arm as they stood at her door.

"I was going to say love." She gave him a big hug, holding on longer than usual. "But a little hard work, preparation and dedication can't hurt."

Chapter 21

Johnny was a spectator for the first three innings of the next spring training game. The Goliaths had a 3-0 lead when his number was called. He didn't need to be perfect. He just needed to do his job and let his defense do theirs. And hope he could lay down a bunt if he got to the plate with a runner on and less than two outs.

He threw his warm-up pitches and bent down to pick up the rosin bag. A ritual he'd performed so many times in his career. He was ten years old the first time he threw a pitch. In the past twenty-five years, he'd honed his delivery to maximize velocity, pinpoint control, and fool the opposing batters well enough to make a decent living at it.

He adjusted his cap, took his position on the mound, and started his windup.

Focus.

Just concentrate on what was most important. For the first time in his life, Johnny realized it wasn't baseball.

Breathe.

He needed Alice like he needed air.

Let it go.

He couldn't let her go.

He'd finish this game. Then he'd figure out how to win her heart once and for all. He wouldn't pitch again for at least four more days. If he couldn't convince her to come down here, he'd fly home. He was entitled to up to three days paternity leave, but since the test had been tampered with, he didn't think it would count.

Besides, it really didn't matter if Zach was his kid or not. He was Alice's son, and a fine young man. The two of them had formed a bond, and unless Zach wanted to know if it was biological, Johnny was satisfied with that.

After three innings, Johnny was done for the day. He'd had a solid outing. Not perfect, but respectable. He'd given up a solo home run in the sixth, but thanks to Baxter's bat, they were up 5-2 and it was up to the bullpen to hold the lead. He'd leave the game feeling like he'd done his job.

He could do this job for one more year. He'd made a commitment to the team. If he remained healthy, he would take the field. Every time he was asked to. He had to set an example for Zach, and for all the kids he worked with. As much as baseball was just a game, it had given him so much more.

Johnny knew what he wanted to do when the season was over. He wanted to open up his own baseball camp. As much as he enjoyed the work he'd done at the minicamp, it was only the beginning of what he wanted to accomplish. He could help a lot of kids. He'd share his experience. The good and the bad. He'd let kids know that no matter where they started in life, where they ended was up to them. With hard work, discipline and perseverance, anything was possible.

The philosophy had served him well on the field. He just hoped it would work in his personal life, as well. He'd find out soon enough. He hadn't known for sure whether he was going to get in today's game or not; otherwise, he would have already booked a flight back to San Francisco for tonight.

Johnny held his head high as he walked off the mound. Bryce Baxter came up behind him, put a hand on his shoulder and then gave his a hearty clap on the back.

"Hey, check out that blonde behind home plate." Bryce chuckled.

"Not interested." He should know him by now. Johnny headed straight for the dugout.

"Trust me. You want to see what she's got to offer." Baxter shoved him just enough, he was forced to stop. Or else topple over in front of the sold-out ballpark.

Johnny looked up in the stands.

Alice stood three rows behind home plate. She held up a large hand-lettered sign that read *I LOVE YOU, JOHNNY SCOTTSDALE!*

The word love was surrounded by a heart and covered in glitter.

When she caught him smiling at her, she turned the sign over. She'd written, *Ask me again.*

Johnny dropped to one knee, removed his cap and shouted as loud as he could into the stands.

"Marry me, Alice. Make my life complete. Make it better than perfect."

The crowd erupted in cheers, whistles and applause. So loud that he couldn't hear her response.

She opened the sign to reveal a Goliath sized *YES!!!!!* covered in glitter and surrounded by hearts.

She made her way down to the edge of the stands. She climbed over the railing and Johnny pulled her into his arms. He leaned down and kissed her long and hard and didn't stop even with the crowd going wild around them. At the moment, he didn't care if there were ten thousand people watching. He didn't care if their picture ended up on Bay Area Sports Net or even ESPN.

The only thing he cared about was having Alice in his arms. And in his life.

"I don't have a ring." He would remedy that as soon as possible. "But I do want to marry you. I mean it. I love you Alice."

"I love you, too." She leaned into him as he escorted her off the field.

"Thank you for coming down here." Johnny pulled her into the clubhouse. "Saved me a trip to San Francisco."

"You were going to come back?" She was glowing, and it had nothing to do with the glitter.

"I need you in my life." Johnny wrapped his arms around her. "I need you and Zach."

"Even though he's not your son?" Her voice quavered, just a little.

"He could be." Johnny hadn't had a chance to tell her. He'd been too upset last night, and then he'd had to prepare for today's game. "The test was tampered with. The nurse who administered it was a fan. A fanatic. She thought she was doing me a favor."

"So, it was a false negative?" She stepped back, looking up at him with a look of disbelief on her face.

"Maybe. But it doesn't matter to me if he's my biological son or my stepson." He reached out, brushed the hair off her face. "I happen to love that kid."

"Yeah. He's pretty fond of you, too." She smiled at him, a look of pure radiance on her face.

"But I'm willing to redo the test." Johnny wanted her to know he'd go through it all again. "It could be important for Zach to know the truth."

"I think he'll want to know." She closed her eyes and let out a long sigh.

"So, what about the other test?" Johnny brought her to his locker, and pulled up a chair for her to sit in. "Is there a player to be named later?"

"I haven't taken the test yet." She looked up at him, her face radiant with love. Hope. Hormones? "I thought you'd want to be there. I thought we could find out together."

"I'd like that." Johnny knelt in front of her and took her hands in his. "So when can we find out?"

"Anytime. Although, I don't suppose there is a ladies' room around here." She laughed as she looked around the locker room. This was definite guy territory.

"Let's go back to my hotel." Johnny would like to be someplace where they could celebrate. In private. Or get working on making a baby if there wasn't one.

"Let's go." She let him pull her to a standing position.

"Do you want another baby?" He hoped she did. But he'd be satisfied with Zach, if that's the way it worked out. "Do you want to have my baby?"

"You know what? I think I do." She slid her arms around his waist. "What about you?"

"I'd love for you to have my baby. And I want to be there." He wrapped his arms around her. "I meant it when I said I'm quitting after this year."

"Are you sure?"

"Yes. For a long time, baseball was my life." He held her even tighter. "But now, you're my life. You and Zach."

"I love you, Johnny. I've always loved you."

"Good. Then let's go find out if we're expanding our roster."

Johnny stepped back so he could change out of his uniform and into his street clothes. He made it quick. He could use a shower, but would grab one back at the hotel. Maybe he could get her to join him.

"You know, you're going to have to work on losing the baseball talk." She teased him as they went to his Jeep. "It's a little cliché away from the ballpark."

"Hey, I've got a year." Johnny hit the button on his keys twice and opened her door. He helped her up into the passenger seat. "Besides, I'd like to stay involved in the game. But with a schedule that's a lot more family friendly."

"So what were you thinking of doing next?"

"I'd like to give a shot at coaching. Not this year, of course." Johnny hoped he was making the right move. "But I'd like to help coach Zach's team next year. If they can make room for me."

"I'm sure any high school team would be happy to have you on board."

"And if it turns out I have a knack for it . . ." He took a deep breath. It was one thing to come up with the idea while he stood on the mound, his comfort zone, but something else to share it. "I'd like to open up my own camp."

"You have the knack." She turned and smiled at him. "You most definitely have a knack for coaching and inspiring young ballplayers."

"Would you be willing to help me run the camp? I'd like it to be more of a year-round thing. Not just one week of the year." Johnny knew he couldn't possibly pull it off without her.

"That sounds like a wonderful idea." She had a slight catch in her voice. "So, where do you think you want to open this year-round baseball camp? Back in San Francisco?"

"And compete with the Harrison Foundation's camp?" He shook his head. This was the part that had him the most worried. She seemed to love San Francisco. It suited her. "I was actually thinking about starting a camp in Reno. There's definitely a need there. We could work with the university, and it's close enough to San Francisco, we could bring the kids to a couple of Goliaths games a year."

"Reno." She leaned back into her seat. Was that a good sign? Was she considering it, or trying to figure out a way to change his mind?

"That way you could still go to school. If you're still planning on applying." He thought she'd be an incredible teacher.

"No. I don't think I need to go back to school." She reached for his hand. "I think I'll have plenty to keep me busy. A husband. A teenager. A year-round baseball camp. And maybe even a baby."

"Yes. Maybe even a baby. Do we need to stop at a pharmacy? For a home pregnancy test?" There were several on the way.

"I have everything I need right here." She patted her purse.

Johnny smiled. He had everything he needed. He had Alice.

Alice followed Johnny to his room. It was a nice suite. A very nice suite. Still, she couldn't imagine living in a hotel for six whole weeks. But then she supposed he was used to that lifestyle.

Would he miss it? He'd lived the life of a ballplayer for so long. "The bathroom is through there." Johnny sounded a bit nervous. Of course he was. They were about to find out if they were having a baby. Together this time. "Is there anything you need?"

"Just a moment of privacy, and then it'll be about three minutes before we know." She took her purse into the bathroom. She opened the package and read the instructions again. Simple. Efficient. And according to the box, 99.9% accurate.

She did what needed to be done, replaced the cap on the stick and placed a tissue on the granite counter to set the test on. She washed up and then poked her head out the bathroom door.

"Well?" Johnny practically jumped to his feet. "Is it positive?"

"I thought we'd see together." She flashed him a nervous smile. "It should take a minute or two for the results to show up."

"Okay." He stepped closer. Took her hand and gave a squeeze. "If it's not . . . I mean, if you're not pregnant, do you want to? Try, that is?"

Did she want to try for a baby? At her age? She'd done the whole baby-toddler-preschooler thing. Now she was barely getting used to having a teenager. If she was pregnant, she was more than willing to do it all again. But to start over on purpose?

She looked up at Johnny. He had a look of such hope and eager anticipation that the answer couldn't have been any clearer if it had been broadcast on the giant scoreboard.

"Yes. Yes, I would want to try." She pulled him into the spacious bathroom and they stared down at the test.

Positive.

"Well, I guess that answers that." Johnny's voice was thick with emotion. "We're going to have a baby."

"Congratulations, Daddy." She placed a kiss on his cheek.

"We're going to have a baby." Stunned, he wrapped his arm around her shoulders and pulled her close.

"That doesn't mean we can't... practice for the next one." She suggested in a low seductive voice.

"Yes. Practice. Practice makes perfect."

Epilogue

"Introducing your San Francisco Goliaths..." It was Opening Day, and Johnny stood with his teammates, each of them tipping their caps as their name was called.

Johnny stood between Bryce Baxter and rookie outfielder, Austin Davis. Baxter had been cracking jokes in the clubhouse, trying to keep everyone loose. Davis was so nervous, Johnny thought he was going to pass out. He'd given the kid advice. Advice he was doing his best to take.

Focus. Pick a spot on the field. For Johnny, it had always been the point where the grass meets the dirt in front of the mound.

Breathe. Slowly, inhaling through the nose and out his mouth. Concentrating on the grass and the dirt. Shutting out all distractions until he couldn't hear the crowd.

Let it go. Remember what he was there for. To play baseball. It was a simple game. Not an easy game, but a simple one.

A good thing to remember, whether it was a guy's first Opening Day or his last.

"Can you feel it? I just know this is going to be the year." Bryce clapped Johnny on the back as he headed into the dugout to retrieve his glove. "We're going all the way, man. All. The. Way."

"We've got a hundred and sixty-two games. Let's make them count." And he planned on enjoying every last one of them.

Johnny Scottsdale had come to San Francisco hoping to earn a World Series ring.

He glanced down at his left hand. He'd gotten something better than he'd ever dreamed of. He had a wife. A son. And a baby on the way. Alice's due date was shortly after Game Seven of the World Series. If they made it that far.

If not, that was okay too. He had so much to look forward to. They'd had a good spring down in Arizona. The Goliaths finished in first place in the Cactus League and everyone was healthy to start the season. More importantly, they'd come together as a team. Learned to rely on one another, to trust one another and pick each other up if someone had an off day.

Johnny had an even more supportive home team. Alice was waiting for him when he got off work each night. And she sent him off to the ballpark with more than just a smile. He was no longer a monk, at least not off the field.

Zach was doing well in school and was getting ready to start his last Little League season. He was going to have a great year. He couldn't help it; it was in his blood. The second DNA test came back positive. And they were in the process of legally changing Zach's name and birth certificate.

Alice gave her notice at the foundation. Mel Sr. would take over as director and she'd be there to provide a smooth transition. The old man seemed to enjoy his new role, but he couldn't quite give up his need to offer financial advice to Johnny. For most of his career, money had been the furthest thing from his mind. He hadn't squandered it, but he hadn't made the most of it, either. It just sat there, collecting more dust than interest.

Mel had helped him set up college funds for Zach and the new baby, life insurance and a retirement plan. Then he'd helped Johnny figure out how he was going to pay for this baseball camp he and Alice had their hearts set on.

Alice had already started looking for property in Reno. He told her what he wanted and she was determined to make it happen. She'd narrowed it down to three possibilities, all with room for indoor and outdoor facilities. He wanted to put in a regulation size field, with room for stands. There would be batting cages open to the public as well as camp participants. He also planned on having plenty of bullpen space, so pitchers could hone their skills. They just needed to decide and then make an offer.

She'd also been looking for a house in the Reno area. That search might take a bit longer. They needed a big enough place to meet the needs of a growing family. One with a teenager and a newborn. They'd need a place with room for a swing set and a batting cage. It had to be in the right school district. Close enough to town, yet with enough space for them to enjoy the peace and quiet.

But to Johnny, it didn't really matter where they lived. Because wherever Alice was, he was safe at home.

Meet the Author

Kristina Mathews doesn't remember a time when she didn't have a book in her hand. Or in her head. But it wasn't until she turned forty that she confessed the reason the laundry never made it out of the dryer was because she was busy writing. While she resigned from teaching with the arrival of her second son, she's remained an educator in some form. As a volunteer, parent club member or para educator, she finds the most satisfaction working with emergent and developing readers, helping foster confidence and a lifelong love of books. Kristina lives in Northern California with her husband of more than twenty years, two sons and a black lab. A veteran road tripper, amateur renovator and sports fanatic, she hopes to one day travel all 3,073 miles of Highway 50 from Sacramento, CA to Ocean City, MD, replace her carpet with hardwood floors and serve as a "Ball Dudette" for the San Francisco Giants.

Acknowledgments

First of all, I'd like to thank my family for their support and their patience with having to share me with the people who live in my head.

To Mrs. A, I never did get to thank you for helping me believe in myself and my writing.

To M.M., if you hadn't teased your little cousin all those years ago, Johnny Scottsdale would never have earned his happily ever after.

Turn the page for a special excerpt of Kristina Matthews'

WORTH THE TRADE

A ballplayer and a team owner would give anything for a championship—even their hearts...

After inheriting majority ownership of the San Francisco Goliaths baseball team, Hunter Collins wants to prove to herself—and the rest of the league—that she's got what it takes to build a champion. Her first move is to trade for a hot left-fielder. He's got it all, speed, power, and a desire to win. Not to mention undeniable charm.

Marco Santiago is tired of being the new player in town. After four teams in six years, he's facing free agency at the end of the season. He wants nothing more than a long-term contract and a World Series win. Hitting on his new owner probably isn't the best way to get it, but love may be the most powerful challenger either of them has ever faced...

On sale now!

Chapter 1

"That's him. Over there." Hunter Collins recognized her new left fielder by the body language, posture, and raw physical power of a professional athlete.

"The guy in the plaid shirt?" The limo driver shook his head in doubt. "Are you sure? He doesn't look like no baseball player. He's too tall."

Marco Santiago was indeed tall. And dark. And—she hated to admit, even to herself—incredibly handsome. The expert tailoring of his shirt emphasized his broad shoulders, long, strong arms, and slender waist. Dark denim hugged slim hips, clung to muscular thighs, and she'd put good money on what they did to his taut backside.

His tattered duffel bag was slung carelessly over his left shoulder. A small leather case lay at his feet. The casual observer might interpret his relaxed pose as lazy, bored, or perhaps a little worse for the wear. But she'd watched him on the field enough to know he could spring into action with panther-like reflexes at the crack of the bat.

"He's the one." Her heart rate quickened. A little more than three months ago she'd inherited forty percent ownership of the San Francisco Goliaths. At twenty-seven, Hunter was the youngest president of one of Major League Baseball's oldest franchises. She brushed off the pain of losing her father, focusing instead on her first official player acquisition. Together they would make their mark on the new era of Goliaths' baseball.

As the driver pulled up to the curb, she noticed the slight change in Santiago's stance. His shoulders straightened and he rocked back on his heels like he was ready to chase down a fly ball. There it was, the instinct that had her drooling over him for some time. As a ballplayer, nothing more.

Her driver got out, opened the passenger door, and Santiago ducked inside.

"Whoa, you scared me. I didn't expect company." He smiled at her, flashing a set of dimples and startlingly blue eyes. He let his gaze travel the length of her body, inspecting her, before nodding his approval. "But this might turn out to be a good trade after all."

Excuse me?

"Are you saying you're not happy about the trade?" He had no idea how hard she'd worked to make this deal happen. For the past few weeks she'd practically slept with her cell phone attached to her ear, when she'd slept at all. She'd tuned out the sports talk show hosts and beat reporters and bloggers who claimed she was too inexperienced to make a deal. As if *inexperienced* was a euphemism for *female*.

Not to mention the embarrassing and insulting offers initially given by the other team. They'd wanted her to give up half her farm system, thinking she didn't know the wealth of talent she had in the minor leagues. But once they realized she actually did know what she was doing, they were able to strike a fair deal.

"It came as a surprise." He settled into the leather seat. "Sure, I heard rumors. But there are always trade rumors this time of year. I really didn't expect to walk into the clubhouse this morning only to be told I was no longer wanted in St. Louis."

"You'll be welcomed with open arms here in San Francisco." Hunter gave him what she hoped was an encouraging smile.

"Is that so?" He looked her over as if she wore something low-cut and see-through. Or nothing at all. "So are you the welcoming committee? If they'd done their homework they'd have known I usually prefer blondes. But I can make an exception, just for tonight."

He cocked one eyebrow up and drew his mouth into a grin that stopped just short of a leer.

"I don't see why my hair color should matter to you." She tried not to roll her eyes. He wasn't the first athlete to assume the only place for a woman in pro sports was underneath him and naked. "Your last owner was fully gray. And the one before him was completely bald."

At his stunned silence, she smiled and held out her hand.

"Hunter Collins. President and Managing Partner of the San Francisco Goliaths Baseball Club." She avoided referring to herself as the *acting* president. A role she'd served in during her father's long illness. Hell, she'd served in that role since she was old enough to read a box score. Unofficially, of course. Henry Collins had always been the face in the meetings, the name on the contracts. But she'd been right there with him, working behind the scenes. This was as much her team as anyone's.

"My new boss." He gave her a firm handshake before sinking back into the seat and letting out a frustrated sigh. "Can we start over?"

He turned toward her, a forced smile on his face. The kind of smile he'd give a reporter after a tough loss.

"Don't bother telling me how happy you are to be here." She had to admit, she was more than a little disappointed. Why wouldn't he want to be here? The Goliaths were a first class organization. Her father had saved the team from being moved to Florida. He'd taken on partners in order to build the state-of-the-art ballpark without using public funds. The fans came out to fill the seats night after night, and the ownership did its best to offer the fans their money's worth, even though they hadn't won it all. *Yet.*

"I am happy to be here. I just . . ." He ran his left hand through his hair. She didn't need to check for a wedding ring. He was single, no family to uproot for the cross-country move. "My flight was delayed. I lost half my luggage. And I haven't had a good night's sleep in weeks. So I apologize if I seem less than thrilled."

"I suppose you'll be happier when you can get out on the field." She'd been around athletes her whole life. Enough to know they were creatures of habit. Rain delays, schedule changes, and especially trade rumors could wreak havoc on their routine. Those distractions upset their rhythm and could only be remedied by getting back to work.

"I wish I could have been here in time to get out there tonight." He leaned forward, resting his forearms on his knees. His thighs trembled with nervous energy. "But maybe a day off will do me some good."

"You didn't have the best series against Philly." She'd followed his career closely. Probably knew his stats better than he did. "I imagine the trade rumors had something to do with it. I know you guys say you don't pay any attention to that kind of thing, but it's got to be a big distraction. Not to mention, a little hard on the ego."

"So I take it you're a hands-on kind of owner." His voice was smooth, rich, sensual. The thought of his hands on her body popped up into her imagination. Not what she needed right now. His hands were going to make good catches, good throws, and big hits. His hands were going to make them a lot of money if they made the playoffs. *When* they made the playoffs.

"I like to keep up with my players. It's good for business." She had to turn away from him, from those blistering blue eyes. Where'd they come from? He had the dark hair, dark skin, dark stubble of a Latino player. He should have dark eyes, too, not neon blue ones.

"Don't worry, I won't disappoint you. You'll get exactly what you paid for." He looked down at his hands. Long, straight fingers. Short, well-manicured nails. Thick, strong wrists.

Oh my.

"My father always thought highly of you. He wanted to trade for you last year, but St. Louis beat us out." She needed to remember why they were both here, in this limo that felt so much bigger before he slid into the seat next to her. Now it felt like they were thrown together into the back of a Smart Car. Not that a Smart Car even had a back seat. "So, I decided to carry out his wishes and make the deal happen. I'm sure you'll prove yourself. On the field."

"Your father?" He edged away from her. "Your father was Henry Collins."

She just nodded, unable to speak past the sudden lump in her throat.

"I'm sorry for your loss." His voice lost all traces of teasing. "He was a class act. The league will miss him."

She chose to take his words as a compliment for her father, not an indication that he thought she wasn't up to the job.

"Thank you." She needed to pull herself together. The last thing she wanted was for him to see her as soft or weak. "Let's get you to your hotel, get you settled in so you'll be fresh for the game tomorrow."

"Is the game over?" Santiago pulled out his phone, scrolled though the screen. "Nope. It's the bottom of the seventh. Goliaths on top three to one. Why don't we swing by the ballpark? I'd like to meet my new teammates tonight."

"Right now?" She hadn't expected him to want to get out there tonight. Especially after a long flight, lost luggage, and his disappointment at her not being a blonde.

"Unless you have something else planned for me." He raised an eyebrow and flashed one of his dimples. He knew all too well how irresistible that smile was. "Because you own me now. So . . ."

"The ballpark it is." Hunter leaned forward to alert the driver of their change of plans. She didn't want to think about what she could demand of him, other than a division title. That was the only thing she wanted from Marco Santiago.

The limo driver pulled up to the players' lot and checked in with the security guard who waved them inside.

"I'll see that your bag is sent to your hotel." Hunter's—Ms. Collins' tone was cool. Very impersonal and businesslike. "I'll send the driver back around when the game is over."

"Aren't you going to stay?" Why that disappointed him, he had no idea.

"No. I've had a long week." She heaved a sigh, sinking back against the seat. "I think I'll go home, take a nice long bath."

Marco closed his eyes, trying not to conjure up the image of her slipping naked into a tub full of warm water. Bubbles. Perhaps some scented oils. Damn. He shifted in the plush leather seat, his jeans becoming uncomfortably tight.

Please don't let her notice. She was his boss. The worst thing he could do would be to get all worked up trying to picture what kind of underwear she wore under her various shades of gray. Her loose-fitting charcoal pantsuit was a little on the drab side. Almost as if she'd borrowed it from her father's closet. Her blouse, the color of fog, was buttoned up to the hollow of her throat. But it was just soft enough to hint at the womanly curves she was trying to hide.

Still, something about her drew him in. Her eyes were a warm, golden brown. Her hair was pulled back in some uptight updo, but a single loose strand that curled behind her right ear looked soft, silky, and entirely too touchable. Like the delicate skin of her neck. He couldn't help but wonder how she'd respond to the lightest brush of his lips, right there. Would she shiver? Sigh? Moan?

He'd made the innuendo about her being his own personal welcoming committee. Talk about stupid. Just put her on the defensive. But it had also injected a charge into their interaction. A sexual energy that might have stayed under control if he hadn't opened his big mouth.

This wasn't the first time Marco had experienced lust at first sight. But usually it was for a woman who had all her feminine assets on display. Showcased in tight, revealing clothing. Flashing tons of makeup and broadcasting her availability for a night or two of fun.

Hunter was the opposite. The way she dressed was the least of it. She wore hardly any makeup. Her lips were bare. Pink, soft, and lush enough to make him wonder what she'd taste like. No artificial cherry-vanilla flavoring, or glossy chemical taste. Just pure, unenhanced woman.

Who was one hundred percent off limits.

"Well, thanks for picking me up." He winced. Every word out of his mouth tonight dripped with sexual undertones. "From the airport. And . . . uh . . . thank you for bringing me to San Francisco. I'll make it worth your while. You'll see."

"I'm counting on it." She glanced down at his lap and quickly turned away, color spreading across her cheeks. Damn. She'd noticed the effect she had on him. "Are you going to get out of the car? Or should I tell the driver you've changed your mind?"

"I'm going. I'm going." He slid away from her. Reached for the door to make his exit, but he couldn't quite pull the handle.

"Have dinner with me?" Maybe it was jet lag. Sleep deprivation. Or some seismic anomaly affecting his brain waves. Maybe going more than six months without sex had been a really bad idea.

"I'm sure you'll find plenty to eat at the post-game spread." Did her hesitation mean she was rattled? "We have an excellent caterer."

"No. I want *you* to have dinner with *me*." He leaned toward her, knowing she'd deny him, but he wanted to linger near her a little bit longer.

"I can't." She squirmed, avoiding his gaze. "It would be a conflict of interest."

"You're only conflicted because you're interested." He kept his smile to himself. He was getting to her. Almost as much as she was getting to him. Even though she wasn't at all his type. Or maybe she was, she just worked so damn hard trying to hide it.

"I'm only interested in winning the division and making a strong run in the postseason." She turned her head to look out the window as if to show she was unaffected by the chemistry between them.

"Aren't you a rotten liar?" He chuckled softly. Oh yeah, he was definitely getting to her. "Don't join in the poker game at the next owners' retreat. You'll be wiped out."

She whipped her head around so fast the car shook. "I happen to be a very good poker player. I can hold my own against anyone. Anytime."

Interesting. Her strong reaction told him two things. She was insecure about her place among her fellow owners. And yes, she was interested in him on more than a professional level.

"That explains your wardrobe." He leaned back, not ready to leave her just yet. "You dress like you do to fit in with the old boys' club. But you can't hide the fact that you are all woman."

"And you can't hide the fact that you don't want to be here." She dared look him straight in the eye, but couldn't hold his gaze.

"I'm starting to come around." He gave her one last smile. "I think I'm going to like San Francisco. I think I'm really going to like it here."

Marco slid out of the seat and headed into the ballpark acting like he owned the place.

The game had ended by the time he got through security and onto the field. The Goliaths had held their lead and a good portion of the crowd lingered, singing along to Tony Bennett. One of the on-field reporters recognized him and rushed over to be the first to interview him.

Showtime.

"Rachel Parker here, with the newest member of the San Francisco Goliaths, Marco Santiago." The crowd cheered, as word of his arrival spread and they played the interview on the scoreboard. "Did you come straight from the airport?"

"I sure did." Marco flashed his million-dollar grin. He earned the rest of his salary with his bat and his glove. "I'm just so happy to be here. In this ballpark. With these fans. And this team... This team has a real good chance of going all the way. I can't wait to get out on the field and make a contribution. To thank the ownership for bringing me here."

"We're happy to have you here in San Francisco." The reporter was friendly, almost too perky. "What does your family think of the change?"

"I'm sure my mother will be happy for me." Guilt hit him at the realization he hadn't talked to her since the trade went down. She had to hear it on the news like everyone else. "But she's always been proud of me."

"You're not married?" Was she asking for herself or all the single ladies who might be watching the broadcast?

"Just to my job." He hoped she would drop the subject of his personal life. He didn't have one. Didn't want one. Not until he was settled more permanently. "My focus is on helping my team get to the postseason. The ownership and management took a chance on me. I won't let them down. I won't let the fans down."

He didn't want to let anyone down.

The rest of the night was a blur. He signed quite a few autographs, took tons of pictures, and introduced himself to his teammates. His manager, Juan Javier, made him feel welcome, as did the coaches, trainers, and support staff. It probably didn't hurt showing up after a victory, when the whole ballpark was buzzing from the win.

The atmosphere had a much better vibe than in his former clubhouse these last few weeks. They weren't officially out of it, but with such high expectations the season had been more than disappointing. When management started trading away all their star players it started to feel like they were giving up. *Rebuilding.* In other words, dumping big salaries and trying to salvage their financial asses.

He knew it was just business. Nothing personal. This trade had nothing to do with how anyone felt about him. The St. Louis owners thought they could make more money without him and the San Francisco group thought they could make more money with him. Hopefully they were both right.

But he felt bad for the fans. They'd embraced him in St. Louis. There were bound to be folks who felt let down. People who worked for a living and spent their hard earned money on seats in left field. It didn't matter whether they made it to one game a year, or all eighty-one. The fans made signs, shouted his name. They bought the T-shirts, jerseys, and bobble heads not to add to the team's profits, but because they loved their team. Because they wanted to be a part of something bigger than themselves.

Maybe he wasn't too crazy about being traded once again. But now that he was here, he'd give it everything he had. For his teammates. For the fans. For the lovely Miss Hunter Collins.

Since he couldn't sleep, Marco pulled out his iPad. Good thing he'd kept it in his carry-on bag. After sending a quick e-mail to his mother letting her know he'd arrived safely in his latest temporary home, he decided to do some Internet research on his new team. Who was he kidding? He wanted to know more about his new owner. He hoped to satisfy his curiosity and move on. Instead, he became more and more intrigued by the woman as he watched her life unfold through a series of pictures, videos, and articles about the little girl who was raised by her single dad and the entire Goliaths organization.

What was he doing? Hunter Collins was his boss. Hadn't his family suffered enough at the hands of an employer who'd taken advantage of his employee? He couldn't risk it. No matter how much he wanted her. He'd be a free agent at the end of the season, looking for a team he could finish his career with. He had to make a good impression. On the field. Only on the field. He didn't need any distractions. Especially not one with the power to end his career right when he was hitting his prime playing years.

Still, he went to a little extra trouble with his appearance the next day before heading to the ballpark. He put on his best semi-casual dress shirt. The one that made his eyes bluer than a summer sky. Or so he'd been told. And not only by the salesgirl who sold him the overpriced garment. He spent a good half hour debating whether to shave or go with the scruffy look. He shaved. Since he was starting with a new team, he decided his face needed a fresh start.

Besides, it's not like they were going to hop into bed right away. No. He liked to take his time. Get to know a woman. Draw out the seduction over a period of weeks. Some guys preferred the easy in, easy out approach to relationships. But a woman wasn't a drive up window. He didn't want to just toss her aside after a quick taste. He liked to savor a woman. Leave her with no regrets tainting the memories they'd made.

He wondered what kind of memories he could make with Hunter Collins. She was different than any of the women he usually dated. For one thing, she wouldn't be impressed by what he did for a living.

She was around professional athletes all the time. She'd surely known too many ballplayers who thought they were God's gift. He'd need to show her how he was different from every other man in that dugout.

What an idiot. He probably wouldn't even see her. It's not like she'd be hanging out in the clubhouse. If she even came to the game, she'd be sitting pretty in a luxury box, looking out over her investment. He'd do well to remember she was an owner. She was only interested in him because he could make her money. He should only be interested in her signature on his paychecks.

He needed to focus on getting ready for his first game as a Goliath. He needed to prove he was worth the trade. This was his fourth team since making it to the majors. He hoped it would be his last. He'd spent far too much of his life moving around. As a kid. Again in the minors. When he was drafted in the second round, he thought he'd finally found a home. Texas would keep him around. People loved the local boy makes good story.

But he'd quickly learned that baseball was more than the national pastime. It was a business. Big, big business. Loyalty only went as far as the bottom line. And the investors were restless. Every team started the season hoping this would be their year. For the twenty-eight clubs who didn't make it to the big dance, someone was to blame. Players were shuffled. Free-agents signed. Salaries taken on and dumped. All in the hopes of a share of the postseason pool.

Marco had been called up, sent down, brought back up, and traded three times in the last six years. In the process, he'd become somewhat of a streaky player. One who could turbocharge the lineup for weeks at a time. Then he'd hit a plateau. His average would dip. Run production taper off. And the pressure would get to him. He tried not to listen to the talk shows or read the blogs. But he knew what they were saying about him. Knew it was only a matter of time before someone else started looking better.

He needed to make sure that for the last two months of this season, the grass was greenest in left field beneath his feet.

GREAT BOOKS, GREAT SAVINGS!

When You Visit Our Website:
www.kensingtonbooks.com

You Can Save Money Off The Retail Price Of Any Book You Purchase!

- **All Your Favorite Kensington Authors**
- **New Releases & Timeless Classics**
- **Overnight Shipping Available**
- **eBooks Available For Many Titles**
- **All Major Credit Cards Accepted**

Visit Us Today To Start Saving!
www.kensingtonbooks.com

All Orders Are Subject To Availability.
Shipping and Handling Charges Apply.
Offers and Prices Subject To Change Without Notice.